All it Takes

a novel

Sadie Munroe

All it Takes by Sadie Munroe

Copyright ©2015 Sara Eagleson

Cover design by Sara Eagleson
Cover Photo: Mikulas Zacok - Miobi Photography
Editor: Danielle Webster
Typesetting: Christa Seeley

ISBN: 978-0-9938942-1-3

For *my amazing family.*

Thank you for always supporting and believing in me.

I won't let you down.

. . . you can all stop reading now. None of you read Romance. So just stop. No, seriously. Stop. Put the book down and just walk away.

I'll know it if you don't.

Chapter 1

Star

Like everything bad that has ever happened in my life, it started with a phone call. But sometimes just a simple phone call is all it takes, and that innocent ring that breaks through the smiles and laughter beforehand can interrupt more than your day. It can change your life.

The first call came when I was five. I was playing in the fort I had made out of the old green sofa cushions and every blanket I was able to lay my hands on. I remember the taste of raspberry jam on my lips as I busied myself with pretending to serve lemonade to my stuffed pony. Awkwardly. There was a lot of splashing and a small puddle of lemonade on the rug that I remember hoping my mother wouldn't notice. My mother was in the kitchen, washing up the dishes from lunch and singing along to an oldies song on the radio. The sound of the phone ringing barely even registered as I trotted my pony up and down the throw-pillow mountain, but the sound of my mother's scream was enough for my entire world to come screeching to a halt.

The first call was from the police station.

That phone call came when I was five years old, and it meant that my father was dead.

The second phone call was from child services when I was nine years old and it was almost immediately followed by a knock on the door, by my mother yelling and crying as she hurled things at the men who entered. They had found out about my mother's hoarding. The second phone call meant that they were taking me away. That was ten years ago, and I haven't been back since, not until now.

Not until the third call.

I had just turned nineteen when the third call came. I'd been laughing with my friends in our dorm's common room. I hadn't even paused when my phone rang. I'd just leaned over and scooped it up off the table, cheeks still aching from smiling so much, and had said hello.

I wish I could say that the third call had held better news, but I should have known better.

Because sometimes a single phone call is all it takes.

It's been over a month, but that third phone call still doesn't feel real to me.

First my father. Then my mother.

God. Even now it's almost impossible for me to say it. For me to even think it.

She's dead.

My mother is dead.

A s h

G oddamn, is it ever good to be home.

I don't know how, but that five-hour car ride somehow felt even longer than the five years I've been away. I don't think I've been so jittery, so freaking excited since I was a little kid. I must have driven Mom nuts the entire drive back, bouncing my leg and fidgeting like a five year old, but I couldn't help it.

This is it. This is my new shot. And there's no way in hell I'm going to waste it.

I'm out of the car the second it comes to a stop in the driveway, racing down the path and up the front steps before Dad has even turned the engine off.

"Bruiser!"

I drop my bag on the front porch and wrench open the screen door, but before I've even laid my hand on the doorknob, I realize something is wrong. There should be a racket. There should be the sound of barking echoing off the hallway walls. There should be the pounding of feet as they rush down the stairs and toward the front door. But there's nothing.

There's silence.

I whirl around, still gripping the edge of the storm door in my hand. The metal is cool in the warm summer air, and I grip it tight, desperate for something to hold on to. My chest is thundering.

Something is wrong.

I stand there as my parents make their way slowly up the path and up the front steps. Mom shakes her head and sighs at the sight of my backpack on the wooden planks of the porch. All of a sudden, I'm five years old again, about to be scolded for tracking mud across the carpet.

Fuck that. I'm twenty-eight.

"Where's Bruiser?" I ask, but instead of answering, Mom just leans over and picks up my backpack by the strap, shaking her head at it like it's offending her somehow. Neither she nor Dad is saying a word.

What the hell is going on? I loosen my grip on the storm door, and let it fall shut as I turn around to face them. I lean my back against it, closing it behind me. They can't ignore me. Not if they want to get in the house.

"Where. Is. Bruiser?" I want my fucking dog. I raised him from a puppy and I haven't seen him in five years. I want my god-damn dog. But Dad just sighs and rubs the back of his neck and looks anywhere but at me. Great. Just great. I turn to Mom. She's still holding my backpack, but instead of handing it to me and ordering me to put it away like I expect, she just sets it down on the porch swing. Huh. The swing is blue now. It used to be red. Wonder what else they changed while I was gone. I raise my eyebrows at her.

Mom sighs and clenches her hands into fists at her sides. She started doing that years ago, right around the time of the mud-vs-carpet incident. Fist clenching is never good.

"Mom," I say, trying to keep my words calm and free of curses—the cussing helps me get my own irritation out before it explodes, but I learned long ago that it just makes her more pissed. "Where is my dog?"

She glances up at Dad, but he's looking over at the stupid hummingbird feeder like it may hold all the answers to life. Unlikely, since they've had it since I was a kid and so far, nada. "Roger," she prompts him, but as usual he's off in his own little world.

Mom gets mad. Dad zones out.

Lather rinse repeat.

Endlessly.

Fuck.

"Mom—" I snap, but she whirls on me before I can get out another word.

"Bruiser is gone," she says. "He ran off not long after your trial."

What. The. Fuck?

I try to take a deep breath, but I've got a rhino on my chest.

"And you didn't look for him?" I yell. It's not even a question. I know my parents. I know what the answer is.

"Of course we looked for him," my mother says, her eyes flashing. Liar. Goddamn liar. "But he was your dog, Ash. He was *your* responsibility."

"I was in prison!" I say. Yell. Whatever. The neighbors are going to be in for a show. It's been a while for them, with me out of the picture. Guess it's time for them to get used to it again. I open my mouth. *You said you'd take care of him,* I'm about to say. *You told me he was fine. Every fucking time I asked, you told me my dog was fine.*

"Exactly," she snaps, cutting me off like she always has. "And I think that's pretty much the height of your irresponsibility, don't you, Ashley?"

Fuck.

Dad's finally showing signs of life. "Maybe we should go inside," he says. "Talk this out."

"Not a chance," I snap, moving to shove back harder against the door.

Just as the words leave my mouth, Mom's head snaps around to glare at him. "We discussed this, Roger. He's not coming in."

What.

The.

Fuck.

Dad's mouth opens, like he's about to argue, but Mom's glare shuts him down. I scoff. It's just like always. Not a damn thing has changed. *Are you ever going to grow a backbone, old man?*

Mom turns to me, and as I watch she takes a deep breath and lets it out slowly. A sick, twisted part of me wonders if they have her on the same anger-management program they had me on in prison.

Raising an eyebrow I cross my arms over my chest. "So you're not going to let me in, Mom?"

She looks me straight in the eye. "Your father and I have discussed it," she says. *Yeah right. More like you said what was going to happen and he caved just like always.* "And we think it would be for the best if you didn't move back in with us."

"For the best," I repeat, trying her bullshit words out in my mouth. I don't like them.

"That's right." She glances over at Dad, but he's off in his own little world again. I wonder how I would have turned out if I was more like him than I was like her. Probably be an accountant by now, have my own little nine-to-five and a goddamn goldfish.

"You mean, it would be better for you," I say. "Whether it's better for me hasn't really been brought up for discussion, now has it?"

"Ashley," she says, but this time it's my turn to cut her off.

"It's Ash," I say. "It's been Ash for the last twenty years. And I think you're more concerned about what the neighbors think of you than about your own son." I'm standing right in front of her now, my own fists clenched at my sides. I don't remember pushing up off the door, don't remember walking across the porch, but here I am, anyway.

I pause, wait for her to argue. Wait for her to tell me she's changed her mind, to tell me that this has all been a big mistake. But instead she just shakes her head and reaches into her purse and pulls out a key chain. There's a bright red rabbit's foot on it. It's my key chain, from before. But it's different. The house key is missing. The only one left is the one to my car. It dangles there, glinting in the afternoon light like a beacon, and my gut sinks down to my toes when I realize what it means.

This is why they didn't fight me when I said I wanted to get my license reinstated, why they told me to do it right away. Why they fucking stood in line with me at the DMV while I jumped through hoops to get it back. They wanted to make sure they could get rid of me.

She reaches out and grabs my hand and slams the keys into it, and glares up at me.

"As far as I'm concerned, my son died in that crash," she says. "You're not welcome here."

Then she pushes past me and yanks the storm door open so hard that it slams against the siding. Then she's gone, disappeared into the darkened house.

I turn to my father. The rhino on my chest is now a goddamn whale, but he just shakes his head and reaches into his back pocket. Without a word, he pulls out a little stack of bills and presses them into my free palm. Then he's gone, too.

Fuck.

Chapter 2

Star

The day I aged out of the foster-care system was the day I got my first tattoo.

Well, tattoos.

I don't know if it's self-serving or if I was just so wrapped up in having my own identity that wasn't Delaney's daughter or foster child or what, but I knew from the start what I was going to get.

All my life, I've just wanted to be me, to be Star.

So that's what I got.

Stars.

Eighteen of them. One for every year I'd been trying, and failing, just to be me.

And I've adored them ever since.

Seeing them there, winking up at me, it was like a light had been switched on. All of a sudden, I felt different.

I was different. I was going to be whoever I wanted, and no one was going to be able to stop me.

I sometimes wish I'd thought it through a little better, gotten them placed with purpose. Sometimes I wish I'd found a constellation to arrange them in, instead of just having them scattered across my skin, any which way. But then again, sometimes I'm glad I got them done that way. They're my own constellation, dancing up the top of my left foot from just above my baby toe, up toward my ankle. Eighteen tiny stars, all in black.

That was the day I found my bravery.

And damn it, I'm going to need it.

I stare down at my computer screen and sigh, trying to figure out what to say.

> **Star2274**: Cleaning out my mother's house now that she's passed away.
> **Star2274**: Had no idea it'd gotten so bad.
> **LuckNGlass**: I can only imagine.
> **LuckNGlass**: My parents house is out of control.
> **LuckNGlass**: Sorry for your loss, btw.
> **Star2274**: . . .

The cursor for the chat window on the hoarding message board blinks expectantly at me, awaiting my response. But I'm stumped.

It shouldn't be this hard.

There are a thousand things running through my mind. I could go on and on to LuckNGlass about what I'd found at my mother's house, the boxes upon boxes, the million articles of clothing still in their original shopping bags, tags intact, the sheer amount of *junk* as far as the eye could see. But I don't have the words.

Finally, I sigh and type you don't know the half of it into the chat window. And then, as an afterthought thanks before logging off and closing my laptop.

I don't know what I was expecting, but it wasn't this.

This is worse. This is so, *so* much worse.

I'm so frustrated, I feel like any second now I'm going to start screaming and crying and throwing everything I can lay my hands on, smashing it against the wall. And if I start, I'm never going to stop.

How did this even happen? How the hell had it gotten this far? Why didn't the lawyer warn me? Why didn't he make *certain* I knew what I was getting into *before* he handed over the keys? I have half a mind to track the guy down and give him a piece of my mind. And a brick through his windshield. He'd mentioned my mother's clutter problem, but he'd brushed it off like it was nothing.

This? This isn't nothing. This is the biggest load of *something* I've ever seen. And he'd let me think I could do it on my own. What a load of crap.

Clutter, he'd said. When I pictured clutter—my mother's own brand of clutter, even—I was picturing the house I'd left when I was nine, the one with the piles of junk that were a little too high, a little too tippy, the ones that could only be navigated by the paths that my mother had left between them. I remember my bedroom being so full with toys that there wasn't any place to play, the kitchen that had too many dishes for my mother to cook in.

I'd thought I was prepared when the lawyer handed me the keys. I'd just nodded along when he spoke, all smiles and reassuring little "I'm sure you'll do just fine"s as he ushered me out of his office like he had a train to catch.

Now I know why he was in such a hurry to get me out of there. Because now I've seen what's happened to the house I spent my childhood in, and it's nowhere close to what I remember.

It's so much worse.

I shove another bite of bacon into my mouth and try to hold back a sigh. The keys to the house are still in my pocket, and they dig into my thigh with every movement I make. They're the goddamn albatross around my neck, and I don't know what to do about it. I've been sitting in this diner for the past hour. Mary-Lou's Place. I *think* I remember it from when I was a kid, but if I'm right, it looked different back then. It was a lot more commercial back then. Almost like it had belonged to a chain of truck stops. Now it's all '50s revival, all gleaming chrome and teal vinyl. There's a juke box in the corner, but instead of 45s it plays CDs. They gleam in the light when they shift around in the machine with every song change. It's all so sickeningly charming. I can't imagine my mother here.

I can't even imagine myself here.

If there was anywhere I didn't belong, this place was it. And it was obvious, apparently.

The waitress who'd taken my order had given me the dirtiest once-over I've ever had, her eyes lingering too long on my eye makeup and the tattoos on my arms. She'd huffed and rolled her eyes at me, and had gotten half of my order wrong when she'd finally brought it out.

I sigh and lean back in my seat, draining the last of my coffee from the bottom of my mug. The vinyl is sticking to the backs of my legs and it's making me itch like crazy, but it's not like I have anywhere better to go. It's either the diner, the house from hell, or the freaky little B&B I checked into when I got into town. The town of Avenue isn't exactly a bustling metropolis. I chose that particular B&B because it was the only B&B in the city limits. If there was another one, I'd have moved already. The owner's this little old lady who never blinks and seems to be a little too fond of her miniature poodle for my comfort. She had the thing up on the counter when she checked me in, and it yapped at me the whole time. It reminded me of one of my old foster moms' Pomeranian, aka *the devil.*

If that poodle was the sign of things to come, then I'm pretty much doomed.

I raise my hand in the air and try to flag down my waitress, but she ignores me and moves across the room to top up the mug of an old man who's sitting in a booth with a little boy. They're playing Go Fish, their discarded cards littering the table between them. It's adorable, but it's no reason to ignore me.

Another waitress, a blonde about my age walks by me with a tray of plates in her arms, and I reach out to touch her arm before she gets too far. She jumps at my touch, but doesn't lose her hold on the tray. It's impressive.

"Sorry!" I say, drawing my hands back before I do any more damage. "I didn't mean to startle you. I was just wondering if I could get a refill." I waggle my empty mug in her direction. Her gaze darts between the mug and my face, and the tray in her arms wobbles a bit.

"Star?"

My heart stutters a bit at the sound of my name. How the hell does she know my name? My gaze darts around the diner. I feel like everyone's looking at me. By now the news about my mother's . . . condition must have made the rounds through town, not to mention her passing. Stupid small towns. I look back up at her, and she's smiling down at me, expectantly. "Star Collins?"

"I'm sorry," I say, baffled, "do I . . . ?"

"It's me!" she says, and lays the tray down on a nearby table before sinking into the seat across from me. "Lacey Kendall."

I blink at her stupidly for a second before the name finally clicks into place somewhere in the back of my memory.

Holy shit. I can actually see it now. Her face has slimmed out since childhood, all that baby fat melted away to reveal the woman underneath. The hair is the same, though, bright blonde just like mine is under all the black dye. I can't believe it.

"Holy crap," I say. It's the only thing I can say. I don't know why this didn't occur to me when I decided to come back here. I spent the first nine years of my life in this tiny town. Of course someone would recognize me. Especially the girl I used to spend nearly every afternoon in the sandbox with.

"How are you?" she says, face breaking out into a smile. She leans her elbows on the table between us, somehow managing to carve herself out a little spot between my giant lunch platter and my abandoned laptop. I'd been trying to email my roommate earlier, to update her on what was happening, but I'm not sure that my email actually went through. Wi-Fi is apparently hard to come by in town, and while the sign in the diner's window boasts its availability, its signal strength left something to be desired. I can only hope that I got through. Otherwise my stay here is going to be pretty lonely. As sweet as Lacey seems, all bright eyes and smiles, I'm not really interested in mingling with the locals. Especially if news of my mother's problem hasn't passed around town yet.

What they don't know won't hurt them.

Or, more importantly, *me.*

I don't know how, but if it's possible, I'm going to keep the house and the hoard under the radar. Just the thought of what the house is hiding has me getting all worked up again. I don't need any other distractions. I just need to get it cleaned out.

Even though I have no fucking idea how I'm going to do that.

I look back up at Lacey, and I realize she's waiting for me to say something, but I have no idea what she just said. My mind's a total blank.

Before I can stop it, a nervous laugh bubbles up out of me. God, I'm so awkward.

"I'm sorry," I say, shaking my head and rubbing a hand over my burning face. "I completely spaced. What did you say?"

Lacey just smiles at me, all bright eyes and tanned skin and super-straight white teeth. God, she's grown up to be the spitting image of a small-town girl, all bubbly and blonde. It's bizarre. "It's okay," she says. "I just asked how you were. I mean—" her eyes dance over me, and I can't help but wonder exactly what she thinks she's seeing when she looks at me "—you just look so . . . so different!"

Yeah, I think. *No kidding.*

When I'd last seen her, Lacey and I had looked more alike than we did different. Long blond hair. Big smiles with missing baby teeth. We'd even been the same height. I've grown taller than her, but I am by no means a giant. She just . . . stopped. She is all tiny and dainty and golden. I . . . am not.

I reach up and tug at the ends of my dark hair. I've been dyeing it for years. I don't think I could go back to blonde ever again. It just isn't . . . me.

"Yeah," I murmur, "I guess I do." Her smile is hesitant even as her gaze darts over the tattoos that wander down my arms, the names inked on the fingers of my right hand, the names of the people who have been a positive influence in my life. *Roth* on the inner edge of my right pinkie, *Autumn* on my ring finger, my old foster brother and first boyfriend *Brick* on my middle finger. The word *climb* I had tattooed on the inside of my wrist when I'd gotten into college. Everything. She wants to say something. I can tell. So I shift back in my chair and wait. I just want to see if she's actually going to mention them.

She doesn't. But that might just be because the diner door swings open, tinkling the little bell that's hanging just above it, a guy walks in who looks like he fits in even less than I do.

If that's even possible.

He's not very tall, not for a guy, at least. He's maybe a couple inches taller than my five-foot-six, and he's wearing ripped, baggy jeans that seem to be holding onto his body by sheer force of will, like at any second they're going to make a break for it and just fall right down. Over that, he's wearing a T-shirt and the ugliest army jacket I've ever seen in my life, and just beneath the cuff, I can see the black ink of a tattoo as it snakes down his wrist to cover the back of his left hand.

His dirty-blond hair is cut short, but not in any particular style. More than anything it just looks like he took a pair of scissors to it and started hacking, and his jaw is covered in a few days' worth of scruff. He has a face that looks like if he'd cleaned himself up, he'd look pretty good. But he has a long way to go.

And judging by the way Lacey has tensed up in her chair as she looks over her shoulder at him, she agrees.

The guy kind of hovers in the doorway for a minute, looking around like he hasn't seen the place in years—*Did I look like that when I walked in?*—then his eyes clap on the waitress behind the counter, the one who'd given me and my tattoos a dirty look earlier, and he shoves his hands into his pockets and kind of shuffles in her general direction.

Lacey whips back around to face me, her pale ponytail slicing through the air so fast I'm amazed she doesn't take her own eye out. She plants the palms of her hands flat down on the table top. "Excuse me for a minute, Star. I'll be right back." Then she's up and out of the seat before I can say a word. She's completely forgotten about the tray of food she was in the middle of delivering to the other diners when she spotted me, but, as I glance around the room, worried that someone is going to call her out on it, I realize that none of the diners seem to care about that.

All their attention is on the guy, the one Lacey is making a beeline toward. I can see her face from here, and she looks like a bloodhound who's just caught a scent, all full of concentration and purpose. It's a little unnerving to watch. The guy only makes it about two-thirds of the way to the counter when Lacey intercepts him with a—I hate to say it, but *really freaking snotty*—"Can I help you?"

Cold. Really cold. And judging by the look on the guy's face, he feels the chill.

"I . . . Could I maybe speak to the manager?" He pauses for a moment, and when Lacey doesn't say anything, he adds an awkward "Please?"

"I can help you," Lacey says, and crosses her arms over her chest.

"Okay," he says, and blows out a breath, slowly, like he's trying his best to ignore her reaction, which, to be honest, is unexpectedly bitchy. He reaches into the pocket of his army jacket, and pulls out a folded piece of paper. "Well, I was just wondering if you guys had any openings." He unfolds the piece of paper and holds it out to her. It trembles a bit in his grip, and as I watch, he starts chewing on his lip. "I'm looking for a job."

I expect Lacey to reach out and take the paper, to tell him that she'll pass it on to the manager for him. But she doesn't. Instead she just stands there, her arms crossed over her chest, her fingers tapping against her arm.

"Sorry," she says, but the tone of her voice makes it clear she's anything but. "We're not hiring."

The guy just kinds of stares at her. I don't think he was expecting that, either. The piece of paper—which must be his résumé, I realize—sort of hangs there in the air between them, and the fact that Lacey isn't even pretending to be interested in it speaks volumes. Hell, it *screams* them. After a moment, the guy's gaze drops to the floor, and he pulls the résumé back. That's when I notice just how worn that piece of paper is. It's half-crumpled and looks kind of soft, like it's been folded and unfolded again and again. This is not the first time he's been turned down, but I'm willing to bet real money that it's one of the rudest. And most unexpected, given the way his face falls. "Oh. Okay," he says quietly, and neatly folds the piece of paper and slides it back into his pocket. "Thanks for your time." He doesn't look up as he leaves, just steps around her and beelines for the door.

Just as he pushes open the door, though, one of the customers lets out a cough.

"Killer."

Even through the fake cough, the word is loud enough that I flinch at the sound. And if I can hear him, the guy at the door can, too. He freezes for a second, then, head down, shoves his way out the door. It slams behind him, bell jangling, and I jump as

Lacey slides back into the seat in front of me.

"Holy crap," she says, her face flushed and her eyes wide as saucers. "Did you see that?"

My stomach twists and something inside me aches for that guy. "What the hell just happened?" I ask, turning to face Lacey. She looks so sweet, but that was harsh. What the hell is going on in this town?

"Oh," she says, and a weird little smile begins to spread across her face. She plants her elbows on the table and cups her face in her hands. Leaning forward, like she's sharing gossip at a slumber party, she says, "Just wait 'til you hear this."

Chapter 3

Star

I can't believe it.

This is just my luck.

The stupid car won't start.

I'm stuck in the parking lot with Lacey watching from the window, and my mother's stupid fucking car won't start. I keep turning the key but the engine just won't turn over. It just sputters and dies. Sputters and dies.

I give it one last shot, muttering every swear word I can think of as I twist the key in the ignition, but once again, *nothing*. Groaning, I slump forward and let my head fall against the steering wheel.

Fuck.

God. Fucking. Dammit.

What next? Just how much more am I going to have to deal with?

I already had to sit through Lacey's entire rendition of the tragic life story of the guy she'd run off at the diner. She'd just sat there and went on and on, completely unaffected, like she was regaling me with the plot of a movie she'd just watched or something. It was shameful.

I don't know if I've changed so much since we were kids, or if she has, but the girl I remember playing in the sandbox with wouldn't have gotten so much joy out of another person's suffering. Or wouldn't have been so oblivious about it, as she seemed to be. Because I don't know how anyone could cause the death of another human being unintentionally and not be suffering.

And, according to Lacey, that's what the guy had done.

He'd killed a man. A father. A man with a family.

He'd gone to a party, had apparently gotten high as a kite and he'd driven himself home. But the party was three towns away, and he only made it back through one and a half of them before the accident. He'd made it nearly all the way through Thurould when his car had collided with the other man's. And that had been that.

Lacey had taken such joy in telling me this that it actually soured what was left of my appetite, and I ended up pushing the rest of my food away. She didn't even notice. She just grinned at me. "It was even bigger news around here then when the Fire Marshall's son decided that he was a she, if you know what I mean. I mean, Avenue's very own murderer. How insane is that?"

"Manslaughter," I mumbled as one of the guys in the booth a little ways away started waving in our direction and calling out to her.

She glanced over her shoulder real quick, as the guy called out playfully, "Can we get some service over here, Babycakes?" then turned back at me, puzzlement in her eyes.

"What?" she asked.

"Manslaughter," I repeated, louder this time. "Murder requires intent. Manslaughter is accidental. Unless he actually went out and tried to run someone down, he would have been charged with manslaughter. Not murder."

"Lacey!" the guy had resorted to yelling by then, the playful tone fading out of his voice.

She twisted around in her seat and yelled "I'm coming! Keep your pants on!" at the guy, and then turned back to me.

"Whatever," she said, waving me off and pulling herself up out of the chair and snagging the tray of food she'd abandoned earlier. "Listen, since you're back now, there's someone I want you to meet."

That's how I ended up getting dragged across the diner by my childhood best friend—who I would have been perfectly happy leaving in my childhood—and meeting a group of three guys who looked up at me like I was an alien that had just crash-landed on their planet. On Christmas. In the middle of dinner. Jesus, I was already sick of this town.

How is this my life?

"This is Preston," she said, laying a plate of steak and eggs in front of the guy closest to her, the one with the blond hair and bright green eyes. Damn, I think. Apparently Lacey isn't the only one that embraced the whole small-town-golden-child thing. I nodded at him, like his name was supposed to mean something to me. "Preston's granddaddy owns this Mary Lou's. Has for years. Preston," she said, turning back to me and waving her hands at me like she was presenting some kind of door prize. "This is Star. We went to elementary school together." He nodded at me, and I felt kind of like I'd just been dismissed by a dignitary or something. Who did this guy think he was? "And this," Lacey continued, oblivious to how uncomfortable I was "is Clay." She set another plate of food on the table, this time in front of a guy who I suddenly realized looked exactly the same as Preston. How the hell had she been able to tell them apart? "Clay is Preston's brother," she said to me, because apparently I was blind on top of being an alien.

"Much to my dismay," the guy said, giving me a little smile before turning to his food. Okay, I liked this one a little better. But beside me, Lacey scoffed and whapped him on the shoulder with the back of her hand. "You be nice, Clayton," she said. Then turned to me. "Preston's my boyfriend," she said. Ah, that explained it. "And Clay is just jealous."

"Of course I am, Lacey. Of course I am."

He clearly wasn't, but Lacey didn't seem to notice that, judging by the grin she had spreading across her face. "And that's Barry," she said, pointing at the other guy at the table who had broad shoulders and close-cropped brown hair. And who, mercifully, didn't look anything like the other two. "He's been friends with Preston and Clay since forever. He's back from college for the summer. He's on a football scholarship. Quarterback," she said, her voice ripe with emphasis, much to my confusion. Did I look like someone who cared about football? I was pretty sure I didn't.

"You know," she said, turning to me with a strange little smile pulling at her lips, "since you're here for the summer and Bear's here for the summer, maybe you two could go out sometime."

That was when my brain clicked back online and I realized I

had to make my escape. I could see where she was going with this and I wasn't about to let myself be led like a lamb to the slaughter of a summer full of bad blind dates. Quarterback or not, I was out of there. Before she could get another word out, I made my excuses, grabbed my stuff and tossed a twenty on my table—more than enough to cover my crappy BLT platter when I'd actually ordered a bacon cheeseburger in the first place—and hightailed it out of there before Lacey could stop me.

Unfortunately, my escape only got me as far as the parking lot where my getaway vehicle is refusing to start and sounds like an old woman with bronchitis and a three-pack-a-day habit. Fantastic.

I'm trying to decide whether screaming or crying would be a better option for venting my frustration before I freaking explode when there's a knock on the window next to me and my entire body jerks.

I whip around in my seat, heart slamming in my chest, and find the guy that Lacey had all but kicked out of the diner standing there, looking at me through the driver's-side window.

Great. Just great.

Ash

I fucked up. I know that.

But for some reason I hadn't expected it to follow me around for the rest of my life.

It's not like I've ever stopped thinking about it. It's hard not to, when your fuck-up costs another man his life. But I'd just assumed that when I got out of prison, it would be over.

It is never going to be over.

No one is ever going to let me forget what I've done.

What they don't seem to realize is that they don't have to bother. I've been living my mistake every single day for the past five years.

It had been stupid, so goddamn stupid, but by the time I'd figured that out, it had been too late. The guy was already dead.

Peter Hanlon-Wright. Father of a son with another baby on the way. His face is burned into my brain, and will be for the rest of my life.

I'd been out at a party that night. And like all the parties I went to back then, there had been booze and drugs everywhere. And if it was there, then so was I. I don't even remember the party itself, only that I'd been there with Gina, my girlfriend. Ex-girlfriend now. I can only remember flashes. Throwing back a beer. Doing a line. The flash of Gina's red hair as she tossed it over her shoulder. Bit by bit, I've tried to piece that night together for the past five years, only to realize that most of it is gone forever.

I'll never know why I chose to do what I did, why I snagged the keys to Gina's car and drove home, instead of crashing on the guy's sofa like Gina had. I don't know why I felt like I just had to get home, why I had to drive through three fucking towns instead of just sleeping it off in the backseat.

But I did. I don't even remember the drive, not really. But I remember the crash. The sound of metal on metal. The screams that I took forever to realize were actually coming from me.

The pain.

The flash of the lights from the police cruiser.

Bit by bit, piece by piece, it's like a goddamn puzzle laid out in front of me, but it's missing half the pieces and it doesn't match the picture on the box.

It doesn't seem right that a night you can barely remember can change your life forever, but apparently fair and right don't apply to a guy who killed a father because he was too drugged up and stupid to keep away from the wheel.

I let out a shaking breath and light my cigarette as I try to figure out what the hell I'm going to do.

No job. People in this town aren't going to give me a shot, and I can't blame them.

No home. Parents kicked me out. Living out of my car.

No girlfriend. Gina kicked me to the curb immediately after the crash. I was still in the hospital when she dumped my ass for good.

I'm fucked. No doubt about it.

I take another drag and lean back against the brick wall of the diner when all of a sudden the diner's front door flies open hard enough to send it slamming against the wall and a figure races out.

I watch as the girl I'd noticed—the really hot one with the long dark hair and the tattoos—rushes out of the diner like she's got a herd of raptors on her tail. She has a kind of ratty-looking bag thrown over her shoulder, and it bumps against her hip as she hustles across the parking lot. Toward the crappiest looking station wagon I've ever seen. The thing is ancient, and a fucking eyesore at best, all beige and peeling. My car isn't exactly in tip-top shape after five years in my parents' garage, but it's a damn sight better than that thing. It's a wreck.

The girl doesn't seem to notice or care, though. She just jerks open the door and throws her bag inside fast enough that I'm starting to wonder if she held up the joint or something. I smirk at the thought. It would serve them right. Also? If it was her, it would be kind of hot. All Thelma-and-Louise old school. Not that I watched that movie or anything. At least, not since I grew out of having TV night with my parents.

I lean back against the brick wall and take another drag from my cigarette, waiting for the girl to gun the engine and peel out of there like a bat out of hell. But instead of the epic getaway, the car just sort of...coughs.

Well, that was fucking anti-climactic, I think as I watch the girl's face fall and hear the car sputter again. Yeah, that's not good.

I watch her for a moment, see the flurry of emotions pass over her face as she realizes that her car isn't going anywhere. Hope. Confusion. Anger. Defeat. She glances back at the diner and I wonder just what made her want to book it out of there like that. I look over myself, glancing over my shoulder as I stub out the butt of my cigarette, and see the blonde peeking through the window. Ah, that makes sense.

I stand there for a moment, running the options through my mind, before I let out a sigh and push myself off the wall and make my way over to her.

What the fuck are you doing? A voice in the back of my brain asks. You weren't welcome in the diner, what makes you think you're going to be greeted with open arms when you approach her, you creeper? I tell the voice to shut the hell up and reach over and tap against the driver's-side window. The girl jerks like she's been electrocuted, and spins around to look at me.

This is such a huge mistake, the voice supplies, and I plaster on what I hope is a nonthreatening smile and motion for her to roll the window down. I sink my hands into my pockets and shift my weight around, because apparently five years in prison has completely killed every ounce of smoothness I ever had. But the girl rolls down the window, anyway, and I'm suddenly struck by the fact that I have no plan here, no idea what I'm going to do or say.

So, even though this is a horrible fucking idea, I blurt out the first thing that comes to my head.

"Car trouble?"

Luckily for me, it was the battery. Because, while auto shop was the only fucking class I stood a chance of passing in high school, I'm more than a little bit rusty. So the fact that the battery just needed a boost was a godsend. Seriously. One look under the hood almost sent me running for the hills, it was such a mess. I don't know what she's doing with that car, but it sure as hell isn't right. It would be merciful to take it out back and shoot it.

But of course, I'm not about to say that to the extremely hot girl, who is apparently the only person in Avenue who's willing to talk to me. Seriously, she's even hotter up close. It's criminal.

"Okay," I say, attaching the booster cables to the battery and pulling my head out from under the hood. I wipe my hands on my already-filthy jeans. Damn, I need to go to the laundromat. With what money, I'm not sure. The money Dad gave me isn't going to last much longer at this rate. "Give it a try."

I'm starting to wonder if staying in prison maybe wasn't a better life plan for me.

The car groans a little, but then the engine turns over and it hums back to life. I grin and remove the jumper cables, letting the hood fall back down with a slam. The girl's eyes widen and a smile breaks out across her face and something in my gut jerks.

Fuck off, I tell it. I've been in prison for five years. Of course seeing a hot girl smile at me is going to get me revving. She's not interested, jackass, I say to myself. *Maybe if you hadn't been such a fuck-up, you might've had a shot. But there's no way now. You're lucky she's even talking to you.*

She leans her head out the window, her long, inky black hair whipping around her face in the wind. "Thank you *so much*," she says, reaching out and taking the cables back from me before dumping them into the passenger foot well. "I don't know what I would have done if I couldn't get it to start."

I've seen pornos that start like this, my mind supplies helpfully, and all I want is to turn around and slam my head against the brick wall behind me. *Dumbass.*

"It's no problem," I say. "I mean, your engine's kind of fucked— *kind of broken*—" What is wrong with me? "So you might want to take it in for a tune-up when you get a chance. But that should keep you going for a bit." *Walk away,* I tell myself. *Just nod and walk the fuck away.*

"Seriously," she says, and I can tell that she's trying not to laugh at me. Which I would appreciate, if I didn't want to go bury my head in the sand for the rest of my life. "Thank you."

I just give her a nod and turn to walk back to my car. I love that damn car, but after living in it for a week, it's starting to lose a lot of its appeal. But I'm only a couple steps away when her voice rings out.

"Hey," she says, and I turn back. She jerks her cute little chin in my direction. "What's your name?"

"Ash," I tell her, reaching into my pockets for my pack of smokes.

"Ash Winthrope." I need something to do with my hands. But as I pull one out and stick it in my mouth, she's leaning out her car window, reaching a hand out to me to shake. "I'm Star," she says, and I can't help the startled laugh before it escapes.

"Of course you are," I say, and watch as her brow furrows adorably. I shake my head, a rush of heat traveling up my neck. "I mean . . . I don't know what I meant," I say, going for honesty when quick-thinking fails me once again. Story of my life. I reach out and shake her hand. It's warm and smooth and kind of tiny in mine, but it's stronger than I thought it would be. "I guess I meant it suits you," I say. "It's nice to meet you, Star."

The handshake goes on a little too long to be comfortable, and we both kind of laugh and drop our hands at once as soon as it gets a little too awkward. I'm left standing by her driver's-side door, shifting my weight from foot to foot, trying to figure out an escape route. Whatever game I once had has been completely erased in the past five years. Now I'm a spaz.

"Well," I say. "I guess I'll see you around, Star." And then I start making for my car again.

"Hey, Ash," she calls out, and I stifle a groan. I'm trying to make a fucking graceful exit here. Can't this girl see that?

"Look," she says, "I get this is kinda awkward, but I heard you talking to the waitress inside." She nods toward the diner. My most recent failure. Fan-fucking-tastic.

"Yeah," I say, and reach into my pocket for my lighter. I light my cigarette and take a drag, and try to resist the urge to fiddle with the lighter. Playing with a flame in a public place probably isn't going to endear me to the hot chick who clearly knows enough of my history to be wary of me. No wonder she'd looked so freaked out when I knocked on her window. Must have scared the life out of her. Shit.

"Listen, your history is your business. Not mine. I'm just wondering if you'd be willing to help me out with something."

Ah, shit. She's one of those girls. The ones that want to walk on the wild side without ever getting their own hands dirty. Crap.

"I'm not into that shit anymore," I tell her. "I'm clean now. Five years."

Her eyes widen and her mouth drops open a little. A beat passes, and I wonder if I should just sprint to my car. It couldn't be any more uncomfortable than what I'm dealing with right now. I glance over my shoulder and . . . yep. The blonde waitress I asked about a job is watching us from the front window of the diner. She's probably getting ready to call the cops if I hang around Star much longer. I need to get out of here.

"That's not what I meant!" Star yells, and I shuffle to a stop before I even realize I've moved. I'm halfway to my car. Well, it looks like the old fight-or-flight instincts are still intact. That's something. "Look," she says. "My mother just died and I'm cleaning out her house. But I can't do it by myself. I need help, and I can't afford to hire professionals. I can't pay much, but I just thought . . . "

I look back at her, and I'm surprised to see that she looks just as freaked out as I feel. But for once, her nerves don't seem to be caused by me. Something else is bothering the crap out of her, and I kind of want to throw my arms up in victory that it isn't me. I'm a bastard.

"Not to sound ungrateful . . . " I say, turning and taking a step back toward her car. I take another drag from my cigarette. I'm going to have to start rationing the damn things soon. Maybe quit altogether. Mom would like that, if she bothered to give a shit. She'd been after me to quit since I was a teenager. "But why me?"

Star's teeth worry at her lower lip, which only makes it look plumper and *fuck*. Not the time. Then she sighed and let her head flop back against the headrest. "My mother was a hoarder," she says, her voice so quiet I can barely hear her over the road noise and the jangling of the bells over the diner door as an old man and his grandson exit. The old man shoots me a bitter look when they walk by, and he keeps the kid on the other side of him, shielding him with his body. Yeah, like I'm going to attack a kid and an old man. In broad daylight. Jesus, people in this town are even more fucked up than they were five years ago.

Then Star's words niggle at something in the back of my mind. "A hoarder," I say. "Like those crazy people on that sho—"

"Yes," she snaps before I can get into all the weird crap I'm imagining, like layers upon layers of dead animals crushed under broken lamps and half-full bags of cat food. Then she sighs again, and lets go of the steering wheel she'd been holding in a death grip to press the heels of her hands into her eyes. When her hands drop back down, I can see that *this* is what's bothering her. And it's bothering her enough to ask me for help, a guy she knows just got out of prison.

Fuck. And *I* thought I had problems.

I'm still weighing it in my mind—the desire to eat and maybe one day having an actual roof over my head versus digging through a garbage dump—but my mouth is already moving and words are escaping without my permission. "How much?"

"Like I said, I can't pay much," she says. "Not even minimum wage. I could manage maybe five–six hundred a month."

A *month?* How long is this gonna take? How big of a mess can one person create? I'm still thinking about it, rolling the idea over and over in my head when she turns around in her seat and starts digging in the purse on the passenger seat. I lean forward, arm braced against the car, curious. Then she's turning back and shoving a crumpled piece of paper through the open window. I grab it. "That's my number," she says. "You can think about it if you want, but I'm going to be getting started right away. I need to get this done by the end of the summer, and I'd really appreciate the help. That is, if you're willing."

I stare down at the phone number scrawled across the slip of paper, at the little scribble underneath that could only be an address, and then I look up at her. Her eyes are all big and brown and earnest as fuck. What the hell is this girl thinking?

"You *do* know about me, don't you?" I ask, and try to pass her the piece of paper back through the car window. "Like, you're not under any delusions or anything, right? I just got out of prison. Aren't you worried I'll get in there and start stealing shit?"

Star stares at me for a moment, completely still. Then she throws her head back and laughs, and goddamn if it isn't the hottest fucking thing I've seen in five years. She just shoves the phone number back at me. "If you steal anything, I'll be eternally fucking grateful, you have no idea" she says, and my gut jerks again at the sound of her cursing at me. She's already a gorgeous chick with kick-ass tattoos and the cutest fucking smile I've seen in years. How she just got hotter, I have no idea. "Just keep the number, okay?" she asks. "And give me a call when you make up your mind."

"What if I can't help you out?" I ask.

She just shakes her head and smiles at me. "Either way," she says. "Just let me know." Then she reaches out and wraps her right arm around the back of the passenger seat to watch behind her, and pulls out of the parking spot.

She's down the road before I can think of anything to say to that. I take another puff of my smoke and stare down at the phone number in my hand. It's a little crumpled, so I grip the cigarette between my lips and use both hands to smooth out the paper against the leg of my jeans. I fold it up and stick it in my pocket, and look up to see the blonde waitress still watching me through the window. I give her a smirk and a little wave—one I'm dying to turn into a one-finger salute, but somehow manage to restrain myself—and head back to my car.

I have some shit to think about.

Chapter 4

Star

I wasn't really expecting Ash to call me. Not really. And when I hadn't heard from him by the time I left my mother's house and got back to the B&B that night, I just kind of let go of the idea altogether and powered off my phone and went to bed.

When I turn my phone back on in the morning, there's still no word from him. The only new messages are from my roommate, Autumn. She'd gone out with our friend Roth last night and had kept up a running commentary of the experience via text that I had missed while I'd been asleep.

Autumn: Drinking with R. I miss you!!!! He's the slowest.
Autumn: Worst dirnking buddy EVER!
Autumn: *drinking

Autumn: Oooooh. Cute boy. Glasses. Geeky t-shirt.

Autumn: I'm in love.

Autumn: OK I'm gonna go talk to him. Liquid courage is a beautiful thing.

Autumn: OK. Gonna do it. Wish me luck.

Autumn: Damnnn. Cute boy turned me down. Heartbroken.

Autumn: I'm gonna be single forever.

Autumn: I'm gonna have to get so many cats. I don't even like cats.

Autumn: Will you be a spoinster wit me?

Autumn: *spinster. *with.

Autumn: OMG!!!! Cute boy is gay! He's eyeing up Roth! It's like the movies!!!!

Autumn: I must watch this FOREVER. *chinhands*

Autumn: Awwwwww. He's so bumbling. Ther'e's blushing. It's SO CUTE!

Autumn: ROTH HAS NO IDEA!!!

Autumn: He's all like WHAT IS HAPPENING RIGHT NOW?!!

Autumn: Favorite things everrrr!

Autumn: If cute boy is successful, I will carry their babies.

Autumn: Cute boy bought Roth a drink and he STILL HASN'T FIGURED IT OUT!

Autumn: WHY AREN'T YOU HEREEE? WE NEED TO DIS-CUSS THIS!!!

Autumn: Fucckkkk. Cute boy has given up. Roth is uselessss!

Roth: I have discovered that Autumn has been updating you with the travesty that is my attempts at socialization.

Roth: Please disregard everything she has told you. She's intoxicated.

Autumn: Roth's a lying liar that lies.

Autumn: I'm finsa;sdfhina;

I laugh and started typing out a reply to Autumn.

Star: I'm sorry I missed it, darling.
Star: You'll have to save your womb for a more worthy opponent.

Then I send one to Roth.

Star: You need to be more aware of your surroundings.
Star: Please make sure Autumn has lots of water and tell her to call me later.

I really am sorry I'd missed it. I love going out with Autumn, but Roth was another animal all together. He'd been our RA last year, when I was a freshman at Climbfield College. So while we saw him all the time and eventually we became friends, we weren't able to actually hang out with him all that much. There were rules he had to follow as an RA. The first and foremost of which was *No Touching Your Charges*. It's hard to hang out with someone when you're expressly forbidden from touching them. So getting to go out with him is new and is actually a lot more fun than I'd expected. He's like the lovechild of a confused puppy and emotionless robot, so seeing him in any kind of social situation is nothing short of fabulous. It sucks that I slept through it.

I've been going to sleep a lot earlier since I've gotten into town. Surprisingly early, really. I'm a college student. I'm used to late nights. But I'd been under a lot of stress lately, what with school and all. And that had been *before* I'd seen the state of my mother's house.

I let out a groan and flop back against the pillows, shifting around on the mattress, trying to get comfortable. Which is an impossible task, apparently. This isn't the Ritz Carlton. This is a shitty B&B in the middle of nowhere, but it had been my only choice. I hadn't had the car when I arrived. The car was my mother's. I'd taken the bus into town.

It is so strange. When I got into town, all I had was my duffel bag, and except for a few things I left with Autumn for the summer, that is pretty much everything I own, which is a pretty big departure from what my mother had built for herself.

From what she'd buried herself under, my brain supplies, but I shake the thought off before it can fully take root.

I don't know if whatever causes people to start hoarding is genetic or learned or ingrained or what. All I know is that ever since I was nine and I was taken away from my mother, I've been doing everything I can to make sure I never *ever* end up like her.

I sigh and press the palms of my hands against my face, blocking out the light that's streaming through the dusty floral curtains.

God, I don't want to go back to the house. It is too much. I've been working on it for days, and I haven't even made a dent.

It takes me ages to get out of bed. Part of me wants to stop at the diner for a big breakfast, but I don't want to risk seeing Lacey again. Not so soon. I know she saw me talking to Ash yesterday, and after the things she said about him, I can only imagine what she'd have to say about me talking to him, let alone trying to hire him. So instead of the diner, I just fill the biggest disposable cup I can find with coffee, and grab as many bagels as I can out of the basket that has been set out on the breakfast bar downstairs. I wrap them in napkins, shove them deep into my bag and hightail it out of there before the owner, the creepy Miss Josephine, catches me. I have no doubt that if she caught me in the act that she'd order me to put them back.

Thoughts of Miss Josephine scolding me dance through my head as I drive across town to the house. She'd set her poodle on me. For sure. I smile as I turn down the tree-lined street and pull into the driveway. But as I do, something catches my eye, and my smile falls away.

There's a red car sitting at the curb.

It's Ash's car.

And he's standing outside, leaning back against it, smoking a cigarette.

I'm a little freaked out, but despite what my gut is telling me—to just shift the car into Reverse and pull back out and drive away—I let out a deep breath and turn off the car. I squeeze my eyes shut for a brief moment, shake off the discomfort and grab my bag from the passenger seat. I slide out of the car.

"I didn't think you were going to show," I call out to Ash as I slam the car door behind me. I clutch the keys in my fingers, letting the metal bite into my palm as I make my way across the grass to where he's standing. "You didn't call." He nods and takes a last puff of his cigarette before dropping it and putting it out with his shoe.

"Yeah," he says as I get close. "Sorry about that. My phone crapped out on me." His pale eyes dart up to meet mine before dropping back to the ground. "Is the job still available?"

I chew on my lip and glance over my shoulder at the house. From the outside, it looks almost normal. It's run down, that's for sure. It's by far the most run down house on the block. But it doesn't look *bad* from the outside. Just like it's fallen into dis-repair.

He has no idea what he's getting into.

I turn back to him, and my heart stutters a bit. He's looking up at me through his lashes. He looks so hopeful. So sad.

Shit. Something inside me lurches. This is such a bad idea. "Look," I say. "Here's the thing. The house . . . it's a mess. I don't know what you're thinking, but I'm going to lay it out for you."

I let out a breath, and I want to kick myself. I'm shaking like a leaf. This is so stupid. It's not my mess. Not really. I didn't make it. It's been thrust upon me to deal with. But still, I feel guilty somehow. Ashamed. Responsible. Like I'm going to be judged and that people are going to think badly of me for it.

Is this what my mother felt, when she thought about her house? Her mess?

Why is this so hard?

"It can't be that bad . . . " Ash says, and it's clear that he's about to continue, so I cut him off before he can get another word out, because he has to know what he's up against before he agrees to anything.

"My mother was a hoarder." The words spill out of me in a rush. "So picture the worst-case scenario that you can possibly think of waiting for you behind that front door, and then multiply it by a thousand, and you'll start getting close to reality." I pull in a deep breath and continue before he can say anything. "So if you don't want to do this, that's fine. Just tell me. No hard feelings. But I asked you because I need help, and if what happened at the diner is anything to go by, your job hunt isn't going so well."

He looks at me for a moment, without saying anything, and I can practically see the wheels turning in his head as he processes what I've just told him. Then he shoves his hands into the pockets of his jacket, even though it's already about a million degrees outside, and takes a step forward.

"I'm in." He says. I raise my eyebrows at him, surprised.

"Just like that?" I ask, because nothing in my life has been that easy. But he gives me a nod.

"Just like that."

I regard him for a second, taking in his slumped posture and his ratty clothes. He's doing about as well as I am, which isn't good. Maybe together we can get a little bit better. Maybe.

"Okay," I say, and hold up the keys for him to see them. "Let me show you the house."

I make it all the way to the front door before my bravado fails me. The knowledge of what's lurking behind that door weighs on my stomach like a ball of lead. I can't believe I'm showing this to another human being. But what I said to him was as true as anything I've ever told anyone in my entire life. I need the help.

I turn to him. "Are you *sure* you want to do this?" I ask.

"Look," he says, pulling his hands out of his pockets and scrubbing them over his face. He looks tired. Even more tired than I feel. That's saying something. "You saw what happened at the diner. That's just the tip of it. I don't know if you know the story, but everyone around here does, so there's no point in me trying to keep it a secret. I fucked up. I went to a party one night a couple towns over. I got high as fuck and I drove home. I killed a guy." He stops there for a moment, like he's waiting for me to respond, but I've already heard it from Lacey, so I stay silent and just nod, and he lets his breath out in a huff and continues. "Like I said, I fucked up. A guy died and I went to prison. I just got out, and no one will touch me with a fucking hundred-foot pole.

"So yeah," he says. "I'm sure. Right now five hundred a month and maybe someone to vouch for me at the end? That sounds pretty damn good."

"Are you *sure?*" The words are out of my mouth again before I can stop them, and I want to kick myself, I'm so embarrassed. I can already feel the heat flooding my face, but luckily a tiny smile tugs at the corner of his mouth and he nods.

"Yeah," he says. "I'm extremely fucking sure. What do you want from me? A fucking pinkie swear or something?" He actually swipes his hand against his jeans and lifts it to me, pinkie held out in my direction.

I laugh, I can't help it. It's the wrong hand, the left one, so it's a song and dance for me to juggle the keys and my bag, but I hold out my own left pinkie to him in response. We link them together and waggle them back and forth a bit before it gets awkward. Then we laugh and let go, our hands dropping back down to our sides.

"Well, okay then," I say, and slide the key into the lock. "I guess we have a deal. But don't say I didn't warn you, okay?"

Ash just smiles, and this time it's a real one, teeth and everything. It's a good look on him.

"Got it."

Ash

Star . . . was not kidding about the mess. This place is fucking ridiculous. Who the hell lives like this?

I mean, yeah, my room was a pigsty growing up, but compared to *this?* Holy shit. No wonder this girl wants help. She needs help. Hell, she needs a freaking army to get this done.

And all she has is me.

That sucks.

I think I actually feel worse for her than I do for myself right now, and that's saying something.

"So . . . " I say, looking past her as she holds open the door to the house so I can see what I'm up against. "Where...where do we start?" Please let this girl have some kind of plan, because I've got nothing. I don't even know where to start. There's barely even enough of a path for me to get into the house. And the path that's there seems to taper off into piles of stuff after less than a dozen feet. The piles inside are taller than I am.

Star just kind of sighs and reaches inside the door. I'm half hoping that she's reaching for a can of gasoline and a lighter, that her plan is just to burn the place to the ground. As much as it would violate my parole, I'm kind of tempted. Not *really*, but shit. This place is insane. How the hell did this end up on Star's shoulders? Other than having a shitty car—which I'm starting to think isn't actually her fault, and that it has something to do with this whole house situation—she seems like a pretty normal girl. She was nice enough to take a chance on me, and I am more than grateful for that, so whatever her plan is, I am *in*. But instead of pulling out a jerry can, she straightens back up with a couple boxes of garbage bags in her arms. They must have been tucked just inside the front door. They'd have to be, any farther in and they'd be lost forever in the hoard.

Before she can ask, I reach out and gently take the boxes out of her arms.

"Thanks," she says, and reaches up to run her hands through her hair, shoving it back from her face. Then she sighs again. I'm getting the feeling she's been kind of emotional lately, that she's been bottling everything up inside and it just keeps escaping bit by bit in sighs and nervous laughter. "Look," she says. "I don't even think we'll get to the house today. I think we need to start in the backyard."

The backyard? Ah fuck, is there *more?*

"The backyard?" I ask, hoping I'm wrong. But she just kind of smiles at me, and the smile doesn't quite reach her eyes.

Crap. There's more.

The backyard is nearly as packed as the house is. It's not stacked as high, but the entire lot is *covered*. And as far as I can tell, unlike inside the house, where every here and there I'd been able to pick something out visually that might actually be *worth* something, the backyard is just garbage. Garbage upon garbage upon garbage, as far as the eye can see. Somewhere, my neat freak of a mother is having a mental breakdown and she has no idea why.

Suddenly the Dumpster out front makes so much sense. But as I look at the mess in front of me, and think back to the Dumpster, all I can think is *it's not going to fit.*

"Now you see my problem," Star says, and I turn to look at her. She's perched on the edge of the porch—which is, itself, covered in enough junk that I'm actually seriously worried that it's going to give out under the weight and take her down with it. She takes a step down, moving toward me. "I know it's a lot of work, and I won't blame you if you hightail it out of here, but I can really use the help. I need to sell this place by the end of the summer, or I'm screwed."

She's standing next to me just as I manage to swallow down my instinctive response of *I hear arson can be fun,* because as much as I can use the money she's offering, this is . . . It's too much. But as I turn to look at her, all I can see is the way her face is already falling, like she can tell what I want to say.

I'm an asshole.

I let out a breath and look around, trying to convince myself it's not as bad as it looks. After a moment, I almost believe it. And I don't know if it's the look on her face or the fact that I need the money to *live,* but I find myself holding out my pinkie—first just like I did earlier.

"Like I told you earlier, I'm in," I say, and link my finger with hers.

Her smile? Is fucking blinding.

So I do the only thing I can. I shrug off my coat and get to work.

Star

I have to hand it to Ash; he is a hard worker. Like, he's a really hard worker. Actually, that doesn't even come close to covering it. The guy worked his ass off. And, mercifully, he didn't complain *once.*

I had seen the look on his face when he first saw the inside of the house. He'd been floored. And as we'd gone through the garbage in the backyard, I could tell just how disgusted he was. But he'd kept quiet about it. He just . . . worked. Picked up a box of garbage bags, asked me if there was anything he should keep an eye out for, and when I shook my head, he just pulled out a bag and shook it out. Then he started filling it up.

After a few minutes, though, we realized that the garbage bag plan wasn't the best one. The entire yard was littered with so much stuff, that it just wasn't feasible to bag it all. So instead, after the first half-dozen bags, we switched methods and started hauling the big stuff into the Dumpster. Waterlogged boxes, huge piles of lawn furniture that had been left out so long it was all broken and faded by the weather. Christmas decorations, most of which were star-themed, which killed me a little bit, were dragged away and dumped. But bit by bit, the piles began to shrink. Hours later, when the sun is just starting to dip, I call it a day and we head inside to wash the worst of the grime off. And that's an adventure in itself, because it's not like the bathroom was miraculously spared from the hoard.

Afterward, finally, we step out onto the porch together, and I close the front door behind us and slide the key into the lock.

"Well," he says, pulling his jacket back on even though it is still really warm outside. "Is it cool if I come back tomorrow?"

I boggle at him. Is this guy *serious?* I was ready to just hand him a twenty and hope for the best.

"Dude," I say, so relieved I'm almost ready to cry. "Of course. You worked your butt off. Of course you can come back."

"So I've got the job?" he asks, but I can already see the grin he's trying to smother as it pulls at the side of his mouth. His eyes meet mine, and I can't help but laugh.

"Oh, shut up," I tell him. "You know you do." And he honestly did. Between the two of us, we must have hauled three or four dozen bags of garbage to the curb, all of them stuffed full to the brim, and put even more than that into the Dumpster. There had just been so much stuff. It had been everywhere, all over the backyard. Bins and boxes, covered with tarps that weren't doing anything to protect them from the elements. Nearly everything that my mother had stored out there had been destroyed by rain and dirt and god knows what else.

It was heartbreaking. I don't even know how long things have been like this. Had the stuff she'd been storing back there gotten to that state of disarray and decay while she was still alive? For all I know, it could have been out there for *years*.

But, together, we'd managed to haul out a good chunk of it. Not a huge amount, not enough for the backyard to be even close to clear enough for me to use it as a sorting area, like my plan had been, but it was still a whole lot better than it had been before. And it was so much more than I could have done in one day on my own. Hell, to be honest, it was more than I could have done on my own in a week.

"Well, I guess I'll see you tomorrow," he says, and pulls one of his hands out of the pocket and gives me a little wave. "Same time work for you?"

"Are you kidding?" I ask. I know this guy's been through some shit, but this is ridiculous. "Get in the car, Ash. I'm taking you for dinner."

"You . . . what?" He's looking at me like I've grown another head. Possibly one that belonged to a lizard. "What are you talking about?"

"Dinner." I say the word slowly, but I smile to let him know I'm teasing him. "Din-*ner*. The last meal of the day. I'm buying you dinner."

"Why?"

"Because you worked really, really hard, dude," I say, starting to get exasperated. "And you offered to come back. And because we didn't even stop for lunch. I don't know about you, but I'm *starving.*"

"But . . . we had lunch."

"No," I say. "We had a couple of crappy bagels that I swiped from the B&B's breakfast buffet. They were dry and gross. Would not recommend. What I want is a big, greasy cheeseburger. So are you going to get in the car, or are you going to follow me in yours?"

It took a lot more cajoling than I expected, but I eventually got Ash into my mother's old station wagon. I figured that way if it crapped out on me again, I'd have him there with me, at least, until I dropped him back at the house for him to pick up his car.

I don't think he realized what my plan was until I turned into the diner's parking lot.

"Uh . . . I don't think this is a good plan," he says as I pull into a parking space right by the front door.

But I just turn off the engine and pull the key out of the ignition. "Come on," I say. "We're going inside."

"No," he snaps, and I kind of jerk in my seat at his tone. I look up at him, and the anger just bleeds right out of his face right in front of me. He sighs and scrubs both of his hands over his face. "Fuck. Sorry," he says. "It's not your fault. I just . . . This is a *really* bad idea. I'm not exactly welcome in there."

"Look," I unbuckle my seat belt and turn in my seat to face him straight on. "I heard what they said to you. But the way I figure it, you have two options here. You either hide yourself away until your parole ends and you can start over somewhere else, or you *make* these people accept you." He's not looking at me. He's just sort of staring off into space. I reach out and hesitantly place my hand on his arm. He doesn't move.

"Why are you doing this?" he asks.

"What do you mean?"

"I killed someone," he says. "I got high as fuck and I killed someone." He squeezes his eyes shut and his head smacks back against the headrest hard enough that it actually looks like it hurts. "And you're just here. Why are you even here? Why aren't you just like everyone else?"

"Look, you messed up," I say. "Bad. I'm not going to pretend like you didn't. But you've served your time, and you're stuck living here until your parole is up. You're trying to do the right thing." I rub my hand against the sleeve of his jacket. *"Illegitimi non carborundum."*

That got his attention. He opens his eyes and looks at me. *Ah, there was the why are you suddenly a lizard-person look again.*

"What. The. Fuck?"

I can't help it. I throw my head back and laugh. One day, one single day of having his help has made the weight I've been carrying on my shoulders feel about fifty pounds lighter. *"Illegitimi non carborundum,"* I say, and shimmy out of my hoodie, which is not an easy trick when you're sitting in the driver's seat of a car. The steering wheel is kind of unforgiving, but finally I manage to get it off. I stretch out my right arm and twist it so that the back of my lower arm, and the dark script that runs down the bone there, is directly in front of him. "Don't let the bastards grind you down."

With a tentative hand, Ash reaches out to touch, but then his fingers stop a hairbreadth away from my skin. "Can I?" he asks, and I nod.

"Of course."

His touch is soft, and it's only there for a second. But he swipes down the words, and I have to stifle a shiver that threatens to run down my spine. "You're a weird girl," he tells me as I pull my arm back, and I smile.

"I'm very aware of that," I tell him. "Now get out of the fucking car. I want a burger."

This time, instead of waiting for him to argue, I tug on my hoodie and hop out of the car.

And mercifully, he follows.

To be honest, dinner could have gone better—we both could have done without the wide-eyed stares from the other patrons—but it definitely could have gone worse. At least Lacey and the waitress that kept giving me dirty looks weren't there. Instead we had a young guy with skinny hips and what looked like purposeful-ly-styled bedhead as our waiter, and though his eyes widened a little when he saw us slide into a booth, he didn't say anything.

I made a point to glance at his name tag when he actually managed to be polite, as opposed to Lacey and that that blonde mean-looking waitress. According to the little plastic tag pinned to his shirt, his name was York, and from the looks of it, it was only him and a heavily-pregnant girl with thick-framed black glasses working that day. And York was doing most of the run-ning around since the girl seemed to be staying put behind the cash counter as much as possible. I didn't blame her. Especially when I saw just how much effort it took for her to pull herself up off the stool back there. But even when some of the other custom-ers were rude to her, calling out for her to hurry it up with their drinks, she didn't utter a single complaint the entire time we were there.

Tough cookie.

We got a few strange side-eyed looks from the other patrons, but unlike the one from the other morning, they stayed silent. Ash looked like he was about to bolt out the front door when we initially sat down, but as time passed, his shoulders slowly began to unhunch themselves and he started to relax.

And by the time our food came, he was leaning back in his seat and actually smiling.

Like I said, it was a good look on him.

Ash

"Well . . . " I trail off as Star pulls the car to a stop in the driveway. I don't know what to say. *Thanks for dinner? Thanks for the job? Thanks for putting up with all the fucking gawkers at the diner? Thanks for not letting me be a complete asshole to you?* I've got nothing.

I used to be smoother than this. I fucking know I was. But all the words are caught in my throat. Jesus. What is wrong with me? The silence between us gets longer and longer to the point where it's so awkward I'm shifting in my seat like a five year old. I want to just mutter *thanks* and then make a break for it, but somehow I don't think that's going to leave the impression I want.

Star glances over at me, and she must see how uncomfortable I am, because she just shakes her head and laughs. "It's okay, Ash," she says, and pulls the keys from the ignition, turning in the driver's seat to face me. "How about this?" She reaches out and offers me her hand to shake. "Thanks for your hard work. I hope you enjoyed your dinner. Hopefully I'll see you tomorrow."

I kind of stare at her outstretched hand for a minute before I manage to shake myself out of my haze. I reach out and clasp her small hand in mine, pumping it up and down twice before dropping it like it's on fire.

Seriously. I *really* used to be smoother than this.

"Thanks," I say. "Ugh, you, too." And then I'm up and out of the car, booking it down the driveway before I can fuck this up any further. I'm pretty sure I can hear Star chuckling to herself as I slide into my car, but I hope it's just her crap car sputtering back to life. I sit in my car and wait as she turns the station wagon back on and pulls back down the driveway. I wait for her to drive down the street, headlights disappearing at the turn, before I let out the breath I've been holding for what feels like forever. "Jesus Christ," I mutter, and let my head drop forward against the steering wheel. Why haven't I thought this far ahead? I can't keep this hidden for much longer. She is bound to figure it out eventually.

I have nowhere to go.

I've been driving my car around Avenue for days, trying to find the perfect spot to spend the night, but in a town as small as this one, it isn't like there are a shit-ton of options. People are going to start noticing. Star is going to notice. And how long am I going to be able to keep the job, as crappy as it is, if she finds out that I am such a fuck-up that I don't have anywhere to live?

At this point, I'm just lucky I don't stink.

With a groan and a muttered *"fuck,"* I stick the keys into the ignition and start up the car. I'm half tempted to just park it in the driveway and sleep there, but Star's mom's house is in a nice neighborhood. My car would stick out like a sore thumb, no matter how much junk we dragged to the curb. With my luck, I would end up getting towed while I was still asleep in the back.

For the millionth time since the crash, I wish I'd somehow managed to grow up to be less of a fuck-up. I wish I'd actually listened to the people who'd told me to smarten up. Maybe then things would have gone differently.

Maybe then I wouldn't be such a fucking loser. I've sunk so low that half the friends I'd had won't even let me couch-surf—and I'd very nearly gotten down on my knees and *begged*—and the other half I haven't bothered with because if my parole officer found out I'd been talking to them, well…it wouldn't be good. But then it wouldn't be good if he found out I was living out of my car, either. Fuck, I *really* need this job.

I drive until I come to the old thrift store just on the edge of town. It's too out in the open, and I know I should keep looking for a better spot, but I'm completely exhausted and I just can't make myself look any longer. I pull into the parking lot, and drive around until I find a spot mostly in the shadows, and park the car. With a sigh, I shut off the engine and wait until everything has gone silent before I turn to look over my shoulder at the backseat.

It's a good thing that Star didn't get a close look at my car, I realize. Because I still have my blanket and pillow back there—snagged from my room when Mom finally relented enough to let me inside to get the last of my stuff—and it's pretty clear what I've been using it for.

With a sigh, I climb over the center console and settle into the backseat, where I lie in the dark and wonder how the fuck my life ended up this way until I finally fall asleep.

Chapter 5

Star

I've managed to make it through just over half my breakfast unscathed when Lacey slides into the booth across from me. She does it so suddenly I actually flinch when I see her sitting there. The girl is like a freaking magician. She's just lucky that my fight-or-flight instincts didn't take over. If they had, the coffee I was holding would have ended up all over her crisp white T-shirt before either of us could blink. I'd been hoping that her whole lecture on the evils of Ash had ended the other day, but by the look on her face, I'd gotten my hopes up for nothing. I glance down longingly at my breakfast plate, empty save for the three slices of overcooked bacon and the last slice of toast.

Damn, I think as she pins me with a look. *So close.*

"What the ever-loving hell is wrong with you, Star?" she says and I cringe. Her voice is so shrill, it's like nails on a chalkboard.

Be cool, I tell myself. Chances are, she's talking about my deal with Ash—which is probably all over town by now, considering just how avidly people had been watching us over the last day and a half—but there's always a chance she could be referring to something else. And since I'm not about to start digging my own grave here, I just paste an innocent look on my face and kind of blink at her, like I'm confused.

I'm not confused.

"What do you mean?" I ask, and I suddenly find myself wishing that I'd bothered to take drama in high school, instead of avoiding it like the plague. Maybe then I'd be a more convincing liar. Well, not *liar,* exactly. Not yet, anyway.

Either way, she isn't fooled. I watch, trying to keep a reaction off my face as Lacey lets out the most dramatic sigh ever made by a human being over the age of five and kind of flops down on the table between us, folding her arms over her head like she's building herself a cocoon. Either she took drama, or this is just some kind of hold-over from when we were little. I'm having flashbacks of the second grade, of us playing in the sandbox together. I remember building lopsided sand castles, and then Lacey, with her tiny blond pigtails blowing in the breeze, acting as though the world were ending because I wouldn't be a princess with her. Because every castle needed a princess apparently. In my defense, who the hell would want to be a princess when they could be a dragon instead? I know I wouldn't. Second-grade Lacey hadn't agreed with my logic back then, so, judging by what is happening in front of me as I calmly drain the last of my coffee, I'm not holding out a ton of hope she'll be swayed by my argument now.

I'd just assumed she'd grown out of using hysterics to make her point—I was wrong.

I look around the diner, frantically. I'm going to need way more coffee for this discussion. The middle-aged blonde waitress from the other day is back, but when I try to flag her down as she passes by, she just glares down her nose at me and keeps walking.

Yep, I think. *Word has definitely gotten around.* That would explain the death glares she's been giving me all morning. But then again, it wasn't like she'd been super friendly to me before Ash and I met, either. Maybe she is just an angry person. Could be.

You'd better cool it with the looks, lady. I think as she walks past me. *Your tip is rapidly dwindling down to nothing.* I turn a little in my seat and shoot her a glare of my own as soon as I see her back is turned, smiling a little when she disappears into the kitchen, and I know I've gotten away with it. At this point, I'll take any victory I can get, no matter how insignificant. I turn back to Lacey, and instantly regret it. She's left the private sanctuary of her arm-cocoon and is gazing at me with huge, almost cartoon-like eyes, like I've betrayed her somehow.

I sigh and gaze down at my empty mug. I definitely need more coffee for this.

"Why, Star?" she asks, her voice cutting through the quiet din of the diner with way more force than necessary. I have to bite down on my own tongue to stop myself from telling her to keep it down. People are already turning to look. Great. Just what I need. More attention. "Why would you talk to him after what he did?"

I pick at the last of my bacon, which is yet another disappointment in itself. They make it way too crispy here. It's almost charred. I shrug and pop a piece in my mouth, anyway, but I've timed it badly and I'm stuck trying to chew like crazy to get it down while the blonde waitress makes another round. I'm not being at all subtle in my attempts to flag her down, but with my mouth occupied all I can do is wave in her direction. Which I'm *doing*. I've got nearly my entire arm flapping about, but even though I *know* she can see me, she still doesn't come over. Instead she just stares at my arm like *it* has now managed to offend her delicate sensibilities somehow, and turns on her heel and walks away.

Swallowing the last of my bacon, I sigh and slump down in my seat, defeated. I'm never going to get out of here. The service here is terrible, especially with the blonde in charge. I miss the waiter from last night, the one with the hipster jeans. He at least acknowledged my existence, even though he looked like he'd been ready to bolt like a frightened deer at a single movement from Ash.

The blonde waitress disappears into the kitchen yet again, taking the full carafe of coffee with her. *And there goes the rest of your tip*, I think and turn back to Lacey. I have to stifle a groan at the sight of her. Apparently ignoring her little outburst just made things worse. She's managed to get herself so worked up now that there are actual *tears* shining in her eyes. Is this what I left behind when I went into foster care? Dealing with a spoiled brat? Child protective services outdid themselves, if that was the case. Because I'm pretty sure that if I had to grow up with her, one or both of us would be dead by now.

Lacey reaches out and grabs the hand I'd laid down on the table and pins me with a look, her fingers digging into mine. "Don't you realize how dangerous that guy is?"

Ugh, I think. *And that's enough of that*. I can't help rolling my eyes this time, and I shake her hand off as gently as I can before leaning back in my seat and crossing my arms over my chest. "Look,

Lacey," I say, trying to choose my words carefully. Very carefully. I don't want any further dramatics. I just don't have the energy for them today. "No offense or anything, but really? Just stop. I have a million things to worry about right now, and Ash isn't one of them. So thanks for the advice, but I'm good. And quite frankly, this is none of your business. This is between Ash and I."

She opens her mouth to protest, but I cut her off before she can get a word out. I'm done. I'm done with the looks and the tall tales and whatever else the people of Avenue want to dole out like candy on Halloween. I'm done.

"Seriously," I say, my voice firm. "None of your business."

We sit there in silence, kind of glaring at each other across the table. It's like something out of one of those Old West movies, like we're facing off at high noon, waiting to see who will blink first.

Luckily for both of us, today is my day, and Lacey's the one that falters.

"Fine," she says, rolling her eyes and hauling herself out of her seat. "I need to get to work, anyway." She's already a few steps away from the table, having tossed her long blond hair over her shoulder in what I'd been hoping was a sign that our conversation was over, when she stops and whirls back around. "But just so you know," she says, "when you wake up dead in a Dumpster some-where, I'll be expecting an apology. A good one."

Oh, sweetie, I shake my head as she flounces off toward the back of the diner and disappears through the door marked *Employees Only. I don't think you thought that sentence through.*

I wait until I'm certain she's not going to come back out to make an amendment to her final words before I turn back to what's left of my breakfast. Shoving the last bites into my mouth, I reach into my purse to check the time on my phone. I've got half an hour before I'm supposed to meet Ash at the house, so I make a quick decision and tug the plastic-covered menu from its resting place behind the ketchup bottle. I flip it open. Since I don't know if we'll be stopping work for lunch, I figure I might as well get Ash something for breakfast. I don't want him to die of hunger midway through the job, and honestly, I feel a little bad for how people keep talking about him behind his back. Besides, the breakfast sandwich looks good, and if he doesn't eat it, I will.

This time, when the blonde waitress walks by, I don't give her a chance to ignore me. As soon as she steps close enough, I reach out and grab her arm. My grip isn't hard, but it's enough to stop her in her tracks. She seems genuinely startled for a second, but then that passes and she shoots me a disgusted look, like *how dare you touch me, you peon*, which is pretty rich considering it's coming from a middle-aged waitress at a crappy diner. But I drop my hand, anyway. *Sorry, lady*, I think. *But if you're rude to me, I'm gonna be rude to you.*

"Can I get the breakfast sandwich please? To go?" I ask. "And the bill," I add quickly, because if I let her go now, she's never going to come back again. At this rate, I'll be lucky if she doesn't hurl both the sandwich and the bill at my head from a distance, judging by the look Leslie—as her name tag reads—is giving me. *Yeah, you're not getting a tip.*

"Fine," she snaps, reaching down and snatching the menu off the table like she's afraid I'm going to use it for evil and keep adding things to my order just to piss her off. Honestly? I'm tempted. "Will that be all?"

She's got such a sour look on her face, I can't help it. I start to grin. I prop my elbows up on the edge of the table and rest my chin on my folded hands and smile at her sweetly. "Yep," I say. "That'll about do me." *You're lucky I don't report you to your manager, you hateful woman,* I want to say. *You're in a service industry. Service means not being a witch to your customers.* But I keep my mouth shut, and just keep smiling at her, even though my face is starting to hurt. Because it seems to piss her off even more.

"Fine," she says, and turns on her heel and stalks away. Just before she gets out of earshot, though, I hear her mutter, "Inked-up little brat," and I can't stop the loud snort that escapes me.

Seriously? That's her problem? My tattoos? I glance down at my arms. Other than the line of Latin that runs down the back of my right forearm and the names on the sides of my fingers, none of my tattoos are even visible. They're all under my clothes, and even then, there's nothing offensive about them. And, come on, this is a diner. It's not like I showed up at church during Easter Mass with full sleeves on display. I don't even have sleeve tattoos.

Well, I think, letting my grin fade into a smirk and tilting my head forward so I can hide it behind my curtain of dark hair. *Why don't we fix that?* I reach into my purse and uncap the black permanent marker I've been using to label boxes at the house. Then, holding out my left arm and resting it on the tabletop, I grip the marker as steadily as I can. And then I get to work.

Ash

I've only been at the house a few minutes when Star pulls into the driveway. She's out of the car, dark hair swinging around her shoulders, and as I watch her walk toward where I'm sitting on the front porch, I wonder if I should mention the package right away or if I should wait. Luckily, her eyes zero in on it before I have to decide.

"It has your name on it," I tell her. "I'm not an expert or any-thing, but if it matters, I'm pretty sure it's not a bomb." I take one last pull from my cigarette before stubbing it out and pulling myself to my feet. She's halfway up the walkway, a confused look playing across her face, and I don't blame her. The box was just *there* when I got here, wrapped in brown paper and twine and absolutely freaking *huge.* It is the size of two of those Bankers' Box boxes my Dad used to haul home from work put together. And it has Star's name on it.

"Jeez," she says, pulling the strap of her purse off her shoulder and dropping it down on the porch with a thud before kneeling down to get a closer look at the box. I'm kind of impressed. Not by the kneeling, I'm not a total freak, but by the fact she's just will-ing to toss her bag around like that. My ex-girlfriend would have killed herself before she let anything happen to her purse. But then, Gina wouldn't have been caught dead cleaning out a house like this, so I suppose that's just the way it is. Different folks, and all that shit. "I wonder who . . . " her voice trails off, and I turn bodily around to look at her, wondering why she stopped talking. As I watch, a grin spreads across her face, and she lights up like fucking sunshine.

"What?" I ask. "You figure out who sent it?"

"Yup," she says, but doesn't elaborate. Instead she just sinks down further until she's sitting cross-legged on the porch, and tugs the box closer.

She looks like a kid at Christmas.

"So . . . not a bomb, then?" I say, but I can't help the smile that I know is pulling at the corner of my mouth.

She turns to look at me. "Definitely not," she says, and then leans over to reach for her bag. But she doesn't actually move or anything, just starts waving her arms at her just-out-of-reach bag, keeping the box close.

"You're so weird." The words are out of my mouth before I can stop them, and I can actually feel the color drain from my face. Fuck, I think. Already I can feel the panic start to rise up in my stomach. *I'm such an ass. She's definitely going to fire me now.* But instead of getting pissed, she just throws back her head and laughs, and, unable to stop myself, my eyes trace down the long column of her neck, down to the neck of her T-shirt, where I can see just the barest edge of the tattoo I'm sure is hiding beneath the fabric.

"Trust me," she says, still grinning, "you're not the first one to tell me that. Not even close." She's still trying to reach for her purse without letting the box get out of reach, and she hasn't canned me, so I figure it must be pretty important. I reach out and nudge the bag toward her, and for the first time I notice the tattoo on her left arm, a flock of birds in flight, scaling the distance between her wrist and her elbow. It's nice. Pretty. She grabs it and gives me a quick "thanks" before dumping the bag into her lap and starting to dig through it with more focus than I've ever seen on anybody.

"What are you looking for?" I ask, because this has become way more interesting than watching the well-paid people of the neighborhood walk their foofy-looking dogs, which is what I'd been occupying myself with while I waited for her. Except it was kind of a shit way to kill time, since seeing the dogs made me miss Bruiser, and seeing the people glaring at me like I was a serial killer wasn't any better. Honestly, I'd been counting down the minutes until Star showed up.

"My keys," she says. "I need something to cut open the box."

I don't even think, I just reach deep into my pocket and pull out my Swiss Army knife, the one Dad gave me when I was thirteen, before I decided the Scouts were lame. I toss it to her and she gives me the biggest smile ever, all bright eyes and rosy cheeks and *goddamn she's hot.* I try to shake off the sudden punch to my gut that just keeps fucking happening around her, and watch as she makes short work of the twine and cuts open the flaps of the box.

Curious, because I've never actually been able to stay out of trouble, I lean forward to take a look.

That . . . wasn't what I was expecting. I'm not entirely sure *what* I thought was going to be in the box, but cartons of garbage bags wasn't it. But Star's still acting like a little kid who just got a pony or something, smiling like crazy as she pulls item after item out of the box. Garbage bags. Twine. And about a million different colors of permanent marker.

"Um . . . " I don't actually know what I'm supposed to say here. "Did you get a care package from rent-a-hoarder or something?" I ask, and then immediately regret it. I need to shut up. I need to just not talk anymore. Why was I never taught that whole *if you don't have anything nice to say, keep your mouth shut* rule like other kids? Why didn't that shit sink in?

But Star just laughs and starts sorting through her new treasure trove. "Not exactly," she says. "It's from Autumn. My roommate. I told her that I had to clean out my mother's house, but never told her how bad it was. But somehow . . . "

"She knew." Must be nice, to have someone like that.

Star nods, and her smile is so big it looks like the fucking sun. "Yeah," she says, grabbing one of the boxes of garbage bags and tossing it to me. "She just knew."

I don't know what it was, whether it was the package or hearing from her roommate or what, but Star's smile just went on and on. Even when we found the giant plastic bin full of comic books—good ones—that had been destroyed by being stored outside, she didn't falter. She just kind of shook her head and helped me dig them out of the bin and junked them. Which was fucking criminal, since hey would have been expensive. And I'd know. I used to collect them when I was a kid, and my mother was always harping on about how much money I was wasting. But at least I took care of my comic books. These? These had been turned into pulp. And the way Star's finger trailed down one of the covers before she threw it into the trash, I could tell it was something she would have liked. Maybe not now, but once upon a time, if things had been different.

Seeing her like that, smiling even though I knew she was having a hard time with it, made me wonder about my own collection, and if my parents still had it kicking around somewhere. I spent a few minutes mentally cataloging what I had left, and wondering if Star would like it before I realized what I was doing and shook the train of thought right out of my head.

Fucking stop it, I tell myself, hauling the empty plastic bin over to the side of the house so that I can wash it out with the hose. *She's not your girlfriend. She isn't ever going to be anything close, so just drop it. You're being an idiot.*

I just have to get through the rest of the summer without fucking up and giving myself away. One wrong move and she'll know I am into her, and I won't be the guy helping her out anymore, I'll be the creepy ex-con who hangs around her house and makes her uncomfortable. And I don't want to be that guy.

You already are that guy, my brain supplies and I grimace and shove that feeling deep down inside myself. This is supposed to be my chance to start over. I'm not going to mess it up because I'm into the girl who is willing to give me a chance to redeem myself. No way in hell.

I reach down and grab another box and heft it up into my arms. I just have to keep working. That's all there is to it. Eventually the feelings that are pulling at my gut will fade. They always do.

I just have to wait it out.

Star

It was almost completely dark out when we finally stopped for the day, exhausted. I was drenched with sweat, and I bid Ash an exhausted farewell as he pulled away from the curb, then headed back to the B&B to grab a shower before making my way over to the diner for a late dinner.

I have my laptop out in front of me by the time my food arrives, my email to Autumn waiting to be sent.

You're ridiculous, you know that, right? I had written.

I can't believe you sent me all that stuff.
How's life in Climbfield? Have you managed to drive Roth
bonkers yet? If so, send pics. I need to see his angry-face.
It's like Grumpy Cat and must be commemorated for pos-
terity.
I miss yooooou.
<3 Star

It is stupid, but even after only a couple of weeks, I miss my roommate like crazy. I've barely known her a year, but we're already
closer than I have ever been with anyone, save for maybe my foster brother Brick when I was sixteen, before he disappeared from
my life. And the fact that Autumn somehow always knows what
I need, well . . . It is good to have someone like her in my life.
Even if keeping in contact with her while I'm in Avenue is starting to become a huge pain in my butt. I still haven't managed
to find good Wi-Fi, and my cell phone is pretty much out as I
am roaming to the highest degree imaginable. I only brought the
damn thing for emergencies. It is probably a good thing that Ash
had just shown up instead of calling me. After all the money I'm
spending trying to get the house cleaned up, I don't need a gar-
gantuan cell phone bill on top of it.

After ten minutes struggling to stay connected to the diner's
Wi-Fi, I finally manage to get my email to go through, and I close
my laptop victoriously and celebrate with a handful of half-decent
fries from my plate.

I need to come up with a better plan than constantly eating at
the diner. I spent a good portion of the past year trying to wage
war against the freshman fifteen—and being only partially successful, but I figure seven pounds isn't the end of the world—and

it would suck to succumb to it now that my first year of college is officially over.

But honestly, at this point, I think the main reason I keep coming back to the diner is because I know I'm pissing people off. And I'm kinda starting to like doing so. God knows it isn't because the food is great. When my grilled cheese sandwich came out, it was cold and hard as a rock. And Leslie has been shooting daggers at me with her eyes ever since I sat down, and she still hadn't brought me out my soda, even though my meal is almost done. So yeah, I am completely okay with pissing her off.

After all, fair's fair.

She's been pissing me off pretty badly, too.

Between the grumpy waitress and my ever-dwindling funds, not to mention the fact that it is freaking *boiling* outside, I've just about reached the end of my rope. Again.

This summer is going to be a test of my mettle, I just know it.

I wait until her back is turned before I pull the handful of permanent markers Autumn sent me out of my bag and line them up on the vinyl seat next to me, hidden from view. Watching for her out of the corner of my eye, I take a deliberate bite of my sandwich and fiddle with my laptop, toggling from page to page until she disappears behind the counter to refill a drink. Then I uncap the first marker with a smile and get to work.

Soon there's a garden of badly drawn but *extremely* colorful flowers growing up the inside of my right arm and line after line of poetry marching halfway down my left thigh.

If people are going to keep staring at me, I'm going to give them something to stare at. I snap the cap back on the pale blue marker I've been using, and drop it back into my purse. I hear footsteps coming up behind me, and I zip my bag closed just in time for

Leslie—she of the constant disapproving glare—to walk up and slam my soda down on the table top hard enough for it to fizz up precariously close to the rim of the glass. I tilt my head back and grin up at her and reach out to wrap my hand around it. Bringing the glass to my lips, I take a long, deliberate sip of it, watching her as she just shakes her head and stalks away grumbling.

There's a snort from behind me, and I turn around in my seat to look.

York, the waiter from the other night—the one with the baby face and the sinfully tight jeans—is clearing dirty dishes off a table and into a plastic bin. And he's looking straight at me. But instead of the glares I've been treated to by everyone else in this place, he's gnawing on his lip, like he's struggling not to smile. And failing. He looks back and forth quickly, checking that the coast is clear, and then he shoves the last of the plates into the bin and hoists it up on his hip. But instead of heading straight toward the swinging door that leads to the kitchen, he veers slightly to the left coming within a foot of my booth, and as he passes by he slyly reaches out with his free hand, offering me a high five.

What else can I do? I give him one.

Chapter 6

Star

We've been working on the backyard for days now, almost a full week, really, and it looks like we're finally making some progress. I can actually see grass again. Well, not grass. The grass is pretty much toast, having been covered with crumbling plastic crates and tarps and a million other little things for God knows how long. But we've got the yard nearly down to the actual *yard,* so that's something.

Except I'm starting to think I'm going to have to rework my plan. I was not expecting it to take nearly as long as it has to clean this place up, even with Ash's help. And considering the fact that the Dumpster I rented is almost full and we haven't even *started* on the inside of the house yet, well . . . I'm starting to get a little concerned.

This is going to take way longer than I'd hoped, especially if this heat keeps up. Seriously, this is the hottest day *ever*. Possibly in my entire *life*. We've been working since dawn, trying to do as much as we can before the air gets too heavy, but it isn't even noon yet and I feel like I'm trying to do push-ups on the surface of the freaking *sun*.

I don't know how I managed to forget just how hot summers can get in Avenue, and at first I think maybe I just blocked it out, because *holy crap*. But when I think back, something tickles at the back of my memory, and I think I can remember my mother having an air conditioner chugging along in the window, coughing like a three-pack-a-day smoker as it worked. I also remember being small and following around the rotating head of the fan as it swept back and forth, trying to cool my little face, laughing as it blew my pale hair back.

Oh god, I think, grabbing a discarded magazine out of one of my mother's bins—why she kept every magazine she ever owned, hell, that she could get her hands on, I have no idea—and start fanning myself with it. I reach back with my free hand and gather up as much of my hair as possible, pulling the mass up off my sticky neck. There are little rivulets of sweat running down under my loose T-shirt, and I'm seriously tempted to go back to the B&B for a shower, just so I can rinse the worst of the sweat off me. But I'm afraid if I go back there, I'll be lulled into complacency by the air-conditioning I know they have there, and just never leave. *An air conditioner sounds so good right now. Or a fan. I'd settle for a fan. A fan would be* incredible.

But unfortunately, when my mother passed away, the power company switched off the juice, so the fan is a no-go, no matter how good it sounds right now. I just can't risk it. With all the expenses I have going on right now, and my second year of college looming on the horizon, I just can't afford the deposit the power company wants in exchange for switching the power back on.

So unless a miracle happens, we're stuck and I get to feel like I'm *dying*.

Now I know how the Wicked Witch of the West must have felt.

Melting.

Melting.

Melting.

Would it be too weird if I snagged the bikini I'd shoved in my purse and changed into that? Would Ash care? Because seriously, I am dying here. It is so damn hot. And I've been carrying it around with me, just in case I ever happen to stumble upon the lake I know is around here somewhere. But I haven't had the chance to go exploring, and I haven't bothered asking any of the locals where it is, since it isn't like I have any spare time and they probably wouldn't tell me, anyway.

"Jesus Christ," Ash's voice calls out from behind me. "I think I'm dying."

I look over, my eyes scanning across the yard, but I don't see Ash. At least, not right away. After a moment, I see movement and I walk closer. Ash is actually lying face-down on the ground in the patch of shade cast by the big oak tree by the back fence. He's got his arms starfished out at his sides, and he even has his bare cheek pressed against the cool dirt. As I walk up, he lets out a muffled groan and raises an arm weakly in my direction, before letting it fall limply to the ground.

I laugh. "You're . . . not kidding." I amble over to stand in the shade with him. It's a little cooler here, but not by much. I crouch down for a minute, and his eyes blink open to look at me. "You okay?" I ask.

"No," he murmurs. "Too hot. Dying."

"Okay, drama queen," I say, standing back up. "Just let me know if you want me to cover your body with dirt when you expire, or if you want me to drag you to the Dumpster instead."

Ash groans and pushes himself up enough to flip over onto his back. I'm momentarily distracted by the movement of his muscles beneath his T-shirt. His back is broader than I had imagined. Not that I've been imagining what he looks like without clothes, it's just . . .

Yeah. Just stop right there, Star.

"Just leave me here for the wolves," he says, and lets his eyes fall shut again. "They'll drag my body away. No Dumpster-chucking needed."

I know he's joking, but something about what he says gives me pause.

"Wolves?" I ask, trying to keep my voice light and playful. Because Miss Josephine's tiny poodle already kind of freaks me out. Anything wolf-size or related would be over the line. Way over it. And I've been away from Avenue for a long time, so I can't say for certain if he's joking or not. It's a small town near a forest. There could be wolves.

But all Ash says is "yeah," which doesn't help me figure out the whole wolf issue at all. Before I can work up the courage to actually *ask*, he continues with, "Holy shit, how can it even be so hot? This shouldn't be possible. Humans wouldn't have survived as a species. We'd all be dead."

"That's why we created air-conditioning," I reply, and reach down to untie my sneakers. My feet are overheated, like the rest of my body, but at least this is one thing I can take care of. "So I guess you're not used to it, either, huh?" I ask, sliding my shoes off my feet. Ideally, I'd be wearing my flip-flops in this heat—well, *ideally* I wouldn't be out here in the heat in the first place, but that's neither here nor there—but I didn't dare, not in this place. Who knows what kind of stuff could be lying around, just waiting to be stepped on?

I press my bare feet into the dirt. It's delightfully cool, and I wiggle my toes, getting the sandy earth wedged between them like a little kid on the beach.

"Yeah," he replies. "The prison had the A/C running full blast. They had to. There would've been a shit-ton of riots if they let us bake like this."

"People do get pissy in the heat," I agree. I'm trying not to think about it, about what Ash went through. Just the thought of him in prison makes my stomach hurt.

Ash turns and opens one eye to look up at me. "You seem to be doing okay," he says. And I grin.

"That's only because you're staying out of my way," I tease. "If you had pissed me off, well, you'd already be in the Dumpster by now."

"Hmmm," he says, and lets his eyes fall shut again. "I don't know. I think I could take you."

Yes, you can, my brain helpfully supplies before I can shut it up.

Nope, I tell it. *Not thinking about that. At all.* I pull my phone out of the back pocket of my shorts and check the time before sliding it back in and kicking my foot out, nudging Ash with my toe. "Come on," I say. "Get up."

"Ugh . . . " he moans. "Why?"

"Because it's too hot to work right now," I say. "And if you get up I'll buy you a slushie."

He opens his eyes and pushes himself up so he's leaning back against his bent elbows. Raising an eyebrow at me, he asks, "Seriously?"

"Seriously," I reply. "Any flavor you want. But you have to get up." Technically I could just go buy the slushies and bring them back, but for some reason that I don't want to think about, I want him to come with me.

A voice that sounds a hell of a lot like my roommate Autumn laughs at me from the back of my mind. *Shut up,* I tell it. *It's not a date.* I turn back to Ash as I slip my sneakers back on my now-dusty feet. "You coming?" I ask.

"Okay," he says, pulling himself to his feet. "But I'd just like to say that I'm not getting up because you told me to. I'm doing it solely for the slushie."

"Duly noted," I tell him, reaching into my pocket for the car keys. "But if that's your attitude, you can stay in the car while I go into the nice air-conditioned mini-mart."

Ash lets out an honestly pornographic-sounding moan and mumbles something that I'm pretty sure was "air-conditioning," but it came out of his mouth like he was addressing some form of deity. He moves to step past me and my free hand reaches out automatically and starts brushing the sandy dirt off the back of his T-shirt. I don't even realize I'm doing it until he freezes under my touch, and as soon as I see what I'm doing, my entire body tenses up in humiliation. Slowly, deliberately, I pull my hand away and brush it against the side of my shorts. Ash is looking at me with an unreadable expression on his face, and my face *burns.* But this time I know the fire I'm feeling isn't from the sun.

"Sorry," I mumble, and do a fumbling sort of wave as I try to gesture to his back. "Dirt."

"Yeah," Ash says softly, and then turns away to stare at the ground somewhere off to the side.

"Okay!" I say, and clap my hands together, because it isn't like I can make it any more awkward at this point. "Let's go." I forge ahead toward the gate. "Car time. Slushies await."

Taking the car was probably the wrong choice. It is still full of junk, so it is cramped as hell—the first thing I am doing when we get back is cleaning it out, I swear—and it is even hotter inside the car than it is outside, if that is possible. It takes nearly the entire drive over to the mini-mart for the ancient air conditioner to kick in, and when it does, it barely gives off a sputter of cold air before it craps out again.

Yeah, I am definitely going to need to get that fixed.

Goodbye, money.

I sigh and drag my overheated body out of the car. Ash is hot on my heels as I hustle into the mini-mart, the doors sliding open automatically in a burst of icy air that leaves me breathless. *Oh, thank god.* I'm tempted to just throw myself onto the Popsicle display face-first, and stay there forever. And I might have, if Ash didn't herd me toward the slushie machine at the back of the store.

We're there for less than a minute; me, trying to decide which flavor sounds most appealing, Ruby Blast or Arctic Blue, while Ash adds layer after layer of different flavors to his cup. He steps back and surveys his handiwork. It looks almost like a rainbow.

"That's going to be disgusting," I tell him, and reach for the machine that's churning Arctic Blue. Arctic-anything sounds good right now. "All the flavors are going to combine into soup."

"You have no idea what you're talking about," he says, and grabs a double-wide straw from the box next to the machine. He stabs it into his drink and takes a long sip. "It's awesome. Also?" He nods toward the machine. "You're going to spill that."

I whip around. "Oh shit!" I yelp, slamming the slushie machine's handle back into place. I've overfilled it. It hasn't spilled, yet, but if Ash hadn't said anything, it definitely would have. As it is, I don't know how I am going to bring my extra-tall slushie to the guy at the counter with a straight face. The thing looks like a freaking *mountain* growing out the top of my cup.

Crap.

But Ash just chuckles behind me, and makes a grabby hand at my drink. "Come on," he says, smiling. "Give it here." As carefully as I can, I hand over my drink, and he hands me his and turns and starts making his way over to the counter. I can't help but smile as I realize what he's doing, and I snag myself a straw before turning to follow him.

He's letting me hold the normal one, so the guy at the counter won't comment. And he actually manages to do it with a completely straight face, even when we get to the cashier and the guy's eyes bug out of his head at the sight of my blue monster.

"Thanks for that," I say, once we're back outside again.

"No problem," he replies, switching our drinks back and taking a sip of his own.

I open my mouth to say something, but he cuts me off with a look and a crooked grin. "Seriously, Star. It was not a problem. Save your thanks for the big stuff."

"And just what are *you* doing here," a voice calls out and we both whip around. I stifle a groan.

It's Lacey's boyfriend, the one who was muttering shit about Ash in the diner the day we met. At least, I *think* it's him. The other twin is right behind him, though, so it's either Lacey's boyfriend or his brother that's being an asshole. Fantastic.

The guy walks up to us, not waiting for a reply, and steps a little too close to Ash for my comfort. And judging by the look on Ash's face, he's not too fond of his new friend, either.

"I guess you weren't aware," the guy says, getting up in Ash's face, "but you're not welcome here." The guy has a good six inches on Ash and is staring right down at him. "So if you know what's good for you, you'll—"

"Hey, Ash," I say before the guy can finish whatever the hell his threat is going to be. What a tool. "We should probably get back to work." I stick the straw into my drink and, as casually as I can manage, take a sip as I reach between the two guys with my free hand and grab Ash's wrist.

"'Scuse us," I say to Preston or Clay or whoever the hell this guy thinks he is, and tug Ash out of the way. For a terrifying instant, Ash doesn't budge under my grip, and I have visions of him shaking me off and him getting right back into this guy's face. But I give one last tug and mercifully he relents and follows after me.

We're halfway to the car when the jerk behind us kind of sputters and I turn back to see him looking between us and his brother in confusion. The other twin doesn't seem to be quite as angry as the first one. He's actually smothering the beginnings of a grin. I hold up my blue monster of a slushie and give them a little salute. "You guys have a good day!" I call out, making my voice as fake and sweet as I can manage.

My favorite foster father used to laugh and tell me I was going to grow up to be a smart ass. I'd been indignant back then, convinced he just wasn't taking me seriously. But I'm starting to think that maybe he was right.

When I look back again, the twins have disappeared inside the mini-mart, and I drop Ash's hand, grinning. But when I look over at Ash, his face is pale despite the summer heat, and his eyes kind of flicker up to meet mine, hesitant.

"Hey," he says, and his voice is soft and I can hear just how much effort it's taking him to get his throat to work. It makes my chest hurt. He clears his throat and tries again. "Thanks . . . thanks for that," he says. "It's just, the fucking people in this town . . . "

"It's no problem," I say, and grin at him while I take a sip of my slushie. He opens his mouth and tries again to get words out, but I stop him before he can. "Seriously, Ash. It wasn't a problem. Save it for the big stuff," I say, throwing his earlier words back at him. He kind of blinks at me for a second, then a smile starts to tug at the corner of his mouth and I know he got it. He snorts at me and takes a long suck of his disgusting drink and after a minute, he's got some color back in his face.

"All right, smarty-pants," he says, and reaches his hand out, palm up. "Give me the keys."

I dig them out of my pocket and hand them over without hesitation, but I have to ask, "Why?"

"Because it's fucking boiling out here, and I'm going to take us someplace cool." He heads to the driver's side of the car, and I follow after him, ready to go wherever he takes me, because right now? *Cool* sounds like the best idea ever.

"You're a genius," I tell him, kicking off my shoes and scrambling down onto one of the rocks on the shore. I sit down, the remainder of my slushie in hand, and stick my feet down into the water. It's gloriously cool, and I sigh with relief. Behind me, Ash chuckles and hops down from rock to rock until he's sitting on the one next to mine.

"I'm pretty sure that's the first time in my life anyone has actually referred to me like that," he says, reaching down to yank off his own shoes. "I think I could get used to it."

"Keep coming up with good ideas, and you'll have to," I say, and lean back to press my back up against the bigger rock behind me. I take another long sip of my drink, and even though it's more liquid than ice now, it's still cool and refreshing. Between it and the lake and the shade from the trees above us, I'm actually starting to cool down. Off in the distance, I can see the beach on the other side of the lake. There are people splashing and swimming, little motorboats zipping back and forth across the water. But it all seems a million miles away. Where we are, it's quiet.

"How'd you even find this place?" I ask, because it's not like you'd just stumble upon it. We had to park the car on a dirt road in the middle of nowhere, and follow a dirt path nearly hidden in the underbrush through the forest before we got here.

Ash smirks and dunks both his feet in the water at once, hard enough that the water splashes back and mists us with cool droplets. "Came down to the lake with my parents when I was a little kid," he said. "They wanted to go to the beach—their friends were having some kind of fancy barbecue or something, I don't know. They told me to go off and play with the other kids, but their friends' kids never wanted to play with me, so I wandered off instead. Ended up here." He looks out at the water, and he's still smiling, but it's not as bright as before. It's almost sad. "I must have come out here a million times growing up. Whenever I just wanted to get away. The path was already there when I found it, but I've never seen anyone else here, so I figure it has to be pretty damn old. I probably wore it even deeper, coming out here so much." He sighs and shifts until he's lying flat on his back, his feet dangling over the side of the rock, staring up at the canopy of leaves above us.

"Have you been back?" I ask. "You know, since you got out?" I shove the straw back in my mouth and force myself to take another long brain-freezing slurp. I can't believe that I'm reminding him of his time in prison. What the hell is wrong with me? But Ash just shakes his head and stays quiet.

Some time later, after I've finished my drink and we've been sitting there long enough to become lazy and sluggish, Ash groans and tugs himself back into a sitting position. "You know what?" he says to me. "Fuck it. I'm going for a swim."

I can feel my brow furrow. "Seriously?" I ask him. What brought this on?

He nods and pulls himself to his feet. "I haven't gone for a swim in five years. Longer, probably. I'm finally back here. I'm not going to let it go to waste."

Then he reaches down and pulls his T-shirt over his head and my mouth goes dry.

Holy shit.

Ash is gorgeous. He's all smooth muscle and wide shoulders and he's got this big solid black tattoo on his left shoulder that snakes down like smoke. My eyes follow it, desperate to figure out what it is, and that's when I see them.

The scars.

Holy *shit*.

Chapter 7

Ash

For a brief, glorious moment, I feel Star's eyes on me, and I think she's checking me out. And I want to throw my arms up in victory. Hot girl checking me out. Awesome.

Then I remember the scars, and I come crashing back down to reality. Shit. That's why I hadn't wanted to take my shirt off in the first place. I glance down at them. She hasn't said anything yet, but I know how bad they look. My entire side is criss-crossed, and there's one jagged one that looks like something tried to tear me in half. The funny thing is, my wounds from the crash look a hell of a lot worse than they ever were. I was messed up, yeah, but nothing vital was hit. I was never in any real danger.

The guy I hit, on the other hand, all he got was a bump on the head, and that was it for him. Lights out. It fucking sucks.

I hate the scars, but they're important to me like almost nothing else ever has been. They're my reminder. Every time I see them, I have to remember what I did, how I fucked up and caused the death of another human being. And I have to live with that.

Shoving down the urge to scoop my shirt back up off the rock and pull it back on, I look over at Star. Our eyes meet, and she looks a little sad.

Fuck.

She opens her mouth, and since I don't want to talk about it, about the crash, about the guy I killed, about any of it, I cut her off before she can say anything. "You gonna join me?" I ask, and nod toward the water. She kind of blinks at me for a second, like she's trying to decide whether or not to let me have my diversion, but then a small smile tugs at the corner of her mouth.

"Maybe I want you to see how cold it is, first."

"Oh, I see how it is," I say, smirking. "You want to see if I'm gonna freeze my balls off when I jump in. Gonna leave it all on my shoulders, huh?"

"Well, swimming *was* your idea," she says, and leans back against the rock.

"Fine, then," I say, and start climbing back over the rocks, away from the shoreline.

"Hey!" she says, turning to watch me go. "Where are you going? I thought you were going in."

"I am," I tell her, and turn back around.

"Hard to do that from way over there. What? You chickening out already?"

I shake a finger at her. "You're going to regret saying that in a minute," I say. Then I drop my arm, bounce a little on the balls of my feet and start running toward the water.

I race through the forest, bare feet pounding against the dirt, and as soon as my feet hit rock, I do what I haven't done in five whole years.

I close my eyes. I jump.

I fly.

In that moment, there's nothing. Nothing but the wind in my face and the feeling of weightlessness before I come crashing down. And this . . .

This is the hardest part, the shock of the cold all around you when you first hit the water. It moves through your body in a jolt, like an electric shock gone wrong.

It gets to me every damn time, and this time is no different. Still reeling from the cold, I feel my feet hit the bottom of the lake bed, and I shove against it, propelling myself back to the surface. I spin around, searching for Star, and find her on her feet, sputtering, dripping with water. I grin. I knew my splash would get her.

"I told you so!" I yell. And she looks over and glares at me.

"You're a jerk," she calls back, wiping her hands down her arms to get the droplets of water off her.

I laugh. "Well, you're already wet now," I call out to her. "You might as well come in." I'm not gonna lie, the sight of Star dripping wet in front of me is doing things to me. Even through the chill of the water, I can feel the heat that courses through my body at the mere thought of her with her soaked clothes sticking to her.

Down boy, I tell myself. *No perving on Star. We've fucking established this.*

"Turn around," Star calls from the shore.

What?

"What?" I yell back. It's weird how loud the water is once you're actually on it. All I can hear is the sound of the waves around me, the echoes of the splashing and laughter from the beach across the way. Why the hell would she want me to turn around?

"Just turn around, Ash," she says, planting her hands on her hips and giving me a little glare that's honestly not doing anything to make the heat in my belly die down.

"Ugh, fine," I say, and swirl my arms around me until I'm facing in the other direction. From here I can see the crowd on the beach, and I can't help but wonder if my parents are a part of it. They could be there, right now, attending another barbecue or whatever the hell they do during the summer now that they're retired. I've never asked. I feel kind of bad about that, all of a sudden. It's been five years, and other than them losing my dog, I have no idea what they've done in all that time, no idea what their lives are like. I tread water for a bit, waiting, wondering what Star's doing back there. With my luck, she'll have grabbed my shirt and shoes and run for the car as soon as I turned around, leaving me waiting here, splashing around like an idiot. That's what my ex Gina would have done. She would have laughed the whole way, and then would have told me to stop being such a pussy, that it was just a joke, when I would be all pissed at her, afterward.

Not that I'm speaking from experience or anything.

But seriously, what the hell is Star doing back there? I wonder if I should turn around, but she told me not to, and technically she's my boss, so . . .

"Okay," her voice breaks through my daydreaming. "You can turn around now."

With a splash, I turn back toward the shore, and I'm kicking myself for not turning around. She would have killed me, but it would have been worth it, because *fucking hell* that girl is wearing the tiniest black bikini I've ever seen, and I'm so freaking glad I'm immersed in cold water right now, because *Jesus Christ*. She's so fucking hot. I can't help it; I let out what I hope is the quietest groan ever, and dunk my head under the water. When I come back up for air, she's making her way down the rocks like a billy goat, arms stretched out at her sides for balance.

The girl has tattoos everywhere and that fact alone is going to kill me.

"Be careful, okay?" I call out to her, because, contrary to popular belief, I'm not a total asshole. "The rocks are slippery."

"You're not kidding," she says, sliding a bit before catching herself with a gasp. I swim closer. Better she fall on me than on the rocks.

"Just get to the edge of that one and jump in," I tell her. "It's deep enough."

"I'm not really the jumping type," she tells me, but she plants her feet on the edge of the rock like she's considering it, anyway. "Normally I just ease myself in."

"Rookie mistake," I say, and now that I'm close enough I start treading water again, holding my position. "It's better to just get it over with." She stares down at the water like she's trying to figure out its secrets, and I want to laugh at the serious look on her face, but I'm too distracted by her tattoos. I've seen the one on her right arm, but it looks like she has an almost matching one on the back of her upper left one, but I can't make out what it says. There's also a bunch of stars trailing up her foot—fitting, I decide—and what looks like some kind of pink-and-white flowers dancing up her ribs.

She's fucking gorgeous. Her eyes dart up to me, catching me

looking at her, and at first I'm afraid she's going to tell me off, but all she says is "you sure?" and I nod.

"Just jump," I tell her. "You'll be fine."

And then she does.

We lose track of time and the sun is starting to set by the time we head back to the car. We're dripping wet and laughing, our clothes sticking to our damp bodies like a second skin, our stomachs rumbling from our forgotten lunch and dinner.

"I'm *starving*," Star moans as we pull up to the house. Her hair is still dripping, and the tiny droplets keep running down her neck and under her shirt, and I really *really* want to follow them with my eyes, find out where they go. But instead, I nod my head in agreement and haul myself out of the car. Instead of heading to the diner for the millionth time, we stopped at the grocery store on the way back and got stuff for sandwiches, and I pull the bag out of the backseat and slam the door. "I forgot how hungry swimming makes me."

"Too bad," I tell her, following her to the backyard. "Because I'm going to eat all the sandwiches. All of them." I wrap my arms around the grocery bag to claim it for my own. "Every last one."

"Not a chance," she says. "You even try and I *will* feed you to the wolves."

I laugh. "Then I'll be full and the wolves will be full, and you'll still be hungry. So that would still be a win for me."

"But you'd be dead," she points out.

"Full and dead," I say, because the *full* part is the important one here.

"Ugh, you're a terrible person," she groans. "Why do I hang out with you again?" She's joking, I know she is. But her words still make something jerk inside me. Because right now, she's the only one I've got, and as amazing as Star is, that still really fucking sucks.

I step forward in the darkness, and go barreling into her unexpectedly. I grab her before we both go tumbling to the ground, and when we right ourselves, my arm is wound tightly around her waist. "Woah," I say once we're steady on our feet again. "Are you okay?"

"Ash?" There's something in her voice that makes me freeze up. Something's wrong.

"Yeah?"

"Were you being serious about the wolves?"

"What?"

She looks over her shoulder at me. Her eyes are like saucers. "Are there really wolves in Avenue?"

"Why?" She takes another step back, until her back is pressed hard up against my chest. She's shaking. Her entire body is trembling in my arms.

"Because I think there's something in the backyard." Her voice cracks on the last word. It takes a second for her words to filter through my brain enough for me to make sense of them. As soon as I realize what she's trying to tell me, I pull her back, putting my body between her and the gate to the backyard.

"Whoa, are you fucking serious?" I ask. I have my hand flat against her stomach, and I keep my arm extended, keeping her well behind me. I can feel her muscles jump beneath my fingers. I take a careful step forward, trying to see into the backyard while still keeping my distance. But it's too dark. I can't see. The only light out now is the glow from the streetlights, and it isn't quite making it to the backyard. Fuck.

I realize I'm still holding the grocery bag, so I hand it back to Star. She takes it without a word, and together we edge closer to the backyard. We're almost at the gate when, out of the corner of my eye, I see something move along the back fence, disappearing into the shadows under the oak tree. "There!" Star hisses, reaching out and jabbing a finger toward the shadow. "Did you see it? It was right there?" She takes a step forward, and I reach out and catch her by the arm, pulling her back.

"I saw it," I say. "At least, I think I did." It is too dark, too fucking dark. I can't see anything clearly. My free hand darts out, and snags the flashlight out of the box that we'd dumped by the side of the house. I flick the switch and a beam of light shoots out. I flash it over the fence, scanning the light back and forth, gazing hard into the darkness.

Where is it? Where the fuck is it?

There!

My eyes catch on it. Yes! I inch closer, squinting at the dark shape, Star's question about wolves looping over and over in my mind.

"Hey!" I yell out, waving the light back and forth, trying to get its attention. "Get out of here!"

But as the words leave my mouth, the thing steps out of the shadows, and I catch it in the beam of the flashlight, and my entire body fucking freezes.

Holy. Shit.

Holy. Fucking. Shit.

Bruiser?

Star

O h. My. God.
I've never seen anything like this.

I thought for sure that the way Ash had tensed up, the way his eyes had darted back and forth across the yard, searching, meant that he was going to turn to me and tell me to get in the house and call animal control. But when his eyes landed on the creature, his grip on my arm didn't tighten, and he didn't start pulling me back to the car. Instead his grip loosened until his hand fell from my arm to hang limp at his side, and his eyes turned into dinner plates.

He murmured something and shot forward, through the back gate, straight toward the animal. I opened my mouth to stop him, to scream, to do *something*. But instead of growling or snarling or backing away—or any number of things the animal could have done—it let out a series of high pitched barks and then raced forward, straight into Ash's arms.

Holy. Shit.

I'm on the back porch now, but even from here I can see the look on Ash's face. He's laughing but at the same time he looks like he's about a second and a half away from bawling his eyes out. He turns and buries his face in the dog's neck, even though its dark brown fur is filthy and probably stinks just as bad as anything we've found in the yard. He's on his knees in the patchy grass, the still-damp fabric sinking into the dirt, but he doesn't seem to notice. He just wraps the massive dog up in his arms, and starts squeezing it like there's no tomorrow.

The dog, on the other hand, is the image of pure joy. It's squirming in Ash's arms like all of its Christmases have come at once, and just the sight of it is making my eyes start to burn.

Fuck.

I didn't cry when CPS knocked on my mother's door and took me away. I didn't cry when I got the call that my mother had died. And there's no way in hell I'm going to start crying over whatever the hell is going on in front of me, no matter how much my throat is choking up right now.

I turn away and scrub my hands over my face, though. Just in case.

Ash starts making his way back over to me once he and the mutt—who actually has a much sweeter disposition than his appearance led me to believe—have calmed down enough for him to introduce us, and I can't stop thinking about it. About how happy they both look.

Ash can't stop grinning, and the dog is staring up at him like Ash is the true source of happiness, like he's got sunbeams and unicorns coming out his butt. It's . . . pretty cute, actually.

I guess this is what people mean when they say they're *dog people*. I'd never seen the appeal before, not after my less than stellar past with my foster mom's Pomeranian. But I have to admit, I'm starting to come around. Especially when Ash walks over to me, the dog plastered to his side, and introduces us with tears still shining in his eyes. He kind of sniffs and tries to scowl them away, like he'd gotten something in his eye, but we both know why they are there.

"So," I say. "Not a wolf."

Ash barks out a kind of strangled-sounding laugh, and scrubs his hands over his face. "Yeah," he says. "Not so much."

I let the smile I've been trying to tamp down start to sneak through, and plant my free hand on my hip. "You know, you still haven't answered my were-you-serious-about-the-wolves question."

"It doesn't matter, anyway." He reaches down to give the dog an affectionate slap on the side. "We've got this big guy to protect us."

"And I'm guessing you know each other," I say, smirking at him.

"Yeah . . . yeah. Star, this is Bruiser," he says, and ruffles the mutt's ears. The dog's entire body shakes with joy. "He's my dog."

The night has cooled down enough that we can actually use the fire pit that we'd unearthed from the ton of junk in the backyard, and Ash tells me the whole story as we get a campfire going. The dog is his, he tells me, as we settle in and start building the sandwiches from the stuff we picked up from the grocery store. He'd left Bruiser with his parents when he'd been put away for the accident—the crash, he called it, because for some reason, he never seems to use the word *accident,* even though I know that's what it was—and they hadn't told him the dog had gotten out and gone missing until he'd gotten back to Avenue.

"I've been so fucking *angry,*" he says, pulling a sliver of roast beef out of his sandwich and tossing it to the dog, who snaps it out of the air like it is nothing. "It's like . . . I *know* I'm a fuck-up, okay? But Bruiser? He didn't do anything. And I just . . . " He trails off, staring into the fire.

I turn my half-eaten sandwich over in my hands and pull my gaze away from him to stare down at it. "You just wanted him to be taken care of."

Ash lets out a kind of half-sigh/half-snort, and I look up to find him looking at me. "Yeah," he says, nodding. "Exactly."

The silence stretches out like a ribbon between us, neither of us knowing what to say. Finally, I can't take it any longer. I take another bite of my sandwich to buy myself a minute, but when I swallow I plaster a smile on my face and look over at him. "So, no offense or anything, but are you sure that he's your dog? I mean . . . he looks pretty feral."

"Pfft, feral," Ash mutters, but I can see the smile tugging on the side of his mouth. "I'll show you feral. Watch this." He reaches down and picks up the bag of potato chips he'd snagged from the grocery store at the last minute, claiming that after all our hard work and all that swimming, mere sandwiches wouldn't be enough for his quote-unquote "manly hunger." He rips the bag open, and the dog is instantly on high alert, pinning the bag with a stare that any body guard would be proud of.

"Sit," Ash says, and before the word has even completely left his lips, the dog's butt hits the ground. His tail's wagging so hard it's thumping against the dirt, drawing dust up into the air, and he watches as Ash pulls out a single large chip and holds it out to him, telling the dog to *wait.* Bruiser looks between Ash's face and the proffered chip over and over again, and I laugh at the look on his face. Half obedience, half betrayal, and one hundred percent *Seriously? You're making me do this right now?* But he doesn't make a move toward it. He barely even breathes.

Finally, after long seconds have passed, Ash says "okay," and the dog darts forward and snaps the chip up. The animated crunching that follows is honestly the cutest thing I've ever seen, and something inside of me is torn between laughing and *melting* at the sight.

"Nope," he says, smiling at me as Bruiser licks his chops and starts rooting around, looking for more treats. Ash just looks down and shakes his head at the dog, grinning, until Bruiser finally gives up and makes his way over to me instead. I'm lost in that moment, that instant of us together in my mother's backyard, sitting by the fire. Because in those long, drawn-out heartbeats, the sight of Ash's smile by the light of the fire is one of the most beautiful things I've ever seen. "He's definitely my dog." He rubs the back of his neck before sinking back down into his seat. "I mean, fuck. He's kinda skinny and he's got more gray fur than I remember, but it's definitely him. It's Bruiser."

I shove down the warmth that's spreading through my chest, and lean forward. "So," I say, reaching out to run a tentative hand down the dog's back. I'm trying to picture a bigger, heartier version of the dog in front of me, and honestly it's kind of terrifying. I feel like the dog's going to turn on me at any moment and snap my fingers off. Just because he seems to adore Ash, doesn't mean he'll put up with me touching him. But Bruiser dashes my fears in about two seconds, as he leans into my hand, squirming, pressing closer, so I continue. "Not dangerous, then."

"Not at all," Ash says, and then reaches out his left hand to me, pinkie out. "I promise." I bite my lip and reach out to link my finger with his.

And while we're mid pinkie-swear, Bruiser sees his opportunity and makes off with the rest of my sandwich.

Chapter 8

Star

I'm settled on the porch steps the next morning, a paper cup of coffee clutched between my hands. It's absolutely boiling—and for once worthy of the *Caution:* Hot label on the side—but I didn't sleep well last night. I was too busy trying to figure out a plan and how to set it into motion, and as a result I ended up getting maybe four hours of sleep. *Maybe.* At this point I need the coffee like I need to live. And even though I was barely awake, Ash was already hard at work when I arrived, and I'm glad that he's finally gotten comfortable enough to just do his own thing.

Progress.

He's puttering around, hauling stuff out to the Dumpster, and at first I think it's just the heat, but after watching him for a few minutes as I wait for my coffee to cool, I realize that what I'm seeing isn't just my imagination. Ash is sunburned.

"You know," I say, trying to force down my smile before it gives me away. "You're looking a little red about the edges, there." My smile breaks free and Ash turns even redder at my words. I can't help it if the guy looks cute with a little pink in his cheeks. He's more approachable that way, somehow.

"Ugh, I know," Ash mutters, scrubbing at his ever-so-slightly sunburned neck. "Curse of the blonds. I was always getting burnt when I was a kid. I was kind of hoping I'd grow out of it."

"I don't think it's something you really grow out of," I tell him, and dig into my purse and pull out a tube of sunblock. "Here." I toss it to him when he turns around. He looks down at it, clutched in his hands.

"You've had this the whole time?" he asks.

"Of course. I need it for the tattoos. The sun messes with them. Also—" I pin him with a smile "—you're not the only blond around here."

His eyes narrow on me for a minute, then he shakes his head and pops open the tube, dumping a pile onto his palm, which he then claps on the back of his neck. "You're messing with me."

I watch as Bruiser twines around Ash's legs like a cat, sniffing away like mad. Probably wondering what Ash has in his hands, and if he can eat it. I've known this dog less than twenty-four hours, and he's already tried to eat *everything* I've laid my hands on. It's a wonder he managed to survive on his own, considering the way he was staring at the station wagon's tires and licking his chops. I look up and Ash is still looking at me like I'm trying to pull one over on him somehow, so I just shake my head at him and settle back down on the porch. It's scorching again today. I can barely take it.

"I'm serious," I say, reaching up and ruffling the roots of my hair. "Totally blonde underneath the dye."

"I can't even imagine what that would look like." He tosses the tube of sunscreen back to me. I fumble it when it hits my hands and it almost goes tumbling to the ground before I manage to get a grip on it. He's gotten a bunch of the sunscreen on the tube itself, and it's all greasy now. I sigh and try to scrub it off as best I can, wiping my gooey hands on my legs. *Boys.*

"It's better if you don't," I say, clicking the cap back into place and dropping the tube back into my bag. Stretching out my leg, I shove Bruiser away with my bare foot, trying to keep him away from my purse. "Stop it. That's not for you." He looks up at me with big puppy-dog eyes and I sigh and reach down to ruffle his ears to ease the sting of rejection. This dog is going to be the end of me.

"No, seriously." Ash steps closer to me, his eyes dancing over my face and hair as a little smirk starts pulling at his lips. "What does it look like?"

"Like Barbie, okay?" I say, exasperated. I can tell he isn't going to let it go. "If I don't dye it, I end up looking like I need a hot-pink car to go shopping in. I hate it."

"That's so bizarre." He laughs and I stick my tongue out at him. "No offense, or anything," he says. "It's just really hard to picture you like that."

"I know. And that's how I want to keep it. It's not me. Hasn't been me for a long time."

Ash sighs and rubs the back of his neck. "I know what you mean," he says, chuckling awkwardly, and I take a sip of my coffee and just *look* at him for a second when I realize he's right. If anyone knows what it feels like, it's Ash. After all he's been through, everyone around him has just decided who he is and what he's going to do, even though he's trying his hardest just to start over. It sucks.

"Well, I figure, fuck it. Right?" He picks up a rake that had been hidden under a pile of boxes just a few minutes ago, its tines stuck deep in the sandy earth. He pries it loose and dusts it off, then uses it as a leaning post as Bruiser sidles up to him and plops down beside him in the one patch of shade. "The people around here, they don't know you. They don't know me, either. So fuck them. I'm trying. They're not. And I just have to accept that. I mean—" he takes a deep breath and blows it out, like he's trying to calm himself down before he gets too worked up "—if they can't accept me, then I just have to live with it, I guess."

I nod, and try to smile even though my heart is breaking for him. "Yeah," I say. "You've paid for what happened. You served your time. If they can't accept that, well, they're not your problem."

"Exactly," Ash says, but his voice isn't as upbeat as I was hoping it would be. Instead, he's just . . . resigned. He tugs the rake free from the ground and walks it over to the shed, leaning it against the siding next to the shovel and all the other gardening tools we've found so far. I don't know why my mother even had all these things. She never gardened a day in her life. Her yard didn't even have room for a garden, not the way it was covered in junk.

"So," Ash says, making his way back over to where I'm sitting on the porch. He draws out the word into three long syllables as I glance up from the box I'm sorting through. I raise my eyebrows at him, waiting.

"Yes?"

"Change of topic," he says, and shoves his hands into his pockets. It's hot enough out today that he's ditched his hoodie, but his

T-shirt is back in place. It's a shame.

A damn shame.

"What's with the other tattoo?"

"What?" I ask, my brain taking a minute to catch up. For an instant I'm terrified that he caught me sneaking looks at him, but when I look at his face, there's no mocking or anger. Just curiosity. He jerks his chin toward me, and I realize he's talking about my tattoos, not his.

"The one on your upper arm," he says. "What does it say?"

When I realize which one he's talking about, I can't help it. I start laughing, because the irony is just ridiculous. He's scowling at me a little, though, so I shake it off and clear my throat before I answer him. "It's an old Polish saying," I say. "It's a saying that a friend of mine used to use all the time." Because Roth made me work for the meaning, even though he said it every chance he got. So I'm just upholding the tradition.

"Yeah," Ash says, rolling his eyes. "I know it's Polish. Well, no, I don't. But I can tell it's not in English since I can't fucking read it. What I want to know is what does it mean?"

I want to tell him, want to see the smile spread across his face when he realizes just what it says. But even though he smiles around me all the time, I know he isn't happy. Not really.

I can change that. At least, I think I can. I hope. But it needs to be one thing at a time. He needs to know that all the good doesn't just come at once and then get snatched away. There's good in life all the time, and he deserves his fair share, no matter how bad he messed up.

"Well," I say, drawing the word out just like he had. "I'll give you a choice." I set my cup of coffee down on the step next to me, and reach for my purse, pulling it into my lap. "You can either have what my tattoo means, *or*—" I pull out the little blue plastic bag I'd shoved in there earlier and hold it up "—you can have the present I got you."

Ash kind of blinks at me for a second, confused. "Present?" he asks, and as I watch, his face goes through half a dozen emotions, from *confused* to *wary* to downright *suspicious* before ending up at *hopeful* in a matter of seconds. But I can still see the caution in his hopeful gaze, and it pulls at something in my chest. How long has it been since the last time he got a present? No strings attached. Just a simple gift from someone trying to put a smile on his face.

Something tells me it's been awhile.

A *long* while. At least five years.

The bag trembles in my hand as I try to swallow around the lump forming in my throat. "Yeah," I say, waving the bag back and forth a little bit, hoping to tempt him. "A present."

Luckily for me, the store is too small to brand their bags, because otherwise it would have given away the surprise. I try not to think too hard about the fact that I really want to surprise Ash.

"You . . . " As I watch, Ash takes a shaky breath and blows it out, reaching up to run a nervous hand through his hair. It sticks up in all directions, and he looks like a little kid. It's awkward and adorable at the same time. If only the rest of the people in Avenue could see Ash like I do. All of his problems would be gone. "You actually bought me a present. Like, actually *went out* and bought me something." He stares at me like he's expecting me to respond, but I think it's pretty obvious that I *did*, so I stay quiet until he breaks and asks, *"Why?"*

I can't quite manage to stifle the groan that fights its way out of my chest. "Because I wanted to, okay?. And I *bought* it because I knew it was the one thing that we'd never find in this damn house." Which is absolutely true. No matter how much random junk and crap my mother had laid her hands on, I knew that this wasn't one of them. My mother *never* wanted anything to do with pets or animals in her house, especially after my dad died. "So what's it gonna be?" I ask, and waggle the bag at him. "The present, or the tattoo? It's your choice."

I know what his choice is even before he makes a move, but I still can't stop the grin that spreads across my face when he steps forward and takes the bag from me. Nor can I stop the warmth that spreads in my belly at the sight of his shy smile. *I knew he'd like it,* I think as he opens the bag and his shy smile turns into a freaking sunbeam. Bruiser is twining around his legs like a puppy, his tail going crazy with excitement as Ash pulls out the collar and leash combo I'd purchased that morning.

"I hope it's big enough," I say, kicking my legs out in front of me so that I can lean back against the wooden deck post. "I kind of had to guess." Which hadn't been easy. Even the pet-store people in this town seemed to have it out for me. The guy in the store had followed me around the entire time I'd been in there, and had eyed me like I was some kind of master criminal who was after his bags of kitty litter. It was unnatural.

Ash looks up at me, and I'm taken aback by the tears in his eyes. "Thank you," he says and then hesitates. He wants to say something else. I know it. But instead he just reaches up with his free hand and scrubs away his tears before they fall. Then he leans down and starts putting the collar on Bruiser.

The silence between us grows until it becomes unbearable, so I pull myself to my feet and wipe my hands against my shorts.

"Come on," I say awkwardly, trying to look anywhere but at Ash. "We should get back to work."

✦

I watch as Ash pulls the loaded-up station wagon out of the drive-way and chugs along down the street. Finally, as it turns the corner and disappears, I let out the breath I've been holding for what feels like forever. *Good. He's gone.*

It had been easier than I thought it would be, getting him out of here for the afternoon. All I'd had to tell him was that I needed him to take a load of boxes to the thrift store on the other side of town. I'd taken a load there myself the other day, and the quite frankly *ancient* guy that ran the place had kept me there *forever*, regaling me with his entire life story. It was torture, but it was more than convenient. It was the only way.

But as soon as Ash is gone, my resolve starts to waver.

This might not be the best idea I've ever had, but I don't have a lot of options. I don't want to tell Ash, but I'm already running out of money. Renting the Dumpster and getting it hauled away cost way more than I thought it would. And I'm not dipping into my college money. I'm just not. So this is my option.

The shed.

And I need Ash gone if I am going to get this to work. Because he'd probably try to talk me out of it if he knew what I am thinking, but really, what other option do I have?

At least it's summer, I tell myself. And while it might be boiling inside the garden shed, it will be out of any rain and elements. Basically, it will be the same as if I'd cleared out a room in my mother's house, since the power is still off in there. Exactly the same.

Except I'll be living in the shed.

Oh god, I can't believe I'm doing this.

We finally managed to get the backyard mostly cleared out, and here I am, about to fill it right back up again.

Ash is going to *kill* me.

"Seriously?" Ash demands when he sees what I've done to the backyard. He catches sight of me and pins me with a look. "Fucking *seriously?*"

"I know! I'm sorry," I say, and I am. I understand his frustration. The backyard is covered again. There was just so much more *stuff* in the shed than I'd been expecting. I couldn't find anywhere to put it. But I managed to get it all out and the mattress I'd scrounged from the house *in* before he got back.

"Seriously? Dammit Star, what the fuck happened?" He's reaching up and raking the fingers of both hands through his hair, looking around the yard like he's never seen it before, and to be fair, that's probably what it feels like. We'd just about gotten used to seeing the same stuff over and over again when we were cleaning before. But all this stuff is new to him. He probably feels like I've set us all the way back to the beginning. "Where did this stuff even come from?"

"The shed," I say, and wave at it over my shoulder.

"Holy crap," he sighs, and wipes his hand over his face. *"Why?"*

Okay, I knew this was coming. I take a deep breath and just hope that I can explain this without sounding like a total lunatic.

Ash

I can't say anything. I know I can't. I live in a fucking car, so if Star wants to sleep in a garden shed, that's her business, but still . . .

"This is a really fucking bad plan," I spit out and then immediately clamp my teeth together to shut myself up. Instead of saying anything else, I just dump the bags of garbage at the curb and turn to walk back toward the yard. Star keeps pace with me, though, dropping the box she was carrying and following me back.

"It'll be fine," she says, and her voice is light but I can tell my opposition to this plan is bothering her. *Good. Maybe then she'll change her mind.*

"What happened to you being afraid of being eaten by wolves?" I ask, shoving the gate open and stepping back into the yard. It's taken us all day to get it back to where it was before, and there's still tons of stuff that we still need to go through. Apparently some of the stuff in the shed might actually be salvageable, ultimately headed for somewhere other than the dump. Who knew? "Or the fact that, *oh yeah*, you'd be living *outside* where anyone could mess with you."

"Awwww," she says, and I whip my head around to look at her, just in time to catch her batting her eyelashes at me dramatically. "Are you worried about me, Ash?" *You little smart ass,* I think, but I can't help it. I smile at her, and she crows with laughter, having caught me.

"Shut up," I mutter, and lean down to haul another box of garbage off the ground. "I'm just afraid of who's going to pay me if you get eaten or dragged off my fucking marauders or something."

"Marauders," she repeats, nodding along like she's humoring me. Like *I'm* the one acting like an idiot here.

I heft the box up, holding it mostly with one arm so that I can use the other to point at her. "Stop being a smart ass," I say, and shake my finger at her. "My point still stands." I drop my arm and use it to support the box. "Maybe I should leave Bruiser here. To protect you."

"Bruiser," she repeats, and hearing his name my dog's ears prick up and he turns to look at her from his seat a couple feet away. She turns to me and rolls her eyes. "You think Bruiser is going to protect me?" she asks, and his tail thumps against the ground at the sound of her voice. She reaches an arm out and makes a finger-gun and points it at him. "Bang," she says, and my dog just fucking *flops* over. The traitor.

I never should have showed her that trick. I've had the dumb dog back for less than a day, and he's already turned against me. She turns back to look at me, a smug little smile tugging at the corner of her mouth. "Somehow, I don't think he's up for the job," she says.

I just glare at her over the top of the box. "Shut up. It's still a bad plan."

But she just smiles at me, and for the millionth time since we met, I'm struck by just how bizarre my life has become.

At least it couldn't get any weirder.

Right?

Chapter 9

Ash

What the fuck?

Diapers? Seriously?

Nothing but stacks of diapers, for as far as the eye can see.

I'm standing in the doorway and there's a wall of diaper boxes in front of me, blocking off access to what should be a bedroom.

This place just gets weirder and weirder.

We finally get to work on the house, and this is the first thing I find when I open a door. It's like I'm working in a goddamn fun house. I feel Star come up behind me and freeze in place, and when I turn to look over my shoulder at her, she looks as fucking baffled as I feel.

"You're an only child, right?" I ask, waving my hands at the mess in front of me. She's never actually said so. I've always just kind of assumed since there's no one else here, cleaning out this shit with us, but I could be wrong.

But she nods her head. So that's that. "Yeah," she murmurs, reaching out to run her fingertips along the side of one of the boxes. Then she shakes her head like she's trying to clear it, and I wonder where her head's at. "I . . . " She stops there, like she can't find the words, and her hand falls back down to her side. I sigh. This damn house has already thrown so much shit at her, I'm amazed she hasn't broken yet.

I reach out and lay my hand on her back, trying to steady her. She looks like she's about to keel over.

"What?" I ask. "What is it?"

She takes a shaky breath, and blows it out slowly.

"I just... I always thought it was because of my dad, you know? The reason she was like this. I thought it started because of my dad's death." It takes me a second, but then I get what she isn't saying. My hand stills on her back, where I was rubbing it. Shit.

"You mean . . . "

She nods.

My brain puts two and two together, and winds up with the worst possible answer.

Shit.

If this pile is anything to go by, Star's mom had probably lost a baby on top of losing her husband.

Fuck.

That really sucks.

Star looks like she's about to cry, like her whole world has been shaken on its axis, and I hate seeing her like that. "Look," I say, "Maybe it isn't what we think. I mean, that was a long time ago, right? These diapers don't look that old. Hell, maybe they're not diapers at all. They're pretty sturdy boxes." I reach out and rap my knuckles on one of them. "Maybe she just liked to store stuff in them."

"Maybe," she says, but she sounds unconvinced. I don't blame her. I know I'm grasping at straws here, so I reach into my back pocket and pull out the utility knife I've been lugging around. I reach up and pull one of the boxes off of the pile, let it thud to the floor in front of me.

"There's only one way to know for sure," I say, and hold the knife out to her, handle-first. "You want to do the honors?"

I can tell she doesn't. Not really. But she squares her shoulders and takes the knife from me and hunkers down in front of the box. Within seconds, the thing is open, like a band-aid that's ripped off quickly, just to get it over with.

Good girl.

She jerks the flaps open, and I have to smother my reaction.

Fuck.

Diapers.

"It might not mean anything," I say before I can stop myself. And she turns to look up at me, questions in her eyes. "Look," I say. "This could have just been one of her things, right? I mean, we found like eighty pairs of gardening gloves in the shed, right? And, not to be mean or anything, but I don't think your mom ever did a lick of gardening in her life. This could just be one of her maybe-one-day things, right?"

Star lets out a shuddering sigh. "Yeah," she says, and flips the flaps of the box closed again. "That must be it." She's saying all the right words, but I can tell she doesn't believe them.

Never in my life have I wanted to wrap my arms around a girl just because. It's always been just a means to an end. But right now it's all that I want, my arms around her.

She's hurting. She's been dealt a load of shit and there's too much for her to shovel alone. Who the hell would do this to their kid?

"So," she says, pulling herself back up and rubbing her palms against her jeans. They're filthy, just like mine, but she's no priss. She's been through hell and back and has yet to do so much as blink. "What are we going to do with all these diapers?"

Yep, I think, and smile. Just a little. Without a doubt, toughest girl I've ever met. I have an instant jerk in my gut, and I just barely stop myself from opening my fool mouth and offering to help her make a baby to solve the whole diaper surplus problem. Just. Barely. Instead I bite my tongue until the urge passes, and shrug. "Why don't we leave this room for now?" I ask. "I mean, it's not like diapers go bad, and we might as well deal with the actual garbage first, right? Give us a little time to figure out if there's anyone who'll take them."

"Yeah," she says, and off in the distance Bruiser barks. Then there's the sound of a chase and a sudden crash coming from the backyard, and she snorts. "Maybe we should check on the damage in the backyard first."

I nod. "Works for me," I say. She nods one last time and reaches out to pull the door to the diaper room shut. As the door clicks into place something inside me cracks, and I reach out and wrap an arm around her shoulders, and give her a squeeze.

It's the most awkward hug ever, and considering how fucking distant and detached my parents are, that's saying something. She kind of freezes up, body going stiff next to me, so I give her a quick slap on the back and step away before I make it even worse.

Then I hightail it to the backyard, muttering something about

Bruiser being a menace.

I need a drink.

Fuck, do I *ever* need a drink.

Star

I'm ripping my grilled cheese sandwich into pieces when Ash pulls his burger off the barbecue. He doesn't even have a plate in his hand, just the bun. And the bun is completely plain. But he doesn't even stop. It's all a single motion. Flipper-barbecue-burger-bun-mouth. There isn't even a pause. I can feel my mouth drop open as I watch, my eyes watering in sympathy at the burns he's inflicting on himself, before I gather myself enough to say something.

"You're kidding, right?" I ask, dropping a too-hot piece of sandwich back on the paper plate in my lap. I wave my fingers around a bit. The cheese is still almost molten hot, and I took my sandwich off way before he did. I'm amazed he isn't dying.

"What?" he asks through a mouthful. "'S good." But judging by the way his eyes start to scrunch up, he's full of shit.

"Yeah, right," I say. "You just let me know when you want me to administer first aid. It's the least I can do." I pick up one of the cooler bits of sandwich and dunk it into the tiny pot of soup I made. Ash had looked at me like I was trying to climb to the moon on a ladder of cheese when I brought out the pot of tomato soup. Apparently, cooking soup on the barbecue isn't socially acceptable, but whatever. I'm running out of money and my mom had stored probably a thousand cans of soup in the pantry. If it hasn't hit its best before date yet, I'm eating it. Bruiser is on the grass between us, looking back and forth all askance, like he's trying to figure out which of us is more likely to give up our food. Joke's on him. I'm starving.

"You're just jealous," he says, and takes another victorious bite. The burger's juice drips down his chin and, dropping the spatula down on the barbecue's little table, he chases after it with his palm. I kind of want to chase after it with my tongue, but that's more about the fact that Ash seems to be getting hotter with each passing day, and less about his burning-hot hamburger. I shift in my seat a little. The wood of the porch steps is digging into the backs of my legs, but for all the junk my mother had in the backyard, a surplus of usable lawn chairs doesn't seem to be part of it. So like always, I am making due. Besides, it means I can keep my tiny pot of tomato soup next to me for easy dipping, and effective guarding from Bruiser, who wouldn't have found the height of a table to be that much of a challenge.

"Jealous of what?" I ask. "The fact that you're cooking yourself from the inside out, or the fact that everything you eat seems to be a random shade of *brown?*"

"What's your point?"

"Well, for one, it's disgusting and you're going to burn the crap out of your mouth, and two, you're going to get scurvy."

He scoffs at me, and takes another deliberate bite of his burger. "Like you're one to talk," he says, and nods down at my lap. I look down. The paper plate still has half a grilled cheese sandwich and the grease is kind of making the plate weak, but there's nothing wrong with my dinner.

"What?" I ask, looking back up at him. I hold up a piece of the sandwich. "It's healthy. I put tomato in it. See?" I waggle the bit at him, showing him the tiny red edge of tomato that's smooshed between melted cheese. I couldn't use much. I'm not able to buy too much fresh stuff, not when we only have the tiny beer cooler we found in the garage. Well, sort of. Beside the garage. We haven't quite gotten around to facing that monster yet. But soon.

I am working up to it.

He smiles and shakes his head. "You eat like a college student," he says, and I narrow my eyes at him, confused.

"Um, I *am* a college student." I thought he knew that. But judging by the way his eyes widen, I guess he didn't.

"You are?" he asks, and he's so distracted by that fact that he doesn't seem to notice Bruiser sidling up next to him, his eyes trained like homing beacons on Ash's hamburger. A smile spreads across my face and I look back up at him.

"What? Why do you look so shocked? Don't you think I'm smart enough?" I'm teasing, but he seems to be taking me seriously, and he begins to turn a little red around the neck.

"Yes," he says. "I mean, no. Of course not." He shakes his head as if to clear it, and he looks down just in time to see Bruiser take a snap at the burger in his hand, and yanks it away before the dog can get it. Bruiser whines and falls back on his haunches, making sad noises at his owner, like he's bemoaning the terrible injustice of it all. It's fabulous. That dog deserves an Academy Award.

"No, I mean you're smart enough. Of course you are. It's just—"

"Just what?" I dunk another piece of my sandwich into my pot of soup, confident in the fact that my food is safe for now, and pop it into my mouth.

"I just didn't realize there were any colleges around here. Like, at all."

"Oh, no," I say. "I don't think there are. No, I go to school in Climbfield."

Ash

Shit. *Shit.* She lives in Climbfield. That's two fucking states away.

Of *course* she does.

I feel like every muscle in my body has tensed up all at once, to haul myself up over the edge of a cliff, only to go limp and fall over the side, anyway. I'm so screwed. I finally find a girl like her, and she's leaving. It's June now. When does college *start* back up, August? September? I don't even know. There's no way she'll want me. I don't even have the smarts to know when college starts, let alone attend one or do anything worthwhile with my life. There's no way she's going to give me a shot, not when she's leaving so soon. And she's got a ton of shit going on in her life, anyway. No wonder she wants to sell the house.

Oh fuck. The house.

That's why she needed my help. So she could get it done in time to sell it before school starts back up.

Fuck.

I look up at her. She's practically glowing in the evening light, skin all golden from working in the backyard with me for the past two weeks. She's smiling from ear to ear, telling me about the program she's in, about the kids she's going to be able to help once she's done.

I barely hear a word of it. My brain has screeched to a brutal halt. All I can think about is the fact that she's leaving.

There's a whine beside me and I look down to see Bruiser gazing up at me with sad eyes. I sigh and take one last bite of my burger before tossing the rest to him. Star stops talking abruptly as he chows it down, and when I turn to look, she's got this little wrinkle between her eyes and I'm so screwed, because I want to lean over, smooth my hands down through her thick, inky hair and kiss that wrinkle away.

"You okay?" she asks, and even though I'm choking on the words, I nod and force them out.

"Yeah," I say. "Just not really hungry, I guess." I'm about to turn to her, to tell her that I should be hitting the road, when my eyes catch on something, something that's been niggling at the back of my brain, bothering me. And it's like a fucking target I can't get out of my sights.

"Can I ask you something?"

"Well, that was *something*," she says, giving me a little smile, "but I suppose I'll allow it."

"You might get pissed." I know I would if someone started questioning *my* ink. Tattoos are fucking personal.

But she just raises her eyebrows at me, and shakes her head, still smiling at me. "Just spit it out, Ash."

"What's wrong with your tattoos?" I blurt out, and then instantly want to kick myself. Because that came out way wrong. "I mean . . . " I need to fix this before she starts thinking I'm a total asshole. "They look like they're fading or something."

The smile slips from Star's face, and she looks down at her arms, brow furrowing. Then she does something completely out of the fucking blue.

She tilts her head back and *laughs.*

"Oh god," she says, reaching up to clap a hand over her eyes. "You scared me for a minute there."

"Okay, I'm really fucking confused," I tell her. What the fuck is she laughing at?

"They're just drawings," she says, voice muffled by her hands covering her mouth. "They're permanent marker."

"What, all of them?" I ask, because if so, they really fooled me. But she just shakes her head and lets her hands fall back to her lap.

"The waitress at the diner kept giving me her murder-face whenever she caught a look at my real ones, so I started adding to them with the sharpies Autumn sent me, just to piss her off." She stands up and reaches out, turning her extended arms this way and that, so I can take a closer look. Without thinking, I squat down so we're at the same level and reach out and wrap my hand around one of her wrists, turning her arm gently. She's right. They're just marker. Now that I'm up close I can see where her real ones end and the drawings begin. It's pretty obvious, actually.

I kind of feel like an asshole, though. But Star just smiles at me, looking up at me through her dark lashes.

"They're kind of shitty, I know," she says. "I'm not a very good artist."

"I am," I murmur, and then freeze when I realize I've spoken aloud. I wait a beat. Then two. Three. Then I tear my gaze away from her arm and look up at her. She's staring at me, a little furrow forming between her brows.

"You are?"

"Shit," I say, and drop her arm and pull myself out of my crouch, trying to put some distance between us. "I didn't mean to say that. Your drawings are fine."

"My drawings look like they were done by a twelve year old on Ritalin," she says, and instead of just letting it go, she stands and turns to face me. "Now what did you say about being an artist?"

"Oh god," I say, and reach up to scrub a hand over my face. I am giving too much of myself to this girl, sharing too much. And the damnedest thing is, I want to.

But I can't. How the hell can I keep my distance when I keep letting her get close.

"Wait here," I tell her, and then walk down the porch, around the corner, and through the gate.

I could just get in my car, I think. *Get in my car and just drive away. Then we'd never have to talk about this, and I'd actually be able to stay away from this girl.*

But I don't. When I reach my car, instead of swinging open the door and sliding into the driver's seat and tearing off down the road, I just lean in and pull out the hardback book I keep on the passenger seat. I don't even let myself think about what I am doing on the walk back. Because if I do, I'll chicken out.

"Here." I thrust the book out to her. She blinks at it, then at me, like she isn't sure what I'm doing. I sigh, embarrassed. "Just take it," I tell her. And she does.

She opens the cover, and immediately sinks back down to sit on the step. "Holy shit, Ash." She says, flipping through pages. "Did you really draw all these?" She goes from page to page, through my sketches. Sketches of Bruiser as a puppy, the yard at the prison I spent five years in, the hallway at Avenue High where my friends and I used to hang out when we should have been in class. They're decent, but they're nothing special. I only picked up drawing because it made girls dig you and simultaneously managed to keep me out of trouble in high school. After all, when I was busy drawing, I wasn't busy doing things I shouldn't have been doing.

It was a damn shame that I let it fall to the wayside after I got with Gina. Oh, I would sketch here and there—after all, it's how I managed to get my ex to go out with me in the first place—but it wasn't anything serious. I only picked it back up for real again after the crash, when I had to do something to keep me busy, or risk going crazy while I was in prison.

But from the look on Star's face, she seems to think they are okay, and I'm not about to argue with her.

I shove my hands into my pockets as she flips from picture to picture. "Yeah," I say, trying to keep the embarrassment out of my voice. She tilts her head back and looks up at me.

"I'm serious," she says. "These are really good." She smiles at me, and I kind of nod—because what the fuck am I supposed to say to that? Thanks?—and she turns back to the sketchbook. She runs her finger down the page with my drawing of my beach hideaway, and lets out a sigh. "My dad used to draw," she murmurs, her voice so low I barely hear her.

She's never mentioned her dad, except for the fact that he died. Not once in the weeks we've been working together has she supplied any other little detail about him. And because I've never developed an adult brain-to-mouth filter that actually works when it's supposed to, I blurt that out before realizing what I've done and then try to kill myself with my brain.

Luckily, Star doesn't seem to notice the fact that I'm an idiot. "Yeah. He died when I was really little." She flips another page. It's a drawing of a lizard this time, one I did when I finally managed to get my hands on some colored pencils in the joint. Greens and reds and yellows. I went nuts. "But the stuff he drew . . . it was awesome, but it wasn't like this. This is real. It looks like it could walk off the page. You're kind of talented, Ash," she says, turning her head to look at me slyly. "I hope you realize that."

Now I'm blushing like a twelve year old. Fan-fucking-tastic. "What did your dad draw?" I blurt out, trying desperately to cover my embarrassment.

Star's face . . . *God*. It just splits into this huge smile, like just thinking about it makes her so freaking happy. "Cartoons. He used to draw me cartoons. Pages and pages of them. There was this one, this little duck. It was so cute. He used to do this crazy duck-voice that didn't fit at all—he made it sound so *angry*." She laughs, and all I want to do in that moment is draw her, all her long lines and gorgeous curves. My fingers start to itch with want. "It was so much fun," she says, but then her face changes, turns sad, and after a moment I realize why. She misses him. She misses him real bad.

"I mean—" she looks down at the sketchbook, runs her fingertips down the edge of the page "—I loved my mother. She was sick and hurting and wasn't able to take care of me, but that doesn't mean I didn't love her. But my dad... All the memories I have of him are good ones. It's . . . it's different, somehow."

"Do you still have any of the drawings?" I ask. But I already know the answer before she shakes her head and flips the sketchbook closed. She hands it back to me.

"If any of them even still exist, they're in there," she nods toward the house. "Somewhere. I was hoping I'd be able to find one or two of them, but honestly..." She sighs. "Honestly, I had no idea that the house had gotten this bad. Even if they're still in there somewhere, I doubt we'll be able to find them. Not when I need to get this done on deadline. We don't have time to sort through every single piece of paper."

"Yeah," I say, because what the hell else is there to say? She's right. It's pretty much impossible. But still, I'm going to try to keep an eye out, anyway. She deserves to have something of her dad. And if I can, I'm going to find it for her.

We sit in silence, until finally the minutes stretch into miles and it turns awkward enough that I can't take it anymore. "Okay," I say, and force out a laugh as I reach up and rub at the back of my neck. "This has gotten pretty fucking grim."

Star chuckles uncomfortably and pulls her knees up to her chest, wrapping her arms around them in a hug. "Yeah," she says. "Sorry about that."

"That's okay," I say, but even now, the silence starts to drag on and on. All I can think about is the fact that Star's leaving, and that, no matter what I do, she's probably going to end up having to leave Avenue without a single good memory of her family to take with her. And it sucks. Honestly, I don't think she's going to have a single happy memory of Avenue as a whole. Not after everyone has been treating her like crap, and I know a lot of that is because of me.

That's when it hits me, and a grin starts spreading across my face. I don't even try to smother it.

"Hey," I say, and Star tilts her head back again to look at me, and every single damn time that happens, I get a punch in the gut. She's so damn beautiful. In another life, maybe things could have been different. If her mom hadn't messed up, if I hadn't been such a fuck-up, maybe we could have been something. Something good.

Coulda, woulda, shoulda, I think. I can't change the past. But I sure as hell am going to make the best of the present. I raise an eyebrow at her and set my sketchbook down on the porch. "Want some help pissing off the good people of Avenue?" I ask.

A smile tugs at the corner of her mouth. "What do you have in mind?" she asks, and I know I'm grinning like an idiot when I reach out my hand to her.

"Give me some of those markers," I say. "And you'll find out."

Twenty minutes later, Star has the lizard from my sketchbook living on her shoulder, and her smile keeps shining long after the ink has dried.

Chapter 10

Ash

There are six sofas in the living room. Six. Seriously. Why the fuck are there six sofas in the living room? Who the hell could ever need that many sofas? And how the hell did Star's mom even manage to get them in here by herself? Because she must have done it somehow. Unless she had a load of friends that disappeared into the woodwork the day she died, she did this all on her own. And I just can't wrap my head around it.

My extreme fucking bafflement must show on my face, because Star just kind of shrugs at me and goes, "Yeah . . . I have no idea."

We found the first one by mistake when we were trying to carve a path through the piles of stuff. Then we found the second one. That's when we started to wonder what we were up against, and started climbing on the piles and digging through shit to figure out what was underneath. The answer? Six goddamn sofas. I'm dumbfounded.

But now that I know they're there, I can't help but eye one of them, trying to figure out how comfortable it is by sight alone. They're all piled high with stuff, but they seem to be okay, and even if they're not, they're still starting to look pretty tempting, especially since I've been sleeping in the backseat of my car for the past *month*. It's not the end of the world—don't get me wrong, I'd rather have the car than have nothing—but for the past week I've been sharing it with Bruiser. And while having my dog back is amazing, and the big lug is awesome in many different ways, he isn't exactly what you would call *small*. He takes up almost as much space in the car as I do.

Also, he fucking *snores*.

"Well," Star says, hands on her hips as she surveys the mess in front of us. The living room is now a maze of paths and mountains of stuff, so while we can navigate it, it isn't exactly welcoming. "The way I see it, the sofas are good news and bad news."

"So, par for the fucking course, then," I say, because every time we seem to catch a break, we get blasted with another setback. I have no idea how we're going to get this done by the end of the summer, if we ever get it done it all. We've only just gotten the backyard done, and all we've managed to do inside is carve out these paths and get the worst of the trash out of the living room. We haven't even touched the kitchen yet, other than to snag utensils and steal canned goods when we can manage to reach them. We're a month in and we've barely made any progress at all.

Long story short, we're fucked.

I groan and scrub my hands through my hair. It's fucking *scorching* in here. Again. It's even worse than it was outside, and that's saying something. "What's the good news?" I ask, because we could really use some at this point.

"The good news is that this means the piles in here aren't as high as we thought they were," she says. And that makes sense. The sofas take up a lot of space so they push everything else up closer to the ceiling. Okay, that's not so bad. That actually means there's a lot less shit in here than I originally thought. That's . . . something.

"And the bad news?" I ask, because I know it's coming and I figure I might as well get it over with.

Star sighs and kind of rolls her neck. It's like she's trying to work the kinks out of it. It makes her hair dance around her shoulders and draws my eyes like a magnet to the glistening skin above the neckline of her shirt. Part of me—a huge fucking part of me—starts hoping that the heat will continue to rise and that she'll strip down to her bikini top like she did the other day. I wince and tamp that thought down as fast as I can, before the heat pooling in my belly can turn into anything real.

Do not perv on Star, I remind myself for the thousandth time since I met her. *She's hot as hell, but she's also your kind-of boss. And she's the only person in this town willing to take a chance on your stupid ass. Don't blow it.*

She runs her hands through her hair, pulling it up off her damp neck and piling it up into a messy bun on the top of her head. Then she lets it go, and it falls like a black tidal wave down her back. I swallow. Hard.

"The bad news," she says, crossing her arms over her chest as she surveys the mountain of stuff in front of us. "Is that there's no way the sofas are going to fit in either of our cars, not unless we strap it to the roof and drive insanely carefully, and I can't afford another Dumpster. Not yet, anyway. So I have no idea how we're going to get them out of here."

Shit.

She's right.

We've been jockeying stuff to the dump between my car and her mom's old station wagon ever since they hauled away the Dumpster when it filled up. And that had been nothing in comparison to this, it had only held the stuff from the backyard. This was a hell of a lot more. I have no idea how much the Dumpster cost her, but judging by the look on her face when she got the bill, well . . . we weren't going to be getting another one any time soon.

Fuck.

I turn to her to ask what the plan is, but the instant I open my mouth the sound of a car horn fills the air, cutting me off. And it's the loudest, longest fucking car horn I've ever heard, and I turn away from the sound with a wince. But as I do, something flashes through my memory, and I feel my body freeze. All at once, I'm back there, the night of the accident. And all I can hear is the sound of the guy I killed as he honked his car horn frantically. I can see it, hear it. It plays over and over in my mind. The sound. The lights. The pounding of my heart as I realize I've lost control of the car. The screech the tires make against the asphalt as I try to stop, but go careening toward him despite everything.

Shit.

I squeeze my eyes shut and shove the heel of my hand into my eye socket, trying to block it all out.

"Ash?" Star's voice cuts through me like a knife and I pull in a deep breath and hold it until my chest starts to burn. Then I let it out slowly, trying to calm the beating of my heart. I drop my hand back to my side and open my eyes. She's staring at me, her

All it Takes

confusion plain on her face. But there's more there. *Shit*, I think. *I scared her.*

"Ash?" she says again. "Are you okay?" She steps closer to me, lays a hand on my arm, and I force myself to nod, to focus on the feel of her skin against mine, clasping onto the feeling like an anchor to hold myself in the here and now.

"Yeah," I say, nodding shakily. I hate what this does to me, the flashes I get. "Just…" I blow out a breath. I don't know what I'm supposed to do here, what I'm supposed to say. All I've ever been able to do is wait it out, and eventually the sounds and the images fade back into half-forgotten memory. I look down at her, and I realize with a jolt just how close she's standing. She's right in front of me, looking up at me with those big brown eyes of hers.

Fuck, I think. *I could just reach out and touch her.* Six inches. That's all it would take. I could just lean forward, close the distance between us and kiss her. I'm moving before I know what I'm doing, and Star's eyes flicker from mine down to my mouth and back up again.

And the car outside blasts its horn again and I jerk away.

"Jesus Christ," I say, pulling back and trying to get my muscles to unclench before I get pulled under again. "What the hell is all that honking about?"

"I have no idea," she says, stepping back. I let myself mourn the loss for an instant, then shake it off. I shouldn't be kissing her, anyway. I shouldn't even be *thinking* about it. She gives me one last once-over with her eyes, making sure I'm okay, and then turns away. I watch as she starts navigating the path we cleared to the front door, and then I follow. I want to find out what the hell is going on out there.

Star jerks open the front door and together we step out onto the porch. Bruiser, who decided that the single sofa we managed to get cleared off now belongs to *him* and has spent the last hour napping on it while Star and I surveyed the rest of the mess, is now hot at my heels. He's sniffing the air, his ears folded low, like all of the survival instincts he picked up over the past five years are suddenly on red alert, and he's waiting for an attack.

He might have the right idea, I realize when I lay eyes on the truck. I take an instinctive step back when I see it.

It's this huge shit-kicker pickup, old and blue and rusty around the edges. It looks like it must belong to some kind of gigantic redneck that goes by the name Bubba.

Beside me, Star stands frozen, and all at once all the muscles in my body have tensed back up again and I feel like I'm about to head into a brawl. Beside me, Bruiser growls low in his throat, and I reach out and grab him by his collar, holding him back. Whatever is about to happen—and something is going to happen, of that I have no fucking doubt—I don't want Bruiser to be the one to start it.

The truck's passenger door swings open suddenly, and Bruiser barks at the movement and lunges forward. I look down and jerk him back before he can make a break for it. Then I look back up, and I *freeze*.

What the hell?

I watch as a plump brunette hops out of the cab of the pickup. She's got a smile on her face so big that she looks like she could light up the night sky with it. There's a slam and a figure emerges from the other side, rounding the nose of the truck and heading for the front path. It's a dude, but he's far from the bible-thumping, squirrel-shooting redneck I'd been picturing. This guy looks more like a Mormon or something. His dark hair is all neatly cut and styled, and he's wearing a pair of khakis that I can see from here have been ironed. Not to mention the dress shirt he's wearing that he's actually *tucked into* the pressed khakis.

Who the hell are these people? I wonder. Beside me, Bruiser lets out another bark and I hiss at him to be quiet. I turn to Star, hoping she has some idea of what's going on.

But what I see when I turn to look is *not* what I expected. At all.

Star . . . The only word that I can come up with to describe the look on her face is *joyous.* She looks like she just won the lottery, and she hasn't had time to decide if she's going to freak out and start screaming or if she's going to start crying. She looks *so happy.* And it makes something inside me lurch.

I can't believe how gorgeous she looks.

Before I can ask who these people are, she's off the porch and racing toward the couple. The girl from the truck all but squeaks with joy, and opens her arms and catches Star as she barrels full-speed into a hug. The guy just stands there, hands in his pockets, smiling at the two girls. But his smile is fond. There's affection there, and I try to make the thought of this straight-laced Mormon-looking dude and badass Star fit together in my brain. But as I'm twisting and turning this information over in my mind, I see Star's hand shoot out, and watch as she grabs the guy by the front of his immaculately pressed shirt and yanks him into a reluctant group hug.

I . . . do not know what's going on here. I glance down at Bruiser and find him staring up at me, his big puppy eyes full of confusion. His tail thumps once against the slats of the porch, as if to say *Well?*

Apparently Bruiser doesn't know what to make of this, either.

Star

I can't believe they're actually here. What were they thinking? This is ridiculous. They drove through two states to get here. Who *does* that?

My friends are un-freaking-believable. I can't believe how much I've missed them. I don't think I even let myself feel it, until they were staring me right in the face.

I smile and shake my head as Autumn leans down and ruffles Bruiser's ears. I can't believe they're here. I honestly feel like if I close my eyes or turn my head or even let them out of my sight for too long, Autumn and Roth will disappear.

I can't remember ever being this happy, except for when I got into college. But that was different. That was my own achievement. That was happiness mixed with pride. This is something different. This is the friendship I've waited all my life for, a friendship big enough to make my chest hurt from their kindness.

This is what Ash felt when he found Bruiser. I just know it.

My smile is so big that my cheeks are starting to hurt, but I can't stop. Bruiser is feeding off the energy, and is racing about like he's having the time of his life, rushing back and forth along the length of the porch, stopping for pets and cuddles, before squirming away and racing off and back again.

Ash, on the other hand, seems kid of . . . wary.

"So . . . " he says, shifting his weight from his heels to the balls of his feet and back again in an awkward little sway. He's got his hands buried deep in the pockets of his jeans, as though he has no idea what he should do with them, so he's just decided to take them out of the equation entirely. "How long are you guys staying?"

"Just for the weekend," Autumn says, giving Bruiser one last pat before she pulls herself back upright. "It's a really long drive, so we're going to have to head back early Monday morning. We're sorry we didn't come sooner," she says, turning to me. "But we figured the long weekend was the best time to do it."

Holy crap. Is it almost the Fourth of July already? I can't believe so much time has passed. It feels like the last time I blinked it was the beginning of June. The realization is like a pit in my stomach. It's already been a month and it's felt like days.

How much longer until I'm forced to say goodbye to Ash. And worse, how much longer will it actually feel?

Crap. I shake my head, trying to rid myself of those kinds of thoughts. My friends are here, and that is something to celebrate.

"What are you guys even doing here?" I ask. Because as happy as I am to see them, it isn't like Avenue is a hopping vacation resort. "I mean, I'm happy you're here, but it's kind of boring. We can show you the lake, I guess, but . . . "

"Ugh, we're here to help you, Star," Autumn groans out, and her words take a second to sink in.

"You mean—"

She motions something between a hand-flap and jazz-hands toward the house. "We're here to help you clean out the house."

"Holy shit. Seriously?"

For a moment, I'm sure it's me that's spoken. Those were the exact words that were floating about in my head. But it wasn't me. It was Ash. I turn to him and his eyes are kind of bugged out of his face, and as I watch they dart between Autumn and Roth. "No, really. Are you serious?"

Autumn and Roth look at each other and sigh. I'm used to that, they do it to me all the time. But it's kind of nice being on the outside when they do it. Watching them do the *are-you-really-so-difficult* look to someone else gives me a sick kind of delight.

They do their silent mind-meld talking thingy and whatever they're duking it out over Roth loses. He gives Autumn a long-suffering look and she grins gleefully as he turns to Ash and holds out his hand. "I'm sorry," he says. "I don't believe we've met. I'm Rothwell Harvey. And you are?"

"Rothwell," Ash repeats, testing it out in his mouth like he's uncertain what he's saying is even a word. I know the feeling. Roth's name is pompous as hell.

"Roth," I say his name like the warning it is. And he glances over at me. *No torturing Ash,* I think at him, hoping that for once I'll finally manage to get through to him like Autumn does.

His shoulders drop a little and he sighs and turns back to Ash. "You may call me Roth, as the girls do," he says, and his voice is still proper enough to belong to an eighty-year-old judge from the Old South, but I'll take it for what it is. Progress.

"Oh-kay," Ash says, and holds out his own hand to shake Roth's. It's like watching some strange kind of bird mating dance. Full of posturing and awkward as hell, but impossible to look away from.

"And I'm Autumn," my roommate interjects as soon as the boys' hands drop, sticking her own in to grab Ash's so fast, I'm wondering if she thinks he's going to make a break for it.

Actually, now that I think about it, he kind of *looks* like he wants to make a break for it. I need to get things sorted out.

Fast.

I reach out and grab Ash's arm so suddenly he actually *jumps* and turns to look at me, eyes wide with *what the hell do you think you're doing* written all over his face. I glance over to my friends, at Autumn who's still holding her hand out to Ash. "We'll be right back," I say, and Autumn just smiles and waggles her eyebrows at me as she drops her hand. "I saw that," I hiss at her quietly, mentally reminding myself just how quiet and shy she used to be when we first met… I am starting to miss shy-Autumn. She gave me a lot less crap.

I see her mouth "I know" and grin at me as I turn and start pulling Ash across the yard. He walks after me obediently, but when I glance over my shoulder at him, I can see a million emotions playing across his face. Most of them are *confusion.*

As soon as we're around the side of the house, out of sight of Roth and Autumn, I stop walking and turn to face him. "I'm so sorry about that," I say. "I swear I didn't mean to bombard you with my friends. I didn't even know they were coming." I can't believe they showed up. No one, in my entire life, has been willing to drive across two states for me. Not even my own mother.

"No big," Ash says, and as I watch he seems to almost *shrink* into himself, hands burrowing deep into his pockets again, shoulders hunched, head down. What the hell?

"What's the matter?" I ask. Is he really that upset that they're here?

"No . . . I mean, it's nothing," he says, but he's shifting his weight from foot to foot and he isn't looking at me. Something's wrong. "Just let me know if you want me to get out of your hair or anything."

Wait. *What?*

"What are you talking about?" I ask. My palms are starting to sweat and my heart is inching up in my chest like it's about to make a break for it. What the hell is going on?

And why is some traitorous part of me acting like he's breaking up with me? We're friends. Barely. Co-workers. I should not be feeling like this.

"No, I mean, your friends are here. If you want me to take a hike so you can spend some time with them, it's okay. I get it. I mean . . . " He sighs and looks at some far-off spot just over my shoulder, like he can't quite bring himself to look me in the eye. "I don't want them to think, you know, any less of you or anything."

I wipe my sweating palms against my shorts and stare at him. It takes me a minute, but finally something clicks in my brain and I get it.

Jesus.

"This is about the prison thing again, isn't it?" I ask, even though I already know the answer. "What the hell, Ash?"

Finally he meets my eye, but his face is confused, like *I'm* the one who's saying things that don't make sense. *Idiot,* I think, but the voice in my head is unmistakably fond, and I can't help but smile. I shake my head at him. "You're an ass," I say, and reach out and snag his arm again. "You're not going anywhere."

He doesn't say anything as I drag him back over to Autumn and Roth, but when we come to a stop, I look over my shoulder at him and catch the secret smile tugging at his lips, even as he tries to hide it. I turn back to my friends and find Autumn looking back and forth between us like there's a puzzle she's trying to figure out. Roth, on the other hand, is kind of staring off into space, something he tends to do whenever he's affronted with too many emotions and needs to tune himself out. I look at Autumn. She's stopped looking back and forth between us and has now pinned me with a look that I can only hope to translate as *you okay?*

I nod, and let her see my smile.

"Okay," Autumn says, breaking the silence clapping her hands together like she's the ringleader of this particular circus. "Where do we start?"

Chapter 11

Star

Ash is a traitor. He's a dirty, rotten, no good traitor and I hate him.

And his dog.

"Really, you guys," I say as the others hover around the pantry door in the kitchen. "We should work on the living room. It needs the most work." I don't know why everyone's so focused on the sleeping-in-the-shed thing. I know for a fact that Autumn used to go camping with her family. It's the exact same thing. Almost. In *fact*, it's better, because it has an actual roof and a door to protect me from the elements. Besides, the pantry can pretty much just stay the way it is when I'm trying to sell it. It may be over-full, but at least it's the one place in the house that's full of the stuff it's supposed to be filled with. I think getting the towering piles of shame out of the living room is a little more urgent then getting the canned goods out of the pantry.

Unfortunately, I've been out-voted.

"Can you hear something, Roth?" Autumn says as she rips open a box of garbage bags, her voice too loud in the small space we're working in. "Because I can't."

I hate her, too.

"No," Roth replies, climbing over a pile of what I'm *hoping* is laundry and not anything mysterious and disgusting because I *would* still like to have friends at the end of this. "Not unless you're talking about an ungrateful girl who doesn't care that we're trying to help her not live like a derelict."

I let out a groan. Yeah. I hate him, too. Everyone. I'm just going to live in the shed and hate everyone from now on. That's the best plan.

"Come on, you guys," I try, for what feels like the millionth time. "It's not so bad. And I really do need to get the living room cleaned out."

"What you need," Autumn says, ripping off a garbage bag from the roll and holding it out to me to take, "is a safe place to sleep. Preferably one that's indoors. Now—" she nods toward the path Roth is carving in the kitchen "—we're going to get the kitchen and the pantry cleaned out as best we can, because let's be honest, we're awesome but we're not miracle workers. The pantry is small enough that we actually stand a chance of clearing it out so that you can sleep in there. Your mattress will fit. And you need a kitchen, Star. That's just nonnegotiable. I can't imagine what you guys have been eating while you're here."

"Diner food, mostly," Ash supplies from behind me, and smirks at me when I turn around to glare at him.

"Traitor," I say, and turn back to see Autumn's disappointed look.

"Diner food? Really?"

"What?" I say, kicking myself for being so defensive. I'm a grownup. I'm allowed to eat what I want. "It's good." *Lies. So many lies.* The diner food is mediocre on a good day.

"Nothing is good enough to eat it every day," she says, and reaches out to push me toward Roth. "Now go help. Your bedroom awaits."

"I feel like you're trying to turn me into Cinderella," I tell her. "Making me sleep in the pantry. It won't work. I won't suddenly turn into a princess."

"You have a better chance than if you're sleeping in the shed," she replies. "Now mush!" She jabs a finger toward the kitchen, where Roth is waiting.

Something inside me jerks, and I sigh and go to follow her orders without further complaint. She has that way about her. I climb over a pile of plastic take-out containers and join Roth in the kitchen. "She's going to make an excellent RA," I tell him. "The frosh are going to be following her around like ducklings within a week."

"She learned from the best," Roth says sagely, and grins down at me. "Now get to work, little duckling."

Yeah, I think, shooting him one last glare before I reach down and start loading empty plastic grocery bags into my garbage bag. *I hate them all.*

By the end of the day, though, things aren't so bad anymore. With Roth and Autumn around, we actually manage to get not only a path through the living and dining rooms cleared out, but we also made pretty good headway on the kitchen, the one area of the house I'd been most worried about. It really is a load off my shoulders, having them here.

Especially when it came to the refrigerator. The thing stood there, huge and overbearing that first day, like a modern-day monolith, foretelling my doom. When I head outside for a water break I say as much to Autumn and she throws her back and laughs like a hyena, loud enough for the boys to hear and to turn at us, questions in their eyes.

"Star, sweetie, I think your brain is melting," she says, reaching up and wiping the back of her hand along her damp forehead. The heat inside the house is slowly killing all of us. "It's just a fridge. Nothing to be scared of." She turns to Roth and shakes her head like I'm being ridiculous.

I take a sip of my water, grateful to the tiny droplets that escape the side of my mouth to go trickling cool and wet down my neck, and raise my eyebrows at her. I can't help the smile that comes through as I recap my bottle and set it aside on the porch railing. *She doesn't get it,* I realize. *She has no idea.*

"*Sweetie,*" I say, mimicking her tone, "just what do you think happens to a fridge full of food for three months, in this heat, after the power company has turned off the juice?" I watch as seconds tick by, and my words slowly begin to sink in. Then Autumn whirls around and looks at me with eyes like dinner plates.

"Is *that* what that smell is?" she demands. "Oh. My. GOD."

Laughter bubbles up from inside me so fast I can't stop it, I just collapse back against the siding of the house and try to catch my breath. Looking up through my tangled hair I see Autumn flapping her hands, disgusted, and I realize she must be picturing what could be growing in the refrigerator and she can't stand it.

From his position on the porch steps, Roth clears his throat and we both turn to look at him. "I think that we may have to find an alternate method of dealing with the refrigerator, if that's the case," he says, and pulls his phone out of his pocket and begins scrolling through it. "I'll make a few calls. Excuse me."

I sink down onto the porch, giggles still bubbling every time I take a breath, made even worse by the way Autumn is glaring at me. As I reach over and snag my water bottle off the porch railing and uncap it, Roth disappears around the side of the house, and Ash turns to look at me. "Uh . . . where is he going?" he asks, eyes wide.

Reaching up, I wipe tears from my eyes and grin at him, my cheeks staring to ache. He's not the first one to try and fail to figure out the mystery that is Rothwell Harvey, and he won't be the last. "Honestly?" I ask before taking a sip of water. "I have absolutely no idea."

It really is a load off my shoulders, having them here.

Especially since, when I get up the next morning, the refrigerator's gone. And, judging by the way Ash is side-eyeing Roth at every opportunity, he's trying to figure out if he's in the mob. It's hilarious.

But honestly? It wouldn't surprise me.

Not one bit.

Ash

You're being an idiot, a part of my brain tells me, but it's drowned out by the louder, much more fucking *insistent* part of my mind that's going, *He made an entire rotted-out fridge disappear like it never even existed. You think he couldn't do that with a body?*

One thing's for certain. Star's friend Roth? Creepy. As. Fuck. The guy looks like he's in the running for the next Hannibal Lecter. The thought of hanging out with him doesn't really appeal. I don't know how Star does it.

And it must show on my face, because Star's brow furrows when she looks up from the box of stuff she's sorting through to look at me.

"What?" she asks.

I want to play it off, to act tough and like there's nothing bothering me, because I'm probably just imagining things. But this isn't just about me. If there's something fucked up about Star's buddy, then she has the right to know.

Grow some balls, I tell myself. *It's time to be a man.*

"Not gonna lie . . . " I say, trying to choose my words carefully. It's not like I have a real shot with this girl, but I don't want her to hate me, either. "Your friend kind of freaks me out a little." There. That wasn't so bad.

But she just tosses her head back, all long hair and gorgeous skin, and laughs. "Who, Roth?" she asks. "Why?"

I groan, and suddenly it's all coming out like word puke. I can't stop myself. "He doesn't blink!" I say, gesturing to my own face with the dust cloth I'm clutching. "It's like he's one of those old-timey paintings. The creepy ones with the eyes that follow you wherever you go."

"That's what makes me so good at my job," a voice says behind me.

Fuck.

I spin around and see Roth standing in the open doorway behind me. Creeper. He's just standing there, staring at me with those freaky eyes, dunking the teabag in his mug over and over, like he's some kind of Bond villain petting a cat. Then, without blinking *once,* he turns and walks away.

"Holy shit," I say, and clutch my hand to my chest. My heart feels like it's trying to beat its way out of there. "Holy *shit.*" Some things deserve repeating. This is one of them. "What the fuck is his job? Cutting people into little pieces and hiding them in the walls?" The dude is a psychopath.

But Star just laughs. "You get used to it," she says. "He's a Resident Advisor. He was in charge of our floor last year. It freaked everyone out so bad. No one on the floor dared do anything where he could see. Guy's got feet like a cat. Autumn and I tried putting a bell on him last Christmas. It didn't go well."

Now I'm picturing probably-a-seriel-killer-Roth with a Santa hat and murder in his eyes. It's scarring. "Oh god," I say, scrubbing my hands over my face. "How are the two of you still *alive?*"

"They have nothing to worry about," a voice says from behind me, and I just about keel over to see Roth standing behind me. Again. Jesus Christ. But he just calmly takes a sip from his mug and stares at me from above the rim.

"Uh, okay," I say. "Can I ask why?" *Just for my own self-preservation.*

"Serial killers generally don't kill outside their own sexual-preference group," he says. "Therefore, Autumn and Star would be quite safe, if I had such urges." He hasn't blinked once during the entire time he's been standing there. What the hell is wrong with this guy? My eyes burn as I try to keep an eye on him, but I, unlike Roth, have the urge to blink. Because I'm human. But luckily, before it gets too bad, he takes one last sip of tea and leaves the room. Distantly, I hear him talking to Autumn, and then there's the sound of the screen door in the front swinging open and then slamming closed again. The metallic rattle echoes through the house, and then Roth's words finally catch up to me.

I whip around to look at Star, but she's already laughing. "What. The. Fuck?" I demand.

She just shakes her head, sending her dark hair tumbling around her bare shoulders. Great. Now I'm terrified and turned on at the same time. Fan-fucking-tastic.

"Autumn and I aren't really Roth's type. If you know what I mean . . . " She waggles her eyebrows at me. It takes me a shameful amount of time to realize what she's trying to communicate here.

"You mean . . . ?" I say, and my hands make a weird gesture on their own before I can stop them, my face burning. Fuck. I don't think I've blushed this much since I was a little kid and my friend Johnny told Katie Jenkins that I wanted to kiss her. Which, whatever. It was true. She was adorable. Didn't want to give me the time of day, though, much to my shame. It sucked being the short kid.

Still kinda does, especially when Star's friend the BTK killer has a good six inches and probably twenty pounds on me. It's a little intimidating. I'm man enough to admit that.

But she just smiles at me. "Gay as Christmas," she confirms, and turns back to the box she was working on, grabbing the flaps and folding them one over the other, so that the box is sealed closed.

"Oh," I say. "Okay." I turn back to what I'm supposed to be

doing, gathering up obvious trash and stuffing it in one of the bajillion garbage bags that are hanging around the house. When I first saw how many she'd bought, I'd laughed, thinking we'd be using them 'til Judgment Day. Now I'm just hoping we have enough. We've already been getting dirty looks from people when we go into town. I don't think that buying out every box of garbage bags in the place is going to endear us to them any further. But as I gather stuff up and shove it into the bag, her words play over and over in my mind, like a record with a skip. I'm missing something. I know I am.

All at once it hits me.

"Wait!" I cry out, louder than I intended to. "How does that help *me?*" If what Mr. Psychopath said about serial killers is true . . .

Star just grins at me. "You've been to prison Ash," she says. "Toughen up a little." Then she throws her curtain of long, inky-black hair over her shoulder, picks up the box she was working on and walks out of the room.

Goddamn, I think, feeling the confusing scared/turned on feeling well up inside me as I watch her body sway as she walks away. *I'm in way over my head.*

Star

"So . . . ?" Autumn sidles up next to me, a smile tugging at the corner of her mouth. I blink at her.

"So?" I prompt, pulling open another box. I peer down at the contents. Old magazines. Again. I sigh and replace the lid and pull one of the permanent markers out of my pocket. I use my teeth to uncap it, and scrawl *garbage* in crooked letters across the top before hefting the box to the side and starting on the next one. The sheer amount of money my mother spent on magazines astounds me. I could have paid my entire first year's tuition just on what I've found so far. And most of it was going straight into the trash. We'd salvaged what we could, and had filled up bin after bin of recycling, but the terrible condition of most of the stuff made it impossible to save.

"Soooo . . . ?" Autumn draws out the word like it's full of syllables, which, considering she's an English major, she should know better. I turn and look over my shoulder at her. She's bouncing on her toes like a little kid with a secret. Oh god. "What's going on with you and Ash?"

My eyes go wide and I scan the room to see if he overheard her, but he's off in the dining room, working his way through the leaning tower of newspapers, and luckily he doesn't look up. I turn back to her. "I don't know what you're talking about," I hiss under my breath, hoping against hope that she'll take the hint and *be quiet.*

Unfortunately, my panic doesn't seem to register, and she keeps going. "I mean the looks between the two of you . . . " She waggles her eyebrows at me, grinning. "It's like there's fireworks going off in the room every time you meet each other's eyes."

"Shut. Up." I mutter as quietly as possible, and look over my shoulder at Ash, just to make sure he can't hear her. But he still isn't looking at us. Instead he's staring down at one of the newspapers, and the sheets of newsprint are trembling a little in his hands. My brow furrows, and I move to take a step closer, to reach out and ask him what's wrong. But before I can take a single step, he shakes his head like he's coming out of a fog and tears the top page off the newspaper. As I watch, he tosses the rest of the paper aside and slowly, carefully, folds up the piece he tore off and slides it into his pocket.

What on earth?

Autumn nudges me, but I don't turn back to her. Not yet. Instead I watch as Ash takes a deep breath and presses the heels of his hands into his eyes for a moment. Then he lets out a sigh and scrubs his fingers up through his hair, leaving the pale strands sticking up in wild tufts.

"Hey, Ash . . . ?" The words are out of my mouth so quickly I can't believe I'm the one who actually uttered them. Ash reacts with a jolt and turns to look at me, and I can see *something* in his eyes for a brief second, something almost *haunted,* before he manages to compose himself and nod at me. "You okay?" But I can see from here that no matter how he answers, the real answer is *no.* He's not okay.

But he just nods and I let it go. Whatever's bothering him, it's not my place to bring it up in front of Autumn. If he wants to tell me, he'll tell me. If not, well . . . that's his decision.

He reaches down and hefts up the rest of the pile of newspaper, a stack about a foot and a half high, and makes his way toward the door. His path brings him right past Autumn and I, and as he passes I reach over and run a hand down his arm. Our eyes meet and we pause there for a second, frozen in our own little world.

"Fireworks," Autumn says, and my entire body jolts and I yank my hand away like it's been burned. I turn and glare at her, but she just smirks at me.

"What's that?" Ash says, confusion lacing his voice.

"Nothing," I mutter, and try to turn away and go back to work

before I'm forced to kill my former roommate in cold blood. My heart is slamming so hard in my chest that it's a wonder no one else can hear it. To me, it's absolutely thundering. *Dammit, Autumn.*

But she isn't done, and I have yet to figure out how to kill people with my brain, so she turns to Ash and I can feel her sunbeam-smile from where I'm standing, even though my back is turned. "Fireworks," she says, and pauses because she's *trying to kill me.* Just as I'm about to whirl around and drag her out of the room kicking and screaming—and probably laughing her ass off—she continues. "I was just telling Star that Roth and I are taking you guys out to see the fireworks tonight."

Wait. What? I turn to look at her, and I'm more than a little concerned when I see the glint in her eye.

"Fireworks," Ash says, like the word is unfamiliar to him and he's testing it out for the first time. I catch his eye and we come to a silent agreement that Autumn is insane. At least, I *think* that's what that look means.

"Yup," Autumn says, her voice light and perky, turning herself into a bouncy cotton-candy-for-brains version of herself, which she always does when she's lying and doesn't want to get caught. I'm going to kill her for this. Dead. Gone. And then I'm taking her book collection.

And burning it, out of spite.

Well, not all of it. There's a bunch I want for myself.

"We saw a flyer when we were heading to the B&B last night," she says. "Apparently there's a big fireworks festival down at the beach tonight, and we thought it'd be fun for all of us to go watch it." She turns to me and pins me with what I'm hoping isn't as super-obvious a *look* as I think it is.

"Together," she adds. Because she's evil.

Ash

I haven't seen fireworks since I was a kid, so I can't be sure, but I don't think I've ever enjoyed them as much as I did tonight. And I barely even looked at the explosions. I was too distracted by Star.

I don't know what it was. Maybe it was how relaxed she was, how happy she was to be around her friends, but she was glowing nearly as brightly as the fireworks themselves.

Autumn had insisted that heading down to the fireworks was *necessary,* and she'd had this look in her eye that even my own mom had never quite been able to pull off with me. The one that said *you're doing this and you will not argue. Or else.* But honestly, until she'd said something, I hadn't even remembered that the town did fireworks every year, even though it made total sense. Who *didn't* do fireworks on the Fourth of July? But if someone had just asked me out of the blue if I was interested, the answer would have been *fuck no.*

But she hadn't asked me first. She'd asked Star. And, after the initial shock on her face had passed, the smile that had spread across Star's face turned my answer from *fuck no* to *hell yes* before I could blink. Before I'd even realized what was happening, all four of us were bundled into serial-killer-dude's truck with a blanket, a bottle of Autumn's homemade wine, a couple six-packs and a grocery bag full of hot dogs and buns. I was going to leave Bruiser tied up in the backyard, but Star had been afraid that the fireworks would scare him off—which, okay, they hadn't bothered him as a puppy, but he'd been on his own for years while I was in prison; I had no idea what would freak him out now—and told me to bring him along.

It was almost worth it for the prissy look on killer-boy's face at the thought of my big, dirty dog in the cab of his truck, but I really wasn't all that willing to push my luck with him. Star seemed to think he was cool, but I still wasn't so sure. So I hopped up into the flatbed with Bruiser for the ride.

But Bruiser is already ass-over-ankles for Star, and the second we get there and she hops down from the cab, he is up and over the side, bee-lining for her. She laughs and ruffles his ears before standing up and tugging her hoodie tighter around her sweet little body. It takes everything I have not to go over and offer to keep her warm.

Instead, I just lean back against a big rock not far from where they have laid out the blanket, and smoke. The beach is already packed with people, even though dusk has barely set, and our little group ended up on the outskirts of the sand, near where the beach met the forest. Even though we are on the edge of the crowd, we still get *looks*. After half a dozen people pass us by and pin me with a side-eyed glare that says they know exactly who I am and what I've done, I almost bail, ready to tell the others I want to head back. But then I see Star, how happy she is, how good her smile and skin look in the fading sunlight, and I can't do it. I stay. I keep myself separate, so that the glares from the good people of Avenue are directed at me and not at the group, but I stay.

Damn, I want to join Star on that blanket, though. And maybe do a little more than just watching the fireworks go boom. But she is laughing and eating and drinking with her friends, and I am happy enough just watching her do it.

They are sprawled across the blanket. Roth on one end, poking at the little fire he got going while doing a fairly fine impression of nursing a beer without actually drinking any of it; Autumn in the middle, all bundled up against the cool night air. And then there is Star. Hot as hell in the little ass-hugging shorts she's been wearing all day, wrapped up in a black hoodie that is about two sizes too big for her. Her legs are all stretched out in front of her, and even my damn dog has weaseled his way in there. He is lying half on and half off the blanket, but his head is resting on my dream girl's upper thigh, and she pets his head between sips of her beer.

Smart mutt, I think with a snort, and take another drag on my smoke, trying to smother a smile.

"You okay over there?" Star calls, and I send a little chin-nod in her direction and blow out a lungful of smoke. She just shakes her head and smiles at me. Then, without another word, she laughs and shoves Bruiser's head off her lap—he gives out a pitiful little whimper and I scoff at him. *You're not subtle, buddy,* I think, but he knows what side his bread is buttered on, and as soon as Star's on her feet, he's already nosing around Autumn, looking for some love.

I watch as Star pulls herself to her feet and brushes the stuck-on sand off her long legs and make her way over to me, fresh cup of wine in hand. She stumbles a bit, and I smile, trying to figure out if it's the uneven ground or whatever Autumn keeps refilling her cup with that's making her move like that. My own cup is half-full of cola I didn't really want, but couldn't turn down when I realized that was the only non-alcoholic drink we had. I'd been a little worried about hanging around the others while they drank, but so far it hasn't been too bad. They sure as hell don't drink like my old friends and I used to. Roth seems to barely touch the stuff, and Star and Autumn seem content to get quietly tipsy, while my old group wouldn't stop until at least one of us was puking our fucking guts out on the sidewalk and laughing all the way through it. This is different.

This is nice.

Star sinks down in the sand next to me and leans back against the rock I'm using to prop myself up. She's holding her cup loosely in her hand, and even from here I can tell that the amount of booze in it is fucking astounding. What the hell is in that wine Autumn makes? Lighter fluid? "Hey," she says, her voice soft, almost husky. It makes me want to reach over and wrap my arm around her shoulders and pull her close. Instead I switch my smoke to the hand closest to her, and bring it to my mouth, just to keep my arm occupied so I don't do anything stupid.

Like touch her.

Don't be a fucking moron, I tell myself, but I can feel the warmth of her skin next to mine, and I can't help but want.

"How are you doing over here?" she asks and sort of sways into me.

Better now that you're next to me, I want to say, but glare at my bent knees instead and stub the last of my smoke out in the sand between us.

"Not bad," I tell her, then glance over at her friends, sure they're watching us. But they're not. The-next-famous-serial-killer is off gathering up more twigs for the campfire, and Autumn is having a wresting contest with Bruiser on the blanket. Bruiser, as always, is losing. But they both seem to be having fun. I look back over at Star, and in the fading light it's hard to make out the lines of her face, but I can feel as much as see that she's smiling. At me.

"Sorry you got dragged out to this," she says, taking a sip of her drink. "I know it's probably not how you wanted to spend your Fourth of July."

"Eh, it's fine." I shrug. I'm fighting the urge to pull out another smoke and light up. I need something to do with my mouth other than talk, because apparently I'm fucking awkward as hell. I used to be smoother than this. I know it. "It's not like I had anything better to do."

"But sti—"

"Ashley?" My body jolts with recognition as I hear a voice call my name. I turn, squeezing my eyes shut for a split second, praying to whoever's up there that I'm wrong, that the voice doesn't belong to who I think. But whoever's in charge up there still has a beef with me, so of course it's exactly who I think it is.

I let out a sigh and reach into my pocket. I *need* that cigarette. Now.

"Hi, Mom."

Chapter 12

Ash

I'm never fucking leaving the house again. The only place in this damn town that's safe is Star's mother's house. And considering the fact I could be crushed to death by the stuff inside it at any second, that's saying something. So just *no*. No more going outside. I'm putting my fucking foot down.

It just isn't worth it.

Mom is staring down at me, Dad hovering at her shoulder like the world's largest, most uncomfortable mosquito, and I'm racking my brain for something to say to make them leave before they realize I'm sitting with Star. Whatever they have to say to me, I don't want her to hear it. I still have some pride. Her gaze flickers down to Star, and she gets this *look* on her face, one that I've seen directed at me a million times. *Disappointment.*

"I don't believe I've met your . . . *friend,* Ashley," she says.

I roll my eyes. *Yeah,* I think, *and you're not going to, not when you say the word* friend *but somehow make it sound like* garbage. I turn to look at Star, whose gaze is darting back and forth between me and my mom. There's a little furrow digging in between her brows.

"Are you okay?" she whispers, low enough so my parents can't hear over all the noise from the crowd on the beach.

I nod once and start pulling myself to my feet. "Yeah," I say back, keeping my voice low. "You stay here, okay? I'll be right back."

I pull myself up and brush the sand off my jeans before turning and facing my parents. "Come on," I say. "Let's take a walk."

My mother shakes her head. "Oh, no," she says. "I don't want to interrupt your evening." *Too late for that. Maybe if you didn't want to interrupt, you shouldn't have, oh, I don't know, fucking interrupted it?* "I just wanted to make sure—"

"You wanted to make sure I was keeping out of trouble," I interrupt. "Well, guess what, Mom? I am."

"I think what your mother meant, son, was—"

"Ugh, save it, Dad," I snap. "She wanted to make sure I wasn't doing anything to embarrass you two. And I'm not. My cup back there? It's filled with cola. I haven't had a drink or anything else since I got out. And I got a job, so I don't need you *checking* on me anymore, got it?"

"Have you been calling your parole officer?" Mom asks, crossing her arms over her chest.

Fuck. This is why I wanted to take a walk. Now people are turning around where they stand, sneaking looks at us. Fucking fantastic. "Yes," I grind out through gritted teeth. And I have. Not that it's been easy without a phone. I've had to drive out to the one pay phone in town, which is—surprise, surprise—just outside the diner, where I'm already a freaking pariah.

"Okay," she says, and for an instant, her gaze drops and I think her shoulders do, too. "Good."

Dad's hand comes to rest on her shoulder. "Come on, Nadine," he says. "I think we should get back."

Mom nods without looking at me, and together, they turn and start walking away.

Something burns in my chest, and I can't tell if it's rage or fucking disappointment, but either way, I can't stop myself from yelling out to them as soon as they're almost back to the crowd.

"By the way," I call out, "I found Bruiser. No fucking thanks to the two of you." Mom stutters to a stop, and turns around to look at me. I raise my arm and point at the blanket where Bruiser is rolling around on his back next to Autumn, who is looking back and forth between my parents and me with eyes as big as dinner plates. Shit. She's probably wondering what the hell is going on, just what kind of guy is hanging out with her best friend.

Fuck.

I let my arm drop and watch as Mom just kind of nods sadly and turns away. I don't even wait for them to disappear into the crowd before I groan and turn back to Star, raking my hands through my hair.

She's got her plastic cup between both her palms, her thumbs worrying at the top lip of it as she looks up at me. "So . . . I'm guessing that was your parents," she says.

I sigh and walk back over to her. Sinking down onto the sand next to her, I nod. "Yeah."

She kind of raises her eyebrows at me, and the edge of her

mouth kind of tugs to one side, like she's trying to smother a smile. "Nice people," she says, and an instant later she loses control and the smirk appears. A laugh forces its way out of my throat and I bump my shoulder against hers.

"Yeah," I say, leaning back against the rock and letting the tension bleed from my body. "They're fucking *great*." I look over at her through the corner of my eye. She's twirling the cup back and forth, pressed between her palms, and is staring down at the tiny whirlpool she's created in her wine.

"I guess parents aren't all they're cracked up to be, huh?"

I shift so I can reach into my pocket for my pack of smokes. "Yeah," I say. "No kidding." The motion makes the side of my body press into the side of Star's, and, much to my surprise, she presses back. The heat of her body seeps into me, warms me like hot coffee on a cold winter's day. I like it more than I should.

But I don't pull away. Instead I stay half-pressed against her as I light my smoke and take a long drag. "Hey," she says, bumping her bent knee against mine. Smiling, she jerks her chin toward the night sky stretched out before us.

"Fireworks."

And together we lean back against the rock and watch as the fireworks begin, and a million colored explosions dance across the dark sky, their thundering sound just barely covering up the thudding in my chest as Star settles down into the sand and leans farther into me. The heat from her skin seeps into mine, and I can't help but grin.

It's the best night I've had in a long, long time.

Star

Roth and Autumn drop us back at the house afterward. In the distance, there are still fireworks going off, but I'm wiped and even though they're heading back to Climbfield, Ash and I still have a long way to go before we're finished.

I hop out of Roth's truck, stumbling a little as my feet slap against the pavement. I'm a little tipsier than I thought. I feel warm all over.

"Are you sure you're okay to drive back?" I ask Roth. I can just barely make out his nod in the darkness.

"I'm fine," he says. "I only had one beer, and that was hours ago. Besides, the B&B is just down the road."

"And we have to get on the road first thing in the morning," Autumn adds, walking around the side of the truck to reclaim the shotgun seat. She reaches out and wraps me up in a big hug that smells like apples, just as she always does. We stumble a little under each other's weight. "Gonna miss you, Starlight," she murmurs into my hair, and I nod, my throat tightening. I hadn't realized just how much I'd missed her until she'd shown up on my doorstep, her and Roth both. I squeeze her back. As hard as I can. And she does the same to me.

"I'm gonna miss you, too," I say.

"Come on, Autumn," Roth calls from inside the cab of the truck. "We need to get going."

"You sure?" Ash says from behind me. I turn and look at him. He's shifting from foot to foot, his hands in his pockets. "I mean, you could stick around for a bit, if you wanted." He drags his eyes from the ground in front of him, and suddenly those blue eyes are all that I can see. That and the little smile tugging at his lips.

My stomach flutters.

Face burning, I dig my key chain out of my purse and pass it over to him. He takes it, and a look of relief passes over his face as he finally has something to do with his hands.

"Sadly, we've been informed by our gracious hostess that the bed-and-breakfast's full service includes a curfew," Roth says, and despite his proper words, his eyes roll to the ceiling of the cab. I scoff.

"Sounds like someone I know," I tease, remembering all the grief he gave Autumn and I as an RA. I raise an eyebrow at Roth through the open passenger-side window. "I don't know where you think you're going—" I step back and open my arms wide "—but I'm not letting you leave here without giving me a hug."

He grumbles as he gets down from the cab, but I can hear the affection in his voice. I've seen the distance he puts between himself and other people, always keeping them away. But somehow, by some miracle, Autumn and I managed to see through all his posturing and grumpy looks and get close to him.

I can count on one hand the number of people I've let get close in my life. I'm not letting him go now. He trudges over and wraps me up in a big hug that lifts me bodily off the ground. I laugh as my feet dangle, from the ridiculousness or the drinks I've consumed, I don't know which. It doesn't matter, anyway. I burrow into his shoulder and breathe his warm, almost spicy scent in. I'm going to miss him. I'm going to miss them both. But even with that knowledge hanging over my head, I'm happy.

"He'd better treat you right," Roth whispers, his voice low enough that only I can hear him. I rub my face into his shoulder and squeeze him even tighter.

"It's not like that," I tell him, even though I want it to be. Sometimes. When I let my guard down and allow that traitorous part of me to *hope*.

He gives me one last squeeze and sets me back down on my feet. Pulling back, I see a small smile tugging at the side of his mouth. "Liar," he mutters through his smirk.

"Come on, big guy," Autumn says, stepping forward and clapping Roth on the shoulder. "Miss Josephine awaits."

Roth lets out a sigh that can only be described as long-suffering and turns to me. "The owner of the B&B appears to be under the mistaken impression that Autumn and I are married. Her behavior to that end is . . . unnerving."

I grin at the sight of his discomfort. It takes a lot to shake him, so it makes something warm bloom inside me at the thought of tiny Miss Josephine, the little old lady with the tiny poodle, setting him so off balance. A million scenarios run through my mind of things she could have done. All of them are hilarious.

"Ah, Miss Josephine," I say, unable to resist. "I think she might be just a tad—" I hold my fingers half an inch apart "—old-fashioned."

Autumn laughs. "She keeps calling me Mrs. Turner. It's *awesome*. Roth keeps looking like he's trying to conjure up a hole in the floor to hide in through sheer force of will." I watch as she hops up into the passenger seat and a zing of sadness rips through me at the thought of them leaving.

"If anyone could do it," I say. "It would be Roth."

Roth just shakes his head and sighs at Autumn's laughter before turning to Ash and holding out his hand. "It was a pleasure to meet you, Ash," he says, and waits patiently as a riot of emotions parade across Ash's face as he tries to decide if Roth is for real. He looks like a robot when he reaches out and shakes Roth's hand, but then Roth steps closer and whispers something in Ash's ear. Whatever he said, it was too quiet for me to hear, but it made Ash's eyes widen a little as Roth steps away. They share a moment of that weird thing guys do when they're silently trying to figure out which one of them is top dog. Then Roth silently turns away, and Ash looks down at his hand once Roth has released it, staring at it like it betrayed him somehow.

As he steps back toward the car, I grab Roth in one last hug. "You take care of yourself, okay?" I say, and then lean forward to whisper in his ear. "What did you say to him?"

"I'll do that," Roth says loud enough for the others to hear, and then whispers in my ear, "Wouldn't you like to know?"

I pull back. "You're evil." He just smiles at me, and doesn't blink.

I hate when he does that. But I can't help but laugh.

"You've got everything?" I ask him, and he nods.

"I have enough ramen to keep my charges fed in the event of a nuclear holocaust. If I need anything else, I don't know what it is."

I smile, but it's kind of true. We found so much ramen in my mother's pantry, it was ridiculous. They'd taken it back to the B&B in the meantime, but once it was packed in the car, it would be stacked up in the truck's backseat so high it would nearly block the back window. Between that and all the other stuff I've foisted off on him, Roth should be set through the rest of his tenure as an RA. Even if he decides to go for his PhD.

The image of him eating never-ending bowls of ramen while he glares at his homework springs fully-formed into my mind, and I giggle out loud before I can stop myself. I clamp a hand over my mouth to stifle the sound but it's too late. I feel my legs sway a little bit under me, and try to right myself without being too obvious about it, but by the looks the others are giving me, I'm failing pretty hard.

I guess the wine is hitting me harder than I thought.

Our goodbyes are brief after that, and Ash and I stand at the edge of the driveway together, Bruiser sniffing at the edge of the grass by our sides, watching as Roth's truck disappears into the night before turning and heading toward the house.

"Ah crap," I mutter, swaying a little as we climb the porch steps, Bruiser happily trotting along after us until Ash nudges him and tells him to go lay down. I sway directly into Ash's side and settle there, even though I can feel my face begin to heat. Or maybe that's just the warmth coming through his clothing. It's nice. I press closer and murmur, "I forgot to pay you," and hope that he isn't going to be too pissed.

His arm wraps around my back, steadying me. I was swaying a little more than I thought, and I tilt my head back to look up at Ash. He's looking down at me and he's got this little furrow digging between his brows. Cute.

"What?" he asks, and helps me forward, though the front door. I hadn't even realized he'd unlocked it. When did I give him my key?

I make it over the threshold gracefully enough, but then my leg glances against a stack of empty boxes we'd put by the door, and they all go tumbling down.

"Oops." I take a tentative step back from the mess. "Why are those still in here? Shouldn't we have tossed them?"

"We were gonna use them in the campfire, remember?" Ash says and kicks one of the boxes out of the way so the path is clear again. "Save us a trip to the dump."

"Oh, yeah. But no. Right." What was I talking about again? Ugh, stupid Autumn with her stupid wine. It always hits me so much harder than anything else. I think hard for a second, leaning against the wall to steady myself as I try to remember what I was talking about. Stupid wine. My thoughts are slipping away from me like the beach sand through my fingers. "What was I . . .h, yeah!" I wag a finger at Ash. "Money." That was it. I look around the room, but it's too dark. "Where's my checkbook?" I know it's here somewhere. It has to be. I'm halfway to the little table we put by the front door when I hear Ash laugh and feel his hand close around my upper arm, tugging me back.

"I have no idea what you're talking about," he says, and even in the darkness I can see his smile. I really, really like his smile. "Come on—" he tugs at my arm again "—let's get you to bed."

The journey through the kitchen feels both epically long and like a sudden whirlwind all at once, and before I know what's happening I'm tumbling down onto my mattress, laughing so hard that I have tears in my eyes.

"Stupid wine." I giggle, and reach up to wipe the moisture from my face. Ash is just looking down at me in the darkness, shaking his head but I can still see his smile. "Seriously, though. It's been a month." The words are coming out of my mouth, but I've half-forgotten what I'm talking about. "Your pay!" I blurt out after a moment, feeling victorious that I've managed to remember. "I need to pay you."

I struggle like an upside-down turtle for a moment, before getting my bearings enough to roll over and make a grab for my purse. It's by the side of the mattress, but there's only the tiniest amount of light coming in through the kitchen windows, so the quest for my checkbook has been upgraded from *difficult* to *mission-freaking-impossible.*

After a couple of minutes or hours or however long it takes, I give up and shove my purse to the side. "I'm such a shitty boss. I'll pay you tomorrow," I say, flopping back down on the mattress. Reaching up, I rub the heels of my hands into my eye sockets and try to make my thoughts make sense. Seriously, what was in that wine? I'm starting to suspect it was closer to moonshine than actual vino.

When I pull my hands down and open my eyes again, my entire body kind of *jerks. Jesus,* I think, trying to get my heart rate back down to normal. *I forgot Ash was even here.* He's standing so still, and he hasn't said a word.

"I'm sorry," I say again as I turn over and reach for my pillow, because Ash definitely deserves a boss that will actually pay him when they're supposed to. It's not his fault that I'm so bad at this. "I really am. I'm a terrible boss. I'm lucky you haven't already quit." I face-plant into the softness of the pillow. Mmmm. Nice. "I couldn't do this without you."

I'm almost asleep when I feel it, a dip in the mattress, a gentle hand on my shoulder, resting there for a second and then trailing down my head, smoothing down my hair.

"Don't worry about it," Ash whispers. "I'm not going anywhere." I smile into my pillow.

The mattress shifts again just as I'm on the edge of sleep, and I feel it as Ash gets up. He whispers "goodnight," and his shadow crosses over to block the tiny bit of light through the doorway, and I wake up enough to turn and look at him.

"Where're you going?" I mumble.

"Just heading home," Ash says. "It's late. Or early, now, I guess. I'll see you in the morning."

I reach out and sort of flap my hand in his direction. "Stay," I say, and then I realize what I've just said. I just invited him to stay the night. Oh god. I can feel my face heat, and I want to smother myself with my own pillow. This is mortifying. Ash must agree, because he's completely frozen in the doorway, and even in the dark I can tell he's staring at me like I've grown another head.

This is what happens when the entirety of your romantic involvement can be summed up with a handful of drunken make-outs and a single boyfriend who disappeared off the face of the earth the second he turned eighteen. Minimal experience; total embarrassment.

"Um . . . what?"

I pull in a deep breath and blow it out slowly. In for a penny, in for a pound. "Stay," I say, turning over completely so I can look him in the eye. "It's late." His silence is killing me, so I hastily add, "You can take the shed or the sofa or whatever. But don't drive. It's too late and you must be exhausted."

"I . . . " Ash starts, then stops for a moment. I watch as he shifts from foot to foot in the darkness, waiting for him to let me down easy, but his rejection doesn't come. "Okay. I'll stay."

"Good," I say, and burrow back down into my pillow before I can do any more damage. Even though I'm turned away and can't see him, I can still feel his presence. He hovers in the doorway for a moment, and slowly but surely, the tendrils of sleep begin to tangle around me once again.

I'm almost lost to them when I hear his quiet murmur of

"thanks," and the soft sound of his footsteps as he walks away, and I can't help but smile.

Ash

I'm a fucking idiot.

Honestly, a punch to the gut probably would have been gentler. It's just a job to her. It always has been.

I'm the one that keeps forgetting that. It's not Star's fault. She's just being nice. I'm the one latching onto her like a fucking octopus.

And the really pathetic thing? I don't see that stopping anytime soon. That's why I'm up at the ass-crack of dawn, in line at the take out counter at the diner to get her breakfast. Because even though she isn't interested, she's amazing and I'm a huge fucking pussy.

If my ex saw me right now, she'd be laughing her ass off.

But then again, Gina never did think very much of my efforts to be a good boyfriend. Not that I *tried* a lot back then, but still. Anything I did to try to be romantic had been shot down. The one time I brought her flowers, she'd laughed in my face and asked if that's what I really thought she wanted from me.

I can't believe I ever actually thought she loved me. I'm such a fucking idiot. Or was an idiot, I guess. I know a hell of a lot better now. I'm not going to be fooled by pretty red hair and a sweet smile, not when there was a fucking heartless shell underneath.

Star isn't like that. I know it.

But it still sucks that she only sees me as an employee, and nothing more.

"What can I get you?" I look up, startled at the voice, and I realize with a start that I've reached the front of the line, and that the waitress—Maisie, her name tag reads—is standing in front of me, pad in hand, eyebrow raising millimeter by millimeter as I stand there, unresponsive. Fuck. I shake my head, trying to clear it of the bad memories, and blurt out the first thing that comes to mind.

"Shit, sorry," I say. "Breakfast sandwiches. Two of them. And coffee, too. Please?"

She blinks at me for a second, then nods and turns away, which is about a million times better service than I got from the blonde waitress the other day. But it's still nowhere close to *welcoming*. I sigh and scrub my hands over my face. Who the hell am I kidding? Star's the only one in this town willing to take a chance on me, and she's leaving soon. I'm going to be miserable without her.

There's nothing in this town for me, not anymore. But I can't leave. I'm stuck here until my parole is up.

Star's going back to school. She's going to make something of herself. And I'll be just some distant memory of a loser she took pity on for a summer. She'll move on.

And I'll be here, in Avenue, missing her. I don't know how I'm going to get over her, or if I ever will. It's not like I have any better prospects coming along. Star's one in a fucking million. Even if I manage to find another girl around here who's willing to give me a shot, chances are she'll be just like my ex, who fucking ripped my heart out. And then stomped on it for good measure.

Bitch. Way to kick a guy when he's down.

"Here you go," Maisie says, handing me a packed-full paper

bag. "Ten eighty-nine."

I take the bag from her and hand over the money. Maybe I should have taken up Star's offer of paying me last night. I'm almost out of cash.

Maisie turns to the cash register beside her, ringing me through as I tilt my head down and start digging through the pocket of my jeans, trying to take stock of what's left of my money by feel alone. Considering all I can feel is coins, I'm going to go with not fucking much.

"Um," she says, her voice so soft I nearly miss it. "Um, I think you need to go outside. Like, right now."

*Fan*fucking*tastic,* I think. *Another one. I can't believe I thought she'd be any different than the rest.*

"What is it?" I sigh. "Suddenly realize who you're talking to?" I've had enough of this shit.

"No," she says, and her head's shaking so fast it looks like it's going to fly right off her shoulders. Her eyes are huge behind her black-framed glasses. She lifts up a hand and points over my shoulder. "It's your car."

There's a crash behind me and I whirl around and look.

Jesus.

I drop the doggie bag on the counter and sprint out the front door.

It's the asshole who called me a killer that day in the diner, the day Star and I met. And he's got a fucking bat.

And he's using it on my goddamn car!

"Hey," I say, afterward, keeping my voice low as I speak into the pay phone's receiver. "It's me."

"Ash?" And there must be something in my voice that gives me away, because Star's voice goes from *sleepy-rumpled-sheets-come-back-to-bed-baby* one second to *danger-danger-high-alert* the next. "What's going on?" she asks, and I can hear the sounds of her getting out of bed and moving around the room. "Why are you calling? *How* are you calling? I thought you didn't have a phone."

"Yeah," I say. "I don't. Look . . . " I let out a long sigh and squeeze my eyes shut. This fucking sucks. "I'm gonna need you to pick me up."

Chapter 13

Ash

"I can't fucking believe this!" Star says as we near the house. "I mean, who the hell would do that? And why the hell didn't anyone stop them?" She slams her palms down on the steering wheel so hard that I start to worry she's going to hurt herself. "What the *fuck* is wrong with this town?"

"Look," I say as the car pulls to a stop—a little harder than normal, but I get it, she's pissed. I am, too. I reach out and grab her wrist gently, pulling her hand away from the wheel before she can attack it again, and before I realize what I'm doing, I have our fingers linked together, and I'm squeezing her hand. I freeze for a second, afraid I've crossed a line, but after a beat she's squeezing back. "They're assholes. But it's . . . whatever. It's fine. I'll deal. I always do."

"Fuck," she mutters, and lets her head fall back against the headrest. Her eyes close and she's silent for a minute. It should be awkward as hell, but for some reason it's not. It's . . . nice.

"It's okay." I tell her, even though I have no idea what I'm going to do without my car. It was all I had left, and now it's busted and broken, and everything I own is covered in little pebbles of glass. The guy from the tow truck had just kind of shaken his head at me when I asked him if he thought it could be salvaged and my shoulders had sagged. His answer had been written all over his face.

Not with your kind of money, it can't. Fuck.

Star had wanted me to call the cops, get those assholes hauled in, but what was the point? It's not like I'd be any better off. I'd just draw more attention to myself, and with the way things are going, it's not like it would do any good. Somehow it'd just get twisted around, be all my fault, and with my luck I'd end up back in prison, having violated some part of my parole. It sucked, but I was dealing with it. In my own screwed-up way.

Which was to say really fucking badly.

I've never felt so out of my goddamn depth in my life.

"No. It's not," she says, and opens her eyes to look straight at me. I shift in my seat, but I don't look away. Even though it feels like she's looking straight down to my damn *soul,* I don't look away. If anyone has earned the right to see it, it's this girl. "It's not okay. This entire town is just so messed up . . . " She sighs. "The only good thing that's happened since I got back is that I met you." Her voice is so quiet I can barely hear her, but her words warm something inside me, something that's been dead and cold for a long time.

"Come on," she says, dropping my hand and unbuckling her

seat belt. She snags her purse from its home in the space by my feet. "Let's go inside. The sunlight is killing me."

A snort escapes me before I can stop it. No wonder she's pissed. She's hungover as fuck. I chuckle and try to suppress the smile that's threatening to break free. Hearing me, she turns and glares, but after a few seconds she cracks and starts smiling. Then we both start laughing.

"Shut up," she says, reaching over and whapping me gently on the arm before swinging open her door and getting out. "My head's about to explode."

Still laughing a little, I unbuckle myself and follow.

We're halfway up the path when I see it, and a smile spreads across my face. A real one this time. I nudge Star with my elbow.

"Hey," I say, nodding toward the porch. "It looks like you got another present."

She turns to me, brow furrowing for an instant, before she turns back to look in the direction I'm jerking my chin toward.

There, on the porch, is another box wrapped in brown paper.

"I can't believe her," Star says as I drop the box onto the kitchen table. "She must have dropped it off this morning before they left town. I must have missed it when I left to pick you up." And that doesn't shock me one bit, the way she'd peeled into the diner's parking lot with fire in her eyes after I called her. I'm amazed she saw anything but red.

The box itself isn't that heavy. She could have carried it herself. But really, anything I can do to help out at this point, I'm going to do. Especially since Star ended up having to pay to get my car towed out of the diner's parking lot. She'd been all apologetic, like somehow this was her fault for not having paid me yet, which is bullshit. Nothing that has happened to me is on her shoulders. Nothing.

She is the one pulling me out of the gutter. I am the one who keeps slipping back down.

"She didn't have to do this," Star says, smiling as she fumbles with her keys to find one sharp enough to cut through the tape.

"Somehow, I don't think Autumn does anything because she *has to,*" I say, poking her in the side as she cuts open the box. "She just does things for you because she wants to."

Just like you, I want to say. Because Star sure as hell never had to help me. But she keeps doing it. Over and over again.

Even though I don't deserve it.

She pulls open the box and starts pulling stuff out. Garbage bags, just like last time. Rolls of twine. More permanent markers, in even more colors. I can't help but smile at that last one. Autumn must have noticed the "tattoos" Star has been giving herself, the ones I've been helping with. So far I've added not only the lizard, but a rainbow with music notes and a pretty impressive green dragon, if I do say so myself. It's a hell of a lot better than the one I have, but then, I'm in a better place now than I was when I got that. Mine is all anger and darkness. The one I drew on Star . . . that one is full of life.

Just like her.

She's grinning down at the box, and it's like Christmas all over again with her. Something warm rises up in my chest and I reach over and snag the package of markers off the still-messy table. We haven't gotten around to clearing it off yet.

I wave them at her. "I think we can figure out something to do with these, don't you?" I ask, and she nods. But then her smile falters and her eyes widen as she stares into the depths of the box.

"What?" I ask. "What's the matter?"

"Nothing!" she says, and grabs the box flaps and slaps them closed before I can take a step forward. She seems to realize what she just did an instant later, and her face flushes bright pink. "Sorry," she mutters, but she doesn't let go of the box, doesn't let me see. Instead she reaches out and hefts the box up into her arms and turns around.

"I'm just going to...yeah." Face still burning, she makes her way over to the former pantry—her new bedroom—carrying the box with her. Before I can ask, she's already on the other side of the door, and it's swinging shut behind her.

And I'm left standing there, wondering what the hell just happened.

Star

By the time I finally get to the diner with my computer that evening—Ash stayed back at the house, not wanting to return to the scene of the crime just yet, not that I blamed him—Autumn must have already gotten back to Climbfield or at least stopped somewhere with Wi-Fi. Because when I open my email, there is already a message there waiting for me from Autumn entitled MUAHAHAHAHAHAHAAAA!!!!

That's it. Just a subject line. No text or attachments or anything. *That little brat,* I think, and open up another message. I quickly type out a subject line and hit Send, feeling victorious for a split second before I realize I have to click through a bunch of confirmations and actually convince the program that yes, I would like to send an email without an actual message. Yes. I'm sure.

Jeez. Doesn't it realize I'm trying to be dramatic?

It finally goes through and to my surprise I get a reply back almost instantly, this time with text.

Re: you are EVIL!!!!

You there? Open chat if you are.

XOXO

A

Smiling, I take a sip of the soda Maisie slides in front of me. I thank her and she grins at me and then turns and does her little pregnant-waddle back to the counter. It's the cutest damn thing I've ever seen, and I've seen Ash on zero coffee, so . . .

I open the email's chat program and click on Autumn's name. But before I can type anything in the little message bar, a line of text pops up.

AUTUMN: muahhahahahaha!!!!!
STAR: I maintain. You are EVILLLL
STAR: Why the hell did you give me condoms?!?!!!
STAR: Ash was standing right there when I opened the box.
He almost saw them!!!
AUTUMN: Good.
STAR: ?????
AUTUMN: Then maybe he would have gotten the hint.

STAR: No idea what you're talking about. Crazy person.

Lies. All lies. Of course I know what she is talking about. But just thinking about it makes me want to hide my blush behind my soda cup. It burns to know that I was being so freaking obvious about it.

Of course, maybe I am reading into this completely wrong. Maybe Autumn sent me condoms for some other reason . . . that I just can not think of at the moment.

Another message pops up on my screen.

AUTUMN: I'm talking about the fact that you want to climb that man like a tree.

Okay. So not another reason.

It was a long shot, anyway.

STAR: Look, thanks and all, but just drop it, ok?
AUTUMN: But whyyyyy?

I grin despite myself. I can practically hear her dramatic whine from here, two states away. And it is ridiculous. When I first met her, she'd been the quietest person *ever*. It had taken me weeks to get her to talk to me like a normal person. But somewhere in the bonding process, we'd kind of lost filters with each other.

Which was good. Autumn had needed to be cracked out of her shell. College had been good for her. Just like she'd been good for me. Whether I liked to admit it or not, Brick's disappearance had left a gaping hole in my life. I'd lost my closest friend and my first boyfriend in one fell swoop, and even though he'd always told me how strong I was because of the walls I'd built up around myself, his leaving nearly shattered me. By the time I'd gotten to Climb-field, all I'd needed was a friend.

What I got in Autumn was a sister.

> AUTUMN: I need to get my kicks somehow.
> AUTUMN: I'm going to end up a virgin for the rest of my life, and it's not like Roth is the sharing type.
> AUTUMN: I have to live through you.
> AUTUMN: LET ME LIVE THROUGH YOU.
> STAR: Sorry. No can do.
> STAR: It's a dead end. I'm not going to start something with Ash.
> AUTUMN: Why not?
> STAR: 1. I don't know if he likes me back.
> STAR: 2. We live a million miles away from each other. It wouldn't work.

All very good reasons, I tell myself as I take another sip of my soda. I should know. I've been repeating them to myself over and over for the past few weeks.

> AUTUMN: And 3?
> STAR: 3?
> AUTUMN: You know, reason #3 as to why you're not mak-ing goo-goo eyes at Ash.
> AUTUMN: Which, btw, you totally ARE.

I sigh.

> STAR: No 3. What? 1&2 not good enough for you?

There is a pause that goes on long enough that I am starting to wonder if the Wi-Fi has crapped out on me again, but then another message pops up.

AUTUMN: Sorry, Roth was talking to me.
AUTUMN: But seriously.
AUTUMN: 1. He definitely likes you back. Don't be redon-
kulous.
AUTUMN: 2. There are these things called phones. And
cars. And planes. And the interwebs.
AUTUMN: 3. (because I have a #3 and you DON'T!) I've
never seen you like this with a guy.
AUTUMN: Take a chance.

I sit there, wondering what I should say to that when the bell over
the diner's front door dings, and the door swings open to reveal
Ash.

Shit.

I resist the urge to slam my laptop shut. Barely. I only manage
because I know it would be super obvious that I was talking about
him if I did.

I type.

STAR: Ash is here.
STAR: Gotta go.
AUTUMN: Give him a kiss for me :D
AUTUMN: AND for Roth.
AUTUMN: Roth totally wants you to kiss him for him. He
said so.
AUTUMN: Yes you did, Roth. Don't lie.

I key-smash out something that looks kinda like *talk to you later*
and log out of the program just in time to see Ash slide into the
booth across from me. "Heeeey," I say, and instantly try to suppress my wince at just how awkward that came out. "I thought
you were staying at the house tonight." He gives me a crooked
little smile.

"Yeah. Changed my mind right after you left so I hoofed it over.

Decided I wasn't going to let them chase me away quite yet. How about you? Everything good with your friends?" he asks, just as Maisie waddles over to drop a glass of water on the table for him. He looks up at her and smiles, and says thanks and she gives him a hesitant half-smile back before turning away. Then, just as suddenly, she stops and turns back.

"Listen," she says, reaching up and pushing her dark-rimmed glasses further up her nose. "I . . . I'm sorry about your car." Ash just kind of blinks at her for a moment, looking like his jaw is about to drop open in surprise, and when she is greeted with nothing but silence, she whips back around and hustles away.

We both watch as she goes, and Ash turns to me and shrugs. "Well," he says, "it's progress, I guess." He's trying to laugh it off. But I can see the sadness in his eyes. Maisie might be an exception, but the rule where the people around here just don't trust him is still in effect. They don't know him and the prevailing opinion seems to be that they don't *want* to know him.

Which sucks. Ash is amazing.

And nice.

And really good looking.

And *shit*. Autumn was right. I do want to climb him like a tree.

Crap.

I'm lucky he didn't see the condoms. Really lucky. I probably looked like a crazy person, slamming the flaps of the box closed like I did, and squirreling the box away in my room before he could take a peek, but I didn't have any other option. What Ash and I have, it is good. I'm not going to ruin it by letting my stupid feelings show.

No matter how strong they are starting to get.

Chapter 14

Ash

It takes me a good minute to figure out what has woken me up. The sun is streaming in through the tiny window of the shed, and that's enough to warm it to really freaking uncomfortable levels, even though it must be ass-o-clock in the morning. I'm sweating my butt off. The sheets are sticking to my skin, even though I'm stripped down to almost nothing. I drop my head back against my pillow with a grunt, and from the ground beside me, Bruiser lets out a little rumble and turns his head to look at me.

"I don't know, buddy," I say. "Just try to go back to sleep." If Star hasn't banged on the door yet, then it's not time to get up. Best boss ever. I turn over and try to will myself back to sleep. That's when I hear it.

Goddamn "Footloose."

I pull myself back up into a sitting position, and crane my head to listen. It's definitely "Footloose." Mom had an obsession with that goddamn movie when I was growing up. I can probably quote the whole thing front to back because of her, and that is definitely the theme song that is being played at eardrum-rupturing levels.

What. The. Fuck?

I haul myself out of bed and step into my shorts, yanking them up and fastening them around my hips. I leave the shirt off. Whoever is playing the music will just have to fucking deal, I decide, and yank open the shed door and step outside into the sunlight. That's when I realize that the music is coming from the house.

What the hell?

I wander over to the porch, scrubbing my hands over my face. It's too early for this shit. Way, way too early. The music just gets louder the closer I get, and when I pull open the back door, it's *blasting.* I stop in the doorway and stare, but it isn't the music that stops me in my tracks. It's Star.

She's *dancing.* She's cleaning the kitchen, piling empty soda bottles into a big plastic bag, but the movements of her tight little body while she's doing it are nothing short of fucking *sinful.* She hasn't seen me yet, and I take a second to admire her as she moves. Hips shaking, hair tumbling. This girl just keeps getting hotter.

It's killing me.

Finally, she turns and catches sight of me. Her movements slow, but she's grinning at me like it's Christmas as she shoves another empty water bottle into the bag. That's when I realize that the music is coming out of the boom box on the kitchen counter, the one that is plugged in next to the toaster.

Holy shit. The power's back on.

I have no idea that I'm speaking out loud until Star laughs. The back of my neck starts to burn. I'm nowhere near awake enough for this.

"It is," she says. "I made a few calls and the power company finally relented. Do you know what that means?"

"I'm still stuck on the fact that I caught you shaking your ass to fucking Kenny Loggins," I tell her. "And the fact that I was woken up by fucking 'Footloose' of all things. I'm not exactly at my best right now."

"Ah," she says. "That's where the good news comes into play. Wait here." And with that, she drops the plastic bag and turns on her heel, hightailing it out of the room.

What the fuck is happening right now? I look down at Bruiser, who'd followed me inside to see what was going on for himself. He looks about as confused as I feel. "I hear you, buddy," I tell him, and he kind of huffs at me, and then settles himself down on the floor, where he's probably a hell of a lot cooler than I am right now.

God, I probably reek. I want to lift my arm back up and check, but before I have a chance, Star's back. And she's carrying a steaming mug in her cupped hands. Her smile is like fucking sunshine when she hands it over, and I moan as I get a whiff of it.

"Is that coffee?" I ask, even though it's goddamn obvious that it is. She nods and presses the cup into my hands. It's so hot that the mug itself is nearly burning me, but I don't care.

"Oh god," I say, and take a whiff of it. Considering all we've had lately is the shitty diner coffee, this smells like heaven. "We have a coffee maker? Here?"

She nods as I lean down and take a cautious sip. It burns like a bitch, but it's so good. "You're a fucking goddess," I tell her. Then, realizing what a sap I sound like, I hastily add, "Even if you *do* have fucking terrible taste in music."

"Hey!" Star cries, but she's laughing.

"Shhh," I tell her, taking another careful sip. "The coffee and I are having a moment."

"Well, then I guess I should leave you two alone. Since you're not interested in the other thing?"

"Hmmm?" I say, looking over the rim of the mug at her. She's looking at me, all playful and shit, leaning against the counter and hemming and hawing, like she's considering not actually telling me what she's obviously dying to. It's cute as shit. And I kind of want to set my mug down on the counter next to her, and block her in with my arms on either side of those cute little hips, just to see if she'd press herself back. But that would lead down a road I can't come back from, so I stay put and just take another sip of my coffee. It's either cooling down enough, or I've burned off all the pain receptors in my mouth. Either way, it's going down easier.

But Star just shakes her head at me and hops forward, reaching out and grabbing my arm. She slides her hand down, until she's got my hand in hers, and tugs me forward, hard enough that I almost go sprawling. "Come on," she says. "You've got to see this."

I'm a little stunned to say the least. We don't touch each other. Not really. It's the only way I've been able to keep a lid on my control around her. Control that's about to go straight to hell if she keeps laying those hands of hers on my skin. But it isn't like I can just brush her off. There doesn't exist a universe where I'd even want to, so I let her lead me out of the kitchen and through the pathways we've made in her mother's stuff, out into the living room.

She drops my hand and looks at me, all expectantly, and that's when I see it. There's a goddamn air conditioner in the window. And it's churning out icy-cold air like a freaking freight train. I can feel it from here, and it's fucking *fantastic.*

I turn to her, one hand still gripping my mug of coffee for dear life, and blurt out, "Marry me."

Her eyes kind of widen at my words, so I plaster a smile on my face and add, "We'll sort out your shitty taste in music after the ceremony," and hide my smirk behind my mug.

Star doesn't say anything, she just tosses her head back and laughs. But as I watch, I see the glint in her eye, the long line of her throat, the way her inky black hair tumbles down her back, and well . . .

I'm starting to wonder if I actually *mean* it.

Star

After Ash finishes his coffee and has woken up a little bit, heading back outside holds absolutely zero interest to either of us. Especially now that the air conditioner is chugging along in the window like its life depends on it. Which, as far as I am concerned, it does. That stupid machine and I shared some pretty passionate words when I nearly put my back out installing it this morning. I made it very clear that it either works like a charm, or it will be taken to the junk heap and be salvaged for parts. If it knows what is good for it, it will keep Ash and I suitably chilled for the rest of the summer. Minimum.

I'm starting to get a little uncomfortable thinking about the summer coming to a close. I had thought I would be thrilled to put this whole experience behind me, but . . . Ash changed all that. Now the thought of finishing the job makes me think about the fact that Ash and I will be going our separate ways, and that makes my stomach start to hurt.

Fuck. I'm going to miss him so much.

"Hey," Ash says, his voice breaking through my reverie. I look up, and see him gazing at me, his eyes soft, concerned. "You okay?" he asks. I nod and rub my hands up and down my arms, trying to warm myself. I'm cold all of a sudden, and I have a hunch that it isn't just because of the air conditioner.

"Yeah," I say, even though I know it's a lie. "C'mon. We should get to work."

There is no use in putting off the inevitable. Time is going to march on whether we finish cleaning the house or not. Either way, my time with Ash is quickly coming to an end.

The days are passing faster and faster, it seems. Now that I have finally accepted that the thing I feel for Ash isn't going away, it feels like every hour is only seconds long, and they slip through my fingers like smoke, evading me as I try to hold onto them, try to make them last.

Soon I will have nothing left but memories. Memories and heartache.

"Seriously," Ash says as we walk down the street together in the fading light, Bruiser trotting along between us, straining at the leash whenever he sees something interesting. "Are you okay? You've been . . . quiet."

No, I think. *I'm not okay. Every day I spend with you, I fall for you a little more, and there's nothing I can do about it.*

But I can't say that, I can't let him know. It wouldn't be fair to either of us, even if he did like me back. I'm leaving in less than two months, and the way things are going, it'll feel like minutes by the times it's over. So I nod instead. It's all I can do.

"Yeah," I say, drawing my arms farther into the sleeves of my hoodie, letting the sleeve edges cover my fingertips. I want to burrow inside and stay there, where nothing and no one can touch me. I want to draw him in with me.

I want a million things I know I can't have.

I want *him.*

"I'm just tired," I say, because he's looking at me again, like he knows I'm lying. We've gone almost all the way around the block with Bruiser now, and a part of me—the stupid, selfish part that makes me want things I can't have—can picture us doing this every night. I can see us taking the dog for a walk, strolling slowly, hand in hand, and then coming home and curling up on the porch swing together. Maybe what I told Ash isn't a lie after all, because the very knowledge that I can't have the things I want is exhausting, and my whole body is drained from it.

I want my bed. I want to curl up on that crappy mattress and close my eyes and pretend that my problems don't exist. But I can't. If I do, it'll mean even less time spent with Ash, and I'm not willing to give that up. Not yet. Not until I have to.

It'll be okay, I tell myself. *You'll go back to college. You'll be with your friends. You'll study and learn and laugh and maybe even fall for someone else. This isn't the end of your world. You're stronger than this.*

I just have to keep telling myself that. Then maybe one day I'll believe it.

✦

We do another lap around the block, now, trying to tucker Bruiser out. But he's still sniffing at every little thing we pass, tail whipping back and forth like he's sweeping for gold or something. That dog's got more energy than I think I've ever had in my entire life, but then again, he didn't just spend his day hauling box after box after box of junk out of what amounted to a minefield. Instead, he slept through pretty much the whole thing.

I'd be perky, too, if our roles were reversed.

Bruiser catches a glimpse of a squirrel and tries to make a break for it. But Ash just laughs and hauls him back. "Woah there, buddy," he says, reaching down and snagging Bruiser's collar in his fingers. I can see the shift of the muscles in his forearm and I curse myself yet again. I have to stop noticing stuff like that. It's not doing me any good. "You don't get to have squirrels for dinner anymore. It's kibble from now on for you."

Bruiser turns around and pins us with the biggest, saddest pair of puppy-dog eyes ever, and I laugh and reach down to ruffle his ears. Except when I do, the back of my hand brushes against Ash's, and I can't help myself. I let it linger there for a second, basking in the feel of his skin against mine before I jerk away with a muttered "sorry."

Ash just nods and gives me a little half-smile before letting go of Bruiser's collar and tugging at his leash to get him moving again.

I stare off into the distance as we round the corner and end up back on my mother's street. I can't keep doing this to myself. I should just cut my losses before I get in any deeper. I should just pack up, get out, hire someone to finish the job even though I can't afford it.

It'd be better than the sweet torture I've been putting myself through; falling for someone I can't have.

"Hey," Ash's voice breaks through our silence, and my first instinct is to ignore it, to just keep walking. But then his hand comes up and snags my arm. His fingers are gentle, but his grip is firm, and I find myself tugged to a stop.

I turn to him. "What is it?" I ask, then I tilt my head up and see the look on his face. Something is wrong.

"Look," he says, his voice low enough to be a whisper, and I turn my head to follow his gaze. There, off in the distance, I can just make out what he's looking at. There's a group of people, three or four of them at least.

And they're standing at the end of my mother's driveway.

Excuse me. Can I help you? I'm about to say it. The words are almost out of my mouth, but as soon as we're within earshot, I hear what they're saying and something inside me freezes up.

"Thank god that crazy woman is finally gone," one woman says, lifting a foot and toeing at one of the garbage bags we'd stacked neatly by the curb. Her motion upsets the pile and the little pyramid we've built comes tumbling down, bags of trash rolling over one another, falling onto the street.

My spine has turned to steel.

The woman lets out a disgusted *"hmph,"* and turns to face her friends. "I mean," she says, her voice loud enough that I'm surprised she hasn't attracted more attention than she already has, "it was bad enough when she lived here, bringing down the neighborhood like she did. I just hope that whoever's flipping this godforsaken place has the good sense to wear a hazmat suit."

I pick up my pace, legs and lungs burning. What the hell is going on? Who the hell does this woman think she is?

"Excuse me." The words are finally out of my mouth, but the pressure on my chest is still there. "Can I help you?" I snap as I come to a stop. Crossing my arms over my chest, I cock out a hip and glare at her.

"Oh," she says, turning on me, a sick little smile touching at her lips. "I'm *sorry*." *Yeah*, I think, *I'm so sure you are*. "Is this . . . yours?" She pokes at the garbage again, scattering it so that it falls even farther onto the street, nearly squashing the tiny white dog by her side, the one I hadn't even noticed until now. She must not be overly concerned about it, since it isn't on a leash and she nearly just crushed the thing with her move. Seriously, what the hell? This woman is old enough to be my mother, and she's acting like a high school mean girl. What is wrong with this town?

"Yes, as a matter of fact, it is," I say, feeling more than seeing it as Ash and Bruiser catch up to me and settle at my side. I take a deep breath and feel Ash's hand land gently on the small of my back. I glance over at him, and something inside me warms to see that his attention is on me. All on me. Not on this stupid woman and her posse. I let out the breath I'm holding as smoothly as I can. I can't show these women how mad I am, how freakishly livid they've made me. Judging by the smug look in their eyes, that's what they want.

I'm not going to give them the satisfaction. Bolstered by the weight of Ash's hand on my back, I raise an eyebrow at her. "Is there a problem here?"

One of the women scoffs. I'm not sure which one, but the sound sends a shot of pure fury up my spine.

The ringleader just plasters on a saccharine smile. "Oh, nothing," she says, reaching up and tossing a lock of her over-processed hair over her shoulder. "I was just telling the ladies here that I was glad that someone was cleaning up the Collins woman's trash, though—" she glances back and forth between me and Ash, a smirk pulling at her lips "—I suppose if this is yours now, that's a little too much to ask for, isn't it?"

And with that she turns to her friends and says, "Let's go, ladies," and the entire fucking group sashays away. My muscles coil under my skin, ready for a fight. I want to lunge after her. I feel wild. I want to rake my nails down her face, claw at her throat, bite at her skin. It's primal, unrestrained.

Vicious. Just like she is. Just like this whole goddamn town is.

It's only the touch of Ash's hand against my back that holds me in place as the hateful woman and her expensive tracksuit-clad posse walk away, a little faster than strictly necessary.

"Jesus *fucking* Christ," I mutter, and jerk away from him to stalk up the porch steps. The boards creek and bang under my boots, and I'm still gritting my teeth as I yank open the screen door. I'm actually *shaking* I'm so pissed off. Shaking so bad that my fingers don't want to close around the key, that it's a struggle to get it into the lock.

How *dare* they? What fucking right do they have to talk about my mother that way? Like she was trash?

She wasn't perfect. But she was never trash.

Who the fuck do these people think they are?

Finally, *finally*, I get the key to slide in, and I twist it with a jerk that hurts my own wrist but I don't give a shit. I just yank open the door and fucking *slam* it behind me.

Assholes.

Ash

I give the women one last glare, and then tug on Bruiser's leash. Together, we head up the front path to the house. As soon as we're on the front porch, I unclip his leash from his collar. He knows what to do, I don't have to worry about him making a break for it, and while I lean over to do it, I steal a glance back at the group. They're walking away, and as I watch, one of them glances back and visibly jerks as she catches me watching. Then she whips her head back around and the group turns the corner and disappears from sight.

Good.

Good fucking riddance. Star has enough shit to deal with, without being judged by some snooty know-it-alls like that.

I should have let Bruiser eat their little fluff-ball. That would have shown them.

Pulling myself upright, I reach for the door, and as soon as I pull it open, I'm greeted with the sound of Star swearing like a fucking sailor, immediately followed by a crash against the wall.

Fuck. She's *pissed*.

I'm in the kitchen before I realize I've moved, and just as I walk through the doorway, Star screams and hurls a frying pan against the wall with both hands. It hits the wall with a crash, sending bits of plaster and drywall into the air before careening away so fast I jump to get out of the way, even though I have no way to know where it's headed.

"Jesus!" I say, and Star fucking *whirls* around to look at me, anger and defiance sparking in her eyes. I lift my hands in the air in surrender. I have never seen her like this. I don't think I've ever seen *anyone* like this. "Are you okay?" I ask, but my voice wavers under her glare, and I hope I haven't just brought her wrath down on me.

"Did you fucking hear what they said about her?" Star demands. "About my mother? Who the fuck do those bitches think they are, talking about her like that, like she was worth *nothing*."

"I know," I said. "Don't listen to them. They don't know anything."

"Goddamn right they don't know anything. Who the fuck even says things like that about someone? Who the fuck are they, acting like she was beneath them?" There are tears streaming down her face, and her face is waging a battle between anger and sadness right in front of my eyes. I take a step forward, raise a hand to reach out to her, but she opens her mouth and lets out a fucking wail, and reaches over to the table, snatches up one of the heavy metal soup pots we'd set there earlier and whips it against the wall. It clangs and ricochets off, just like the frying pan.

"Goddamn them. And her. And this fucking stupid useless house!"

She turns away from me and starts grabbing the mason jars off the counter and smashing them into the sink. As soon as I realize what she's doing, what damage she could do, I race forward and grab her. But it's too late.

There's already blood trickling down her hand.

"Fuck!" she spits, and grabs at it just as I catch her in my arms.

"Hey. Hey hey hey, it's okay." I pull her hand away from her wound. I need to see the damage. She's shaking in my arms, her chest heaving with sobs, and she leans back against me. "It's okay," I tell her again, and wrap myself around her as best I can, pressing my mouth against her ear through her hair. "It's okay."

"No, it's not," she says, and turns around in my arms. She presses her face against my shoulder.

"No," I say, bringing my arms up around her, pulling her close. "But it will be."

I'll make sure of it.

Chapter 15

Ash

"Hey," Star whispers to me, and I turn from my seat on the front step to look at her. She's all wrapped up in a hoodie now, the sleeves tugged all the way down to cover her hands. Only the dark-painted tips of her fingers are visible. She shifts from foot to foot, and I can see the muscles shifting beneath the tanned skin of her long, fucking gorgeous legs.

"Hey," I say back and take another drag of my cigarette. I'm down to my last one. I blow out the smoke slowly, watch it as it dances in the night air.

"Can I . . . I mean . . . Is it okay if I join you?"

God, she looks so scared now, like she expects me to say no.

I don't think I'm ever going to say no to this girl.

I slap the palm of my hand down on the step next to me. "Pull up some wood," I tell her, and turn back out to look at the road. I only barely hear her footsteps as she approaches. She sinks down onto the step next to me, and stretches her legs out in front of her. Her feet are bare, I notice. Her toenails painted white, her star tattoos dancing up her left foot. I want to reach out and touch her, but I won't.

I can't.

So instead I tuck my own hand into the pocket of my hoodie, leaving only the left one, the one farthest away from her free to hold my smoke.

We sit there in silence for a few minutes, watching as the streetlights start to blink on as the darkness finally arrives, covering the neighborhood. I hear Star's intake of breath beside me, and I know she's about to speak, about to talk about what happened. And I'm just not ready for that yet, so I spit out the first thing that comes to my head.

"How's your hand?"

She kind of blinks at me for a second, as though she has no idea what I'm talking about, but then she looks down and tugs up the sleeve, and I can see the stark white of the gauze against the black fabric of her hoodie. It's tinged a little with blood. I shove my smoke back between my lips, and reach out for her hand. "Let me see."

"It's fine," she says, but holds out her arm, anyway, sitting quietly as I turn it this way and that. It's only bleeding in that one spot, and by the looks of it, it's slowed way down. So that's good. When she'd first cut it, I'd been worried she'd snagged an artery or something, or that she'd need stitches, it had been bleeding so bad. She'd stood there, wincing and swearing as I held her hand under the running water of the tap—thank god that hadn't been turned off like the power had been, otherwise I'm not sure what I would have done. When I'd been certain it was clean, I'd pulled it away to examine it, only to have the blood just well right back up again.

I had grabbed a stack of paper napkins out of the package we'd left on the kitchen counter, and pressed them against the cut, telling her to hold it there good and tight, as I went rooting around for the first-aid kid we'd found earlier and had thrown . . . *somewhere*. I finally found it in the dining room, sitting on one of the tucked-in chairs like it was a guest at some fucked-up dinner party. I'd gone a little overboard with the gauze when I began wrapping her up, but it wasn't like I had any stellar first-aid skills. Plus, I figured that too much was better than not enough. At least it looks like the bleeding has stopped.

I tell her so, and she kind of smiles at me, but it doesn't quite reach her eyes, and pulls her hand back.

"Is it still hurting?" I ask, and she shakes her head.

"It's a little sore," she says, picking a little at the edge of the gauze. "But I'll be fine. It's my pride that has taken a beating more than anything."

I can believe that. She's always been so cool and collected. Having me see her like that must really be messing with her head.

She lets out a sigh. "I'm really sorry, by the way. About what happened in there."

I take a long drag on my cigarette and reach over to tap the ash into the little empty soup can that Star gave me when we couldn't find a single goddamn ashtray in the house. "You have nothing to be sorry for," I tell her. And it's the truth. "It's those assholes who should be sorry for talking about your mom like that."

"Yeah," she says, and turns away from me to look out at the

street. It's quiet right now, not that this block ever really bustles with activity. I suppose people pay a premium to live in a neighborhood like this. Not that the one I grew up in was so different. The houses were a little smaller, the cars a little older. But overall, not so different. "But the worst part about it is that they were right."

I turn to look at her. She lets out a breath and tugs the sleeves of her hoodie back down over her hands, covering them completely this time. She wraps her arms around herself, and pulls her legs up, planting her feet on the step directly in front of her. She leans forward, and it almost looks like she's curling herself into a ball. God, she was really affected by that shit.

"I loved my mother. I really did. It's just...when I was little, things were great," she says. But she's chewing at her lower lip, and staring off into space, like just the act of remembering is wearing on her. "But then my dad died and...my mom, she just stopped, you know?"

"Stopped?"

She sighs and reaches up to tug at the end of a lock of hair. It's distracting, all long and half-curled. I keep wanting to bury my hands in it, to see what it feels like for myself. "Stopped being a mom," she says. "I mean, she was there. She didn't abandon me or anything. I was still fed and clothed and dropped off at school on time. But it was like she'd just checked out, you know? She was there, but at the same time she wasn't." She drops her hand back down, and her fingers curl into fists. "That's when she started bringing home the stuff."

Shit. It *had* been her dad's death that had set her mom off. That made sense. She'd lost not only the guy she'd loved, she'd also lost the one person who would have actually been able to stop her from bringing all this shit into the house in the first place.

"And at first it was great," she says. "I had all these new toys to play with, and all this new star stuff. I loved it. But . . . "

"But then it didn't stop," I say, because that's what happened. It just kept coming and coming, burying Star and her mom alive.

She nods. "And soon it didn't matter that I had the newest toys, because there was nowhere to play with them. There were these paths through the piles, and my mom tried to pretend it was a game, like we were living in a maze or something. And that was fine at first, too, but eventually people noticed. And then she had to choose between having me and keeping her things and, well . . . " She's still staring off into space, and I can't help but wonder what she's seeing, if that day is playing over and over in her mind in full color. "Well," she says after a moment, seemingly shaking it off, "you know the rest."

I can't help it. I reach out and wrap an arm around her shoulders and tug her just a little bit closer. "That blows," I tell her, and take another pull on my cigarette before I can say anything else.

I can feel her nod against my shoulder, lean into me, just a little. "Yeah," she says. "It really does. It's just . . . She was a shitty mom. I know that. She chose her stuff over her daughter, over me. But . . . "

"But she was still your mom," I say. And I get it. I do. Because even after they kicked me to the curb, my parents will always be my parents, and I don't think there's anything they could do that I wouldn't forgive them for, at least a little bit. They're the reason I'm here.

Star shifts against me, and I'm doing everything I can to not pull her closer. "Yeah, but it's more like she was a *person*, and people keep forgetting that. They just keep talking about her like she wasn't. Like all she was was *this*," She reaches a hand out and kind of waves it around us, gesturing to the house, the car, all the stuff. Everything.

"Look," I say. "Screw them. Seriously. Those people? The ones from earlier and anyone else who says that shit? They don't matter. Not to you and not to me." I take one last puff of my smoke and finish it off, dropping the butt into the soup can.

Only you matter, I want to say, but I keep my mouth fucking shut. She doesn't need my problems, not right now.

We sit in silence for a minute, just breathing in the night air, until finally Star turns to me. "Come on," she says, pulling out of my embrace and getting to her feet. "We missed dinner and I don't know about you, but I'm *starving*."

I don't even think. I just follow her inside.

I'm pretty sure I'd follow that girl anywhere.

Now that we have the power back on, dinners are less of the *college food experience extravaganza* and a bit closer to the *look at me, I'm a grown-up* kind of thing. The meals aren't fancy, but they are tasty. Spaghetti and meat sauce, tacos, chicken and potatoes. Simple stuff, really. But considering I have no clue what I'm doing in the kitchen, I still think it's pretty damn good. I'm even starting to reconsider my stance on vegetables. When Star adds them to stuff, they taste good. I'm starting to think that it's not veggies I hate, but my parents' cooking. After all the drama we've been through lately, it feels good to just sit down with Star and eat. And she was right. I was ravenous.

But eating dinner with her, cleaning up afterward . . . it's nice.

I'm not used to having *nice* in my life. I'm used to *shitty*. I'm used to *disappointment*. I'm used to people being let down by me, by the way I act and speak and fucking *look*. Everyone's just always so disappointed in me and with me and just—*ugh*.

But when I look at Star, I don't see disappointment in her eyes. Not when she looks at me.

She's standing next to the counter now, drying the last of our dishes from dinner. It was my job to wash since she couldn't with her injured hand. And she's just smiling at me, talking about something that she'd seen Bruiser do today when I'd been out taking a load of stuff down to the dump. But I can't even make out the words she's saying.

I don't even hear them.

All I can do is look at her, at how fucking gorgeous she is. How her eyes fucking light up when she smiles at me, when she tells me about her day. And suddenly all I can think of is the way she looks at me, and the *chance.*

The chance that she feels the same way about me as I do about her. The chance that we could be together. That it could be *good*.

The chance that I keep letting pass me by every single fucking day that I don't open my mouth and say something, don't do something about it.

My heart is racing in my chest, and the thoughts that are racing through my brain must show on my face, because Star's voice trails off and just looks at me, that same little furrow digging deep between her eyebrows.

"Ah, fuck it," I say suddenly, striding toward her. I grab the dishtowel from her hand and toss it on the counter beside her as her eyes widen with surprise.

"Ash, what—" But that's all she gets out before I surge forward and press my mouth to hers.

For a minute, she stands there frozen, and all I can think is that this is the end. I've fucked everything up. But just as I'm about to pull away, her hands come up and I feel her fingers against my face. It's the softest damn thing I've ever felt, and I can't stifle the moan that rises up out of me as I press forward, and slant my mouth against hers. My tongue glances against her lip, and then she's pressing back against me, her mouth opening beneath mine, her fingers tightening in the fabric of my shirt.

Fuck.

My arms come up around her, my palms flat against her sides, my fingers touching, trailing everywhere I can reach. And she fucking *whimpers* and starts writhing her hot little body against mine, and what little control I have *snaps,* and I'm wrapping her up in my arms and leaning her back against the kitchen counter.

Star

H*oly crap.*
     Holy.

Crap.

This is actually happening. God, for *weeks* I've wanted Ash, wanted to press myself against him, touch him all over. Now that it's actually happening I don't even know where to start.

So I do the only thing I can. I touch him everywhere. Up his arms, under the hem of his shirt, feeling the heat of his skin against mine. I reach up and wrap my arms around his neck, tugging him closer. I slide the fingers of my good hand through his hair.

A million years pass; a single second. I can't tell anymore.

And then all of a sudden, we're moving.

His hands are rubbing up and down my sides as we kiss, making our way, together, step by step, toward my makeshift bedroom. When we're just inside the door, Ash spins us so that my back is up against the door jamb, and his hands smooth down my sides to my legs. Then, without warning, his hands clasp behind my thighs and he hauls me up. The jamb digs into my back and I wrap my legs around his waist without thinking, a rush of heat shooting through me. I rake my fingers through his hair and jerk his head closer as he presses against me. His body rubbing against mine. Back and forth. Back and forth. It's driving me crazy.

Moaning, I lick into his mouth one last time, getting lost in the kiss before I pull away enough to drop my legs back down and push him toward the mattress. He stumbles back a bit, grinning at me all cocky. But I can see the way his chest is heaving, the way the muscles of his chest shift and move beneath his skin.

He wants this as badly as I do.

I reach down and grasp the hem of my tank top, and begin pulling it up over my head. The cool air against my overheated skin is delicious and I shiver a little as I shake my hair free and drop the shirt to the floor.

There's a whimper, and I freeze.

That sound wasn't from either of us.

I whirl around and find Bruiser just outside the door, staring at me with big eyes.

Ash lets out a laugh behind me, and I look over my shoulder and glare at him before turning back to the dog.

Bruiser's tail wags back and forth, his doggie smile widening as he realizes he's gotten my attention. His tail thumps against the wall beside the door, and he pulls himself up out of his seated position just as I smile down at him.

Then I reach over, grab the door and close it gently in his face.

Ash

I bark out a laugh as Bruiser lets out a tiny whimper of confusion on the other side of the door, and turn to Star, raising my eyebrows.

"What?" she says, leaning back against the door, all long limbs and glistening skin. "I'm not letting your dog watch us, you perv."

"Hey," I say, and take a step toward her. I want to touch that skin, run my hands all over it. It's irresistible. "I'll have you know that Bruiser is a gentleman and a scholar. He would never—" But Star cuts me off before I can finish bullshitting.

"I caught him trying to hump the blow-up Santa in the back-yard yesterday," she says. She's rolling her eyes but she's still reaching for me as I get closer. The second my hands touch her skin, rub against it, she seems to almost melt. I press my lips against her throat and her fingers tangle in my hair, pulling at it. God. Damn. This feels good. But it's Star, and like hell I'm going to give up a chance to bullshit with her.

"I have no idea what you're talking about," I say, kissing my way up her neck, lingering at her jaw. "Bruiser would never do such a thing."

She tugs harder on my hair, hard enough that I pull back to look at her. She's smirking at me. "I also caught him humping the stuffed frog you threw out on Tuesday. Your argument is invalid. Now take off your pants."

Okay. Maybe I'll let the bullshitting go. Just this once.

I reach for my belt. "Aye, aye, Cap'n."

"Wait," she says, and suddenly my hands aren't alone, they're tangled with hers, and her sweet mouth is pressing against my throat. "Let me help."

I groan and let my head fall back. Fuck. This girl is going to be the death of me. My belt loosens and my jeans drop to the floor next to her shirt. I tilt my head forward and catch her mouth with mine again, tangling my tongue with hers as I reach up and slide my fingers into her hair. It's thick and silky and it twists between my fingers, almost like it has a mind of its own, like it's drawing me in. And *goddamn,* she tastes good. Like the lemonade she was drinking with dinner, and the spearmint gum she chews until it seems like her jaw will crack from it. And something that's just Star and Star alone. I've never tasted anything like it. I've always been shit with words, but I'm pretty sure this is what *intoxicating* means.

It's rivaling every high I've ever fucking had.

Goddamn.

My cock is hard enough to pound nails, and I know she can feel it, the way she's rubbing her belly against it. I just want to reach down and pick her up, toss her on the mattress behind me and fall down there after her. But she's two steps ahead of me, and I've just barely felt the brush of the mattress against the back of my ankle when I'm suddenly horizontal and she's standing over me, looking gorgeous and goddamn triumphant.

Jesus.

"So," she says, reaching down and popping open the button of her cutoffs. I want to chase her fingertips with my teeth, but she seems to be enjoying putting on a show for me, so I lean back on my elbows and watch instead. Her hips wiggle a little as she tugs down her shorts. They slide down her legs like magic and I can't help but fucking groan at the sight. She's in her bikini top, her little nipples sticking through like hard candies, and she's wearing these little panties that look like undies that I wore when I was little, all blue and white with stitching made to look like the front flap. They're riding low on her hips and look so hot on her I could bust. "Any preferences?"

I raise an eyebrow at her. "That's a loaded question," I say and she laughs, taking a step and moving forward until she's got one knee on the mattress, directly between my damn thighs.

Yeah, I'm definitely going to bust. But if I'm lucky, I'm going to make her bust first. I'm reaching for her before I can even decide where to touch, flat on my back, wrapping my hands around her face and tugging her down so I can press my mouth against hers. She's leaning over me now, her body pressing down against mine, and I can feel her pulse hammering as I slide my hand up her neck. Goddamn. If this is what sober sex is like, I just found another reason not to touch a drop ever again. My hands are in her hair again, and she's kissing and rubbing up against me like her life depends on it. That's when my fingers touch the little bow at the back of her neck.

The bikini top.

I grin against her mouth and start working the knot apart with my fingertips. It loosens way easier than I was expecting, and the strings fall from her shoulders without me even having to touch them. I want to touch, though, so I slide my hands down her neck, down her shoulders, until I have my arms wrapped around her. I want to see her. I want to see every single inch of her, but I suddenly feel like it's a choice between holding onto her or dying, and I can't make myself stop touching enough to pull back to look.

She's a million miles ahead of me again, and her other knee shifts so it's pressing into the mattress at my side, and she's clutching at my shoulders, pulling me with her as she rolls over.

Suddenly I'm on top of her, pressing down into her hot little body, and somehow that feels better. Like if I pull away she won't disappear on me. Like she wants me there, on top of her. And I'll be damned if I'm not willing to give this girl whatever she wants.

Getting my knees under me, I pull back, smiling as she leans into me, chasing the kiss, and look down.

God. Damn.

Her tits are amazing. I'm leaning down and pressing my mouth to them before I can even think. By the way Star moans and arches into me, she has no problem with my actions. She presses closer to me, and I lap at her breast and suck the tip into my mouth as I reach around her body to tug at the knot at her back. I can feel it come loose, feel her bikini fall away, but she's moaning and writhing, her fingers pulling at my hair as I suck at her, and I'm so hard I'm dripping through my boxers.

I'm going to die from this.

But goddamn, what a way to go.

SADIE MUNROE

Star

We kiss, chest to chest, and it feels like too much and not enough, all at the same time. I run my hands over his shoulders, cup my palms over the back of his neck, thread my fingers up through his hair. I want to touch *everywhere*. And all at once.

I'm torn between touching forever and rushing full force to the main event, and I press against him as we kiss and kiss and kiss until I can't stand it anymore. I press my palms against his chest, reveling in the warmth of his skin against mine, and push him away.

He blinks down at me, confused, but I smile and shove him a little farther away, so I have room to move. I turn over onto my belly, and reach across the mattress for the box that I've stashed on the other side, the box my no-good interfering roommate sent me. Who I shall love forever and will be given cookies the next time I see her.

I shove the package of markers out of the way, dig past the package of labels and the box of garbage bags, fingers searching and fumbling as I feel Ash's warm palms cup and squeeze my ass, sending a bolt of heat racing through my entire body. Then finally, *finally* I lay my fingers on what I'm looking for, and snatch it up. I pull myself up to my knees and turn around to face Ash, holding the condom out to Ash in victory.

"*That's* what was in the box from Autumn?" Ash asks, laughing.

My face is on fire. "Shut up," I say, and toss the condom at him. It hits his chest and falls into his lap before he can catch it. Leaning forward, I press my mouth against his one more time.

"You can either laugh at me," I say, letting my eyes flutter shut, "or you can put that to good use. What's it gonna be?"

Suddenly, he's not laughing anymore. I open my eyes and find him staring down at me, an intensity in his gaze I've never seen before. My heart thuds in my chest, heat coiling in my belly, and he reaches out and wraps an arm around my waist, hauling me closer, drawing me into his lap.

This is such a bad idea, a voice in the back of my mind reminds me. *It's not going to last. All you'll wind up with is a handful of memories and a truckload of heartbreak if you let this happen.*

Shut up, I tell the voice as I press my mouth to Ash's, tangling my fingers in his hair again. He flips me back over so I'm on my back again, his weight a solid, heavy warmth pressing me down into the mattress as he runs his hands over my body.

"You are so fucking hot," he murmurs against the skin of my neck, trailing kisses as he begins to trace a path down the front of my body. I squirm beneath his touch, fisting my hands in his short hair and *tugging.*

"Yeah," I say. "God. Yeah, you, too." I can't get enough of him, of his skin against mine. We're a tangle of hands and arms and flesh gliding hot against flesh, whispered words spoken against sweat and skin.

Then he grabs the condom from where it has fallen in the tangle of blankets, and tears it open as I pull his boxers down his hips. He kicks them off and they go flying over the edge of the bed and disappear from sight just as he reaches down and rolls the condom on. .

And then he's pressing into me, and it's hot and slick and a million different feelings all at once.

"Yes." I breathe the word against his mouth, and as we move

together, his lips claim mine once again.

There is no more talking, after that.

"So . . . " Ash says as we lay there afterward, flopped on our backs on the mattress. I'm panting so hard, I can hardly catch my breath. I turn my head and watch as he shifts around so that he's lying on his side, gazing down at me.

"Mmmhmmm?" This . . . this was amazing. This wasn't the adolescent fumblings I'd shared with Brick, or the handful of drunken hookups I'd had during freshman year at college. This . . . This was better.

He trails the backs of his fingers up my side. I'm still buzzing with sensation. It feels *amazing.*

"I just wanted you to know, that this wasn't . . . that this wasn't just . . . you know . . . a one-time thing. At least, for me." He's staring down, straight into my eyes, and I feel a warm rush through my chest, giving my heart a little lurch. "It wasn't for me," he says again, and reaches up and cradles the side of my head with his hand.

I raise my hand and let my fingertips slide across his cheeks, up to his hairline, to tangle behind his head. And I can't stop smiling as I pull him down to me. I kiss him, and tug him closer to me, press my body up against him as our mouths move together.

Our lips part and my eyes open and I'm looking straight at him when I answer. "It wasn't just a one-time thing for me, either."

A little smile tugs at the corner of his lips. "Promise?" he says, but it's hesitant. Unsure. And his eyes drop from mine. His body tenses. And suddenly I realize that he's bracing himself for me to shake my head or laugh it off. He's bracing himself for rejection. My heart does something traitorous in my chest, and I struggle to swallow over the lump that's forming in my throat.

"Hey," I say, reaching out and touching the edge of his jaw, tugging his face back up so that he's looking me in the eye. His gaze flickers back and forth across my face, catching my eyes over and over again as I do the same. I want to look at every bit of him, all at once. I feel like I could look forever, and it still wouldn't be enough. I lean forward and press my mouth to his. "I promise," I whisper as we part, and he smiles but even then it doesn't quite meet his eyes.

"Hey," I say again, because he's not getting it. He doesn't believe me. So I do the only thing I can; I bring my left hand up between us, holding my pinkie out to him. *That* makes the half-smile he was sporting turn full-fledged, and we're both grinning like idiots as he reaches up and links his finger with mine and we waggle our linked hands back and forth, cementing the deal.

Then I kiss him again, just to make it official.

Chapter 16

Ash

This...this is nice.

Fuck. There's that word again. *Nice.*

Before the crash, before everything that happened and all the shit that followed, I'd never really thought about what I wanted my life to look like. And when I did, what I brought to mind sure as hell wasn't this. I always thought I'd be some famous goddamn artist, drinking and doing whatever drug I could get my hands on, living my life in the moment.

But this moment, this single snapshot in a day with Star, it's *nice.* Spending our day together, fucking in her bed, dozing off next to each other. It's nothing I'd ever thought I'd want for the long term. But now that I have it, I don't want it to end. Five years ago, if someone had told me that this would be the fucking highlight of my life, I'd have laughed my ass off. I was an idiot five years ago. Star, these moments I have with her? They make me want *more*. They make me want to do better. To *be* better. Hell, just being here with her, walking my stupid mutt down the road with her next to me, it makes something in me *tug*. Like there's a fishing hook looped behind my navel, and every time she turns her head and smiles at me, I feel drawn toward her, like she's reeling me in.

We'd woken up this morning like we had for the past two weeks, in bed next to one another, me trailing my hands over her body, though her hair, her nuzzling into my chest, clinging to me like I'm something important. Something special. I've never felt special to anyone before. I kissed her head and run my fingers down her naked skin, over all the colors and designs she'd let me mark her with after we'd had sex. Her body was this gorgeous canvas, covered in my sketches. She was fucking *beautiful*.

Then she'd yawned and pressed her lips to mine, mumbling something about coffee before pulling herself up and wandering naked into the kitchen, and I'd been struck like lightning with a single thought.

She's fucking *perfect* for me.

And she is. She really is, and there's a war waging in my chest, because I know she's leaving and it's tearing me up inside.

I've finally found the perfect girl for me, and I'm going to have to let her go.

It fucking sucks.

That was hours ago, and I'm still reeling. I don't know what I'm going to do.

Luckily, though, if Star notices I'm acting different around her, she isn't saying anything. Instead she smiles at me as we make our way down the street, our fingers tangled together. As we turn the corner, Bruiser tries to make a dash after a giant orange cat that crosses his path, jerking on the leash hard enough that I have to drop Star's hand and use both of my own just to keep him from racing off after that freaking *giant* cat. Seriously, that damn thing is easily twice the size a cat should be. Apparently the good people of the neighborhood don't know the word *restraint* when it comes to feeding their pets. The thing practically waddles as it walks. Its tail whipping back and forth in the breeze, almost as if it's mocking us, and Bruiser starts losing his shit, barking his fool head off as the cat trundles away like it doesn't have a care in the world. Like it didn't just almost run out of luck and meet its damn maker.

"Stupid cat," I mutter, shaking my head as I pull back on Bruiser's leash. "Yeah, yeah, yeah," I tell my dog. "You want to chase the pussy. I don't blame you."

Star throws back her head and laughs, and that damn fishing hook sinks into my navel again, tugging me toward her at the sound. I don't know if it's the sound of her laugh that does it, or the sight of her dark hair tumbling down her back, or the long pale line of her throat, but either way, I can't stop myself. I have to touch her. I reach out to snag her hand with my free one again. And she lets me, but then, an instant later, she shoots me a little grin and twists our hands around so that only our pinkies are linked.

Pinkie swear, I think, and duck my head for a moment, flashing back to our mornings in bed, and how our hands almost seem to gravitate toward each other's, how our fingers link together in our own little promise, again and again.

I don't know how I'm ever going to be able to let her go.

Suddenly Star stops walking, and I jerk to a halt beside her.

"Shit," she murmurs. "Not again."

My brow furrows, and I glance over at her. She's staring down the street, toward her mother's house, face torn between anger and sadness. What the hell?

I turn to look.

There, standing at the end of her mother's driveway, is a couple. Nosy assholes, just like a few weeks ago.

Star was right. It's happening again.

Shit.

Before I realize what I'm doing, I'm already moving. My legs are pumping and I can feel my jaw clench as I approach the intruders.

"Hey," I snap as soon as I get close. *What the hell do you people want?* The words are on the tip of my tongue along with *fuck off*, but as soon as the *hey* is out of my mouth, the couple turns to look at us, and the words die before I can get them out. I recognize them.

They're from the diner. The skinny waiter and the pregnant waitress. And judging by the looks on their faces, they aren't here to start trouble like the stuck-up women in the overpriced track-suits. In fact, now that we're closer and I can really see them, they actually look a little . . . scared.

Oh, *fan-fucking-tastic,* I think. *More people who think I'm going to run them down in the streets.* But . . . no. Scared isn't the right word. More . . . timid. Nervous at the very least.

"Can I help you?" I say instead, tugging Bruiser to a stop and twisting my hand around so I can link my fingers properly with Star's.

"Uh, hi," the guy says, his gaze darting between me and Star and then finally, after a few passes, back to the pregnant girl beside him. She gives him a wide-eyed *look* from behind her thick-framed glasses that speaks volumes. He shuffles his feet and clears his throat before turning back to us, sinking his hands into the pockets of his hoodie. "I'm York, and this is my sister. Um. Maisie."

He jerks his elbow back toward the girl, who raises a hand and waves awkwardly with a murmured "hello."

"Um . . . " I can see how nervous this kid is from here. It's ridiculous. He's shaking so bad I could knock him over with a cough. "We were just wondering . . . " He glances back at his sister, who finally rolls her eyes and tilts her body to look past him, toward us.

"We were wondering if we could take the sofa."

It takes me way longer than it should to figure out what she's talking about. Then I realize they're not looking at the house itself, not pointing and laughing and looking down at it like those women had. Instead they're looking at the sofa that we'd set out on the curb that afternoon.

"Oh," I say, and glance back at Star. She's got her free hand clapped over her mouth, so I can't see her smile, but it's shining through clear as day in her eyes. I smile and sink my teeth into my bottom lip, trying to stifle it. The last thing I need is for them to think I'm laughing at them, even though I kind of am. I turn back to Maisie and York, and beside me Bruiser wags his tail so hard I'm sure I'm going to have a bruise on my thigh where it's thumping over and over. "You want it—" I turn slightly to catch Star's gaze. She nods and I feel the smile spread across my face as I turn back to Maisie and York. "—it's all yours."

One sofa down. Only five more to go. Maybe this wasn't going to be as bad as I thought.

After that, the tension slowly dwindles and then dies, and we stand there talking and laughing together as the sun sinks below the horizon.

"Look, man," York says, shifting from foot to foot. I've only known this kid for maybe an hour all put together, and I can already tell that he never really settles down. He is always in motion. It is making me fucking dizzy. I want to reach out and grab him by the shoulders and tell him to stay fucking *put*. "I heard about the shit that went down at the diner when you applied. And what happened to your car. I just wanted to say, you know. Sorry."

"Don't worry about it, kid," I say, taking a drag of my cigarette and ashing it onto the sidewalk. "Not your fault."

"Still . . ." he says, trailing off and bouncing a little bit on the balls of his feet, hands still in his pockets.

"What my brother is trying to say, and *failing*," Maisie says, shooting the kid a dirty look before shaking her head and turning back to me, "is that we're sorry you were treated that way."

"Not super surprised, though," York adds, helpfully.

We all turn to look at him, and his eyes widen. He pulls his hands out of his pockets and holds them up in front of him, in defense. "Hey, woah, no. No. Not like that." He turns to me. "I didn't mean like you *deserved* it or anything. Seriously. I just meant that the people at the diner suck, that's not news. It isn't shocking that they'd treat you like that. That's *all*," he says, and glares at his sister like *way to throw me under the bus, sis.*

I chuckle and take another drag, turning away and blowing the smoke out as far away from the pregnant girl as I can, realizing that smoking in front of her probably isn't cool. I drop the cigarette onto the ground and stub it out with my toe, hoping that no one notices. I feel like an idiot often enough. No need to draw any more attention to it. Besides, they're kind enough to take one of the gazillion sofas from the house off our hands—apparently they're renting a trailer on the other side of town and they need furniture. I don't want to make things any harder for them. They seem okay in my book.

Star rolls her eyes at us, and turns to say something to Maisie, who has her hands folded on top of her round belly, and I'm halfway through turning back to York to give him a little shit, just for kicks, when I get a jolt.

"Wait," I say, turning around to face Maisie as the idea turns over in my head and clicks neatly into place. "You're knocked up, right?"

Jesus, the fucking *looks* all three of them pin me with. Like *you think, dumbass?* I wave my hand at her belly and roll my eyes. "Okay, not actually the point," I say. "I'm not stupid. I know you aren't hauling around a beach ball under there." Though, to be honest, it's starting to look like it. The girl's kind of tiny and her belly is getting huge. She looks like she's at risk of tipping over at any minute.

"What's your point then?" York says, crossing his arms over his chest.

Good, I think. *Stick up for you sister. God knows I'd do anything to have family do that for me. Pretty sure Star would, too.*

I glance back at Star, and give her a little wink before turning back to the siblings.

"How would you like some diapers?"

✦

"Thank you for this," York says again, after we've unloaded the last of the stuff we brought over for them, settling it all into the trailer. "Seriously. Thank you."

"Seriously, kid. Shut up about it. It's not a big deal," I tell him and jerk a thumb toward Star just as she disappears into the other bedroom with Maisie to look at some of the baby stuff or some shit. I don't know. *Women.* "There was an entire *room* of this shit at her mom's place."

"Look," he says, dumping the last box into the trailer's second bedroom and shutting the door. "It may not be a big deal to you, but it is to us. My sister can barely afford this place as it is. They pay shit at the diner. I have no idea how she's going to be able to afford this baby, even with me helping her out. So, no. Not gonna shut up about it. 'Cause it means a lot."

I can't help it, I look around the place. It's kind of a dump, but then, so is the entire trailer park, so for all I know, this one is considered a palace by comparison. Except for my five years away, I've spent my entire life in Avenue, and I've never set foot in the trailer park before. Everyone pretty much knows it is a shit-hole and stays away.

My mom would be having kittens if she knew I was here.

I can't even imagine trying to raise a kid here.

"If you don't mind me asking, where's the dad?" I say. "I mean, isn't he going to pitch in?"

York just sort of boggles his eyes at me, like I'm speaking in fucking Chinese or something. "The dad." He repeats, like the word doesn't make sense or something, like he's trying the words out for the first time, seeing how they feel in his mouth.

"Yeah," I say. "I'm pretty sure your sister didn't climb on top of herself and get herself pregnant."

He scoffs, and I can tell I've touched a nerve. "The dad," he says, like he's trying to wrap his mind around just how to put his anger into words. I know the feeling. Anger management helped with that. A little. Mostly it just stopped me from taking my anger out on the few possessions I'd been allowed to keep in prison. Destruction wasn't the most helpful of coping mechanisms, I was told. "The dad is a fucking piss-ant bitch," he snaps, and I can't help the smile that image brings up. This kid is pretty creative with the insults. "Maisie won't even tell me who it is, you know that?" His eyes are wide and I can see the hurt that lingers behind them.

"Dude, really?" I say, because I've seen the lengths this kid will go to for his sister, and the fact that she won't even tell him who the daddy is, well that's gotta hurt. "That sucks, man. I'm sorry."

"It's not like I'd even care," he says, throwing his hands out, and *wow*. This kid has been keeping this bottled up for a long-ass time. He's pissed. He looks like he's about to start pacing around the trailer. "But she doesn't want me to know, which means that either she doesn't want him to find out she's pregnant, and she's afraid I'll go hit the guy up for child support on her behalf or something. Or—" he scrubs his hands over his face and lets out a sigh. "Or, the guy already knows and doesn't give a shit, which means he's the biggest bastard on the planet and she's afraid I'll try to kill the guy. Either way, you're right."

I look at him, wondering just what the hell I could be right about. The corner of his mouth quirks up and he shrugs helplessly.

"It sucks," he says, and burrows his hands into his pockets, his shoulders hunching down again, and all at once I'm struck by how fucking *young* he is. How young they both are. And he's right. This really fucking sucks.

We stand there awkwardly for a minute until the silence gets so fucking loud that the kid apparently can't stand it anymore. "I'm going to go return the truck," he says, bouncing on his heels and looking at me like he's waiting for me to say something. Finally I realize he's waiting for my permission or say-so or some other dumb shit, so I nod at him and he's out the door like a flash the second my head stops moving, leaving me standing there in their living room wondering how the hell is this my life?

But still, it could be worse. I could be living where they are, a kid myself with a baby on the way, stuck living in a shitty trailer on the bad side of Avenue. But they seem to be making the best of it. The trailer is . . . Well, it's better than I thought it would be, I'll admit it. On the outside, it looks pretty run down, but compared to the inside, it's like night and day. The place is neat and tidy, even if it's barren of pretty much anything personal. I can't help but wonder just how fast Maisie's parents kicked her out when she told them about the baby. There are a few warm touches here and there, but nothing that could really identify it as belonging to either her or York. To be honest, it looks like they left in a hell of a hurry. And as nice as they've tried to make it, just looking at it causes a pit to form in my stomach. At least my parents packed my shit up for me. At least they didn't kick me out at eighteen like Maisie's parents. Yeah, she has her brother, and York apparently doesn't care that his big sister had gotten herself up the duff, not when he'd followed after her. I don't know how they did it. At eighteen I was a fucking dumbass. I would have died.

For the first time since I got out of prison, I realize just how worse off some of the other people in Avenue are than I am. At least I have my stuff. And Bruiser.

And Star.

Thank fucking god for Star.

But even though it makes me sad, the place is decent, for a trailer. There are little blue checkerboard curtains hanging in the windows, a couple of mismatched pillows on the sofa they got from us, and an ultrasound photo taped to the fridge. It's definitely better than what I'll have once Star leaves.

Shit.

I don't even want to think about that. Not yet.

I'm not ready.

And the really fucked up part? I don't think I ever will be.

Shit.

I shift the stack of boxes I've been building, so that the tower of diapers isn't in the way if Maisie or York need to get at anything in the kitchen. One of the old guys in the trailer park had let them borrow his pickup truck to get the sofa, and we'd been shuttling it back and forth all day, bringing over everything we thought they could need. I settle the last box onto the stack and wipe the sweat off my brow with the back of my hand before heading over to take a seat at the table, listening with half an ear to Star and Maisie chatting away in the back bedroom. Hauling out one of the mismatched chairs I settle in to wait until they're done, but as I do my eyes catch on the bowl in the middle of the table. It's filled with cherries, ripe and red and awesome-looking. It's also absolutely fucking *huge*. It's like if someone had asked the freaking big friendly giant if he wanted some cherries, and then had to keep filling the bowl until the fucker said *when*.

The door to the trailer jerks open with a clang and York bounds up the stairs. He must catch me staring at it, because he laughs and settles into the seat across from me. "I wouldn't touch those if I were you, man," he says, nodding toward the bowl. "They're

Maisie's. She's been craving them like mad ever since the start of her pregnancy."

"Seriously?" I've heard of pickles and ice cream and crap for pregnant women. But cherries?

He nods, all grave and shit, but his eyes are full of mischief. He reaches out and kind of spins the bowl around, showing off the fruit. Watching it is almost hypnotic. I'm fucking starving. Hauling stuff around all day is hard work.

"It was all she talked about for ages, man," he says. "Cherries. She didn't want anything else, but they were super expensive and the grocery store ones were terrible since they were out of season."

"These ones look pretty good," I say, mouth watering, and he nods.

"They are. Season just started. But man, it's not worth it. I tried to steal some the other day, and I swear to god, I thought she was gonna cut me." He looks up at me and grins. "I'm kinda thinking I might steal some now, and blame it on you, though."

"Fuck, throw me under the bus, why don't you?" I laugh as he spins the bowl around again. "I'd rather not be the focus of a pissed-off pregnant chick, if it's all the same to you."

"And why would I be pissed off?"

York and I both jerk violently in our chairs at the voice, and I spin around. Maisie's standing in the hall, hands on her hips, belly sticking out, eyes darting back and forth between me and York, but she doesn't look mad. Not really. Instead she look like she's caught halfway between glaring and laughing at us. Star, on the other hand has gone straight to laughter. She's standing directly behind Maisie and she looks like she's about to piss herself, she's trying so hard not to laugh.

Guess she doesn't want Maisie pissed at her, either.

Little Mama's gonna be a force to be reckoned with, I think, and grin as Maisie steps forward and scoops the gigantic bowl of cherries off the table and cradles it to her chest like a bear protecting her cubs, glaring at each of us in turn as we burst out laughing.

It is weird, but after that, cleaning out her mom's stuff seems to be less of a chore for Star, and more of a treasure-hunt. All of a sudden, it became less about getting rid of stuff, and instead turned into searching for stuff to give to Maisie and York and the baby.

"York could use this to fix up the trailer."

"Oooh, Maisie would like this, don't you think?"

"This would be great for the baby,"

I hear it a thousand different ways about a thousand different things that Star collects and puts aside, and every couple of days we take a new load of stuff out to the trailer park for them. They are always thrilled, and that makes Star grin like a kid at Christmas.

"You know," I say, as she drags another box with the word BABY scrawled on the top flap across the room, heading for the front porch. "You can't save *everything* for York and Maisie. Otherwise their trailer is going to end up looking like this house. Or worse, considering the fact that this place is a hell of a lot bigger than theirs." I light my smoke and breathe it in, mentally grinning at the thought of their tiny trailer literally bursting at the seams. But Star isn't laughing.

Instead, silence fills the space like a balloon, and I look back over my shoulder at Star. She looks absolutely *wrecked.* "What?" I ask, panicked. "What is it?"

She's not even touching the box anymore. It's sitting on the porch, abandoned, as she backs away from it like it's on fire. She's got her hands over her mouth, and her eyes are *huge*. She's freaking out, and I have no idea why. "Star?" I ask, moving toward her. "What's the matter?"

As soon as I touch her, she breaks. Her hands drop from her mouth and she's reaching for me. "Oh god," she says, and I drop my smoke and wrap her up in my arms. She buries her face in my neck. "I'm turning into my mother."

What?

I pull back enough to see her face, but she's still burrowed into my neck. "Hey," I say, and reach up to tilt her chin so that she's facing me. "What are you talking about, baby?"

"I'm turning into her," she says. "I'm doing the same thing she did."

"Baby," I say, reaching up and cupping her face in my hands. She's actually *shaking* in my arms, and it's freaking me the fuck out. "You're not turning into your mom. You're trying to get rid of stuff. That's the opposite of what she did."

"You don't understand." There are tears in her eyes now. "I've done research into this, okay? Into hoarding. It's a mental disorder, and it all starts with the mentality. The idea of saving stuff that isn't useful, but convincing yourself that it is. It's saving stuff even if it's not useful to you, you convince yourself that it can be useful for someone else."

"Hey. *Hey,*" I say, leaning over to press a kiss against her mouth before she can say anything else. "Listen to me." I rub the tears that have leaked from her eyes away with my thumbs as I look down into her eyes. Goddamn, she's beautiful. "You're *not* like your mom, okay? This stuff you're giving away? It's good. You're doing good. Maisie and the baby need this stuff. It's not like you're going out and buying everything and keeping it forever. You're trying to get rid of stuff, and you've found someone that needs what you have. This is fucking generosity, baby. It's not hoarding. And trust me—" I give her a little smirk because I know she fucking loves it "—after working on this with you, I'm pretty sure I can pick out the signs of hoarding. If you start showing them, I'm going to fucking tell you, okay?" I tug her close again, rubbing my hands up and down her back.

She nods against my shoulder. "Okay," she whispers.

"Okay."

Chapter 17

Ash

Holy shit.
Holy.
Fucking.
Shit.

It's a car.

And it's not just any car. It's a fucking 1967 Pontiac Le Mans Coupe.

I'm in love.

I don't care what anyone says. The 1967 Pontiac Le Mans Coupe was the shit, and yeah, this one is barely a skeleton of one, but it has the potential to be amazing if someone put a little effort into her. God, I can just picture it. Clean up that engine, new tires, fresh coat of paint. Cherry red. Or maybe blue. Damn, this thing would be amazing.

I can't believe it's just been sitting here, all this time.

I'm still holding the edge of the tarp in my hand when Star sidles up behind me. Her brow's all furrowed, little wrinkles between her eyes.

"What's the matter?" she asks.

Matter?

Oh. Right.

So maybe my mental outburst wasn't as strictly mental as I thought.

"Sorry. Nothing's wrong. Did you know about this?" I can't imagine she did, or she would have put the garage at the top of her little list. Even without fixing it up, this thing's probably worth some money.

"What is it?" she asks, and takes a step closer. I pull the tarp up higher so that she can see. But when she looks, there's no recognition playing across her face, so I'm gonna have to fill in the blanks.

"This," I say, tossing the tarp back to reveal as much of the car as possible, "is a 1967 Pontiac Le Mans Coupe." My voice gets louder and louder with every word, but I can't seem to stop it. I'm just so fucking excited. This is an amazing find. I can't believe Star's mom had this in here.

"You're really excited about this," she says, a little smile spreading across her face.

"This is a fucking cherry ride, babe," I tell her. "This is amazing."

"Do you think it's worth anything?" She looks back down at it, but she's pressing her tight little body up against me, and I grin and wrap my arm around her and tug her closer. She's all warm, and my fingertips sneak under the hem of her tank top, stroking the smooth skin of her belly. She twists a little under my hold, squirming against me, and I grin. My girl is ticklish. Good to know.

"It's gotta be," I tell her. "I don't know how much or anything, but I think I can find out." I might be able to track down Mr. Bremner, my old auto-shop teacher. Everything I knew about cars, I learned from that man. He might even be able to help Star find a buyer. The thought of letting such a sweet ride go kind of sucks, but what can I do? It's not like I have any money, and I know Star's bank account is pretty much burned out. So even though I have visions in my mind of fixing it up myself, when it comes down to it, it's her car. And it's her choice. So I tell her I'll try to give Mr. Bremner a call. She smiles at me in return, and presses her lips against mine before turning and heading back into the house.

I watch her go, her hips swaying to and fro as she moves, and all I can think about it how hot she'd look sitting in the Le Mans after it's all fixed up.

Not gonna happen, I remind myself, and turn back to the open garage. *You've got less than a month left with that girl, then it's gonna be a wave in the rearview mirror and a* thanks for the memories. *She isn't gonna stick around and wait for your dumb ass to be able to treat her right. You're lucky you got as far with her as you did.*

Grimacing, I kick out in frustration and send a grocery bag full of grocery bags out of the way.

I only have a few weeks left with Star *max.* I have to make them count.

Now I just have to figure out how the fuck to do that.

Star

I had to go all the way across Avenue to find the tea shop Maisie had told me about when we'd dropped off the diapers, the one with the good Wi-Fi. But it's *so* worth it. I have my laptop out, full bars on my Wi-Fi, and a steaming hot cup of caramel-flavored tea by my side, so decadent and rich that I think Maisie was right about the whole tea-is-just-as-good-as-coffee thing after all. I take a sip and the warmth flows through me, and I sink down into my seat happily, letting my eyes flutter shut.

I feel like I'm back at college.

I've missed this feeling so much.

But at the same time, it just reminds me how soon the summer is ending. How close I am to losing Ash. *God,* I think, reaching up and running my hands through my hair, *what the hell am I going to do?*

I miss college like crazy, and I have to go back. But leaving Ash behind . . . Just the thought of it makes my chest ache.

I need to figure out what I am going to do. What even are my options? Do I just go back to school? Do I try to transfer somewhere closer? Do I ask Ash what he wants? I want to stay, but I don't even know if that's possible. I can't take time off without losing my scholarship. And without the scholarship, I can't finish college.

Does he even want to continue with . . . things? I don't even know what to call it. We've barely talked about it. Our relationship has changed surprisingly little. It's the same as before, that easy friendship, that underlying attraction. Except now, there's sex. And not only that. There's . . . affection. There's a warmth to how Ash treats me, and it builds something up inside me. I'm not sure I can let that go.

I only have a month of the summer left. I need to figure things out. And honestly, I have no idea what I'm going to do.

It's like I'm balancing my heart in one hand, and my future in the other, when in fact I don't want to be balancing them at all. I want to grab on to both and hold on to them for dear life.

I'm screwed.

Sighing, I take another sip of my tea and bask in its heat. I came here to email Autumn, to explain what has happened between me and Ash, to ask for her advice. But now that I'm sitting here, laptop out in front of me, my mind is blank. How am I supposed to ask someone else to help me decide the course of my life? Would that be fair to anyone? The cursor on my blank email just blinks at me. No help there, either.

It's funny. I'm surrounded by people. I have more people in my life, who care about me, than I've ever had at one time before. But at the same time, I've never felt so alone.

Somehow, I am going to have to decide what I want. And I am going to have to do that all on my own. And I am going to have to do it soon. I need to be back at school in less than a month. If that's what I choose. I just don't know anymore.

Giving up on my email to Autumn, I close that window and open another. Click by click, I navigate over to the hoarding website that had been my oasis in the span between my mother's death and meeting Ash. It has been nearly two months since I've been on it, and it feels strange to be browsing through the once-familiar links and logging into my once-avid profile.

YOU HAVE 3 NEW MESSAGES

Brow furrowing, I click on the message folder and I'm accosted by a wave of guilt as I realize that all the messages are from LuckN-Glass, the girl who'd been so helpful when I first realized that I had to clean out my mother's hoard.

> TO: Star2274
> FROM: LuckNGlass
> June 2
>
> Hey, haven't heard from you lately. How's the cleanout going?

I can't believe so much time has passed. It's gone by like a whirl-wind. Feeling bad for leaving my hoarding-buddy hanging for so long, I click on the next message.

> TO: Star2274
> FROM: LuckNGlass
> June 29
>
> Hey, I know you're probably super busy, but when you get a chance, I could use an ear. My parents' house is getting out of control.

That had been almost a month ago. Biting at my lip, I click on the last unopened message.

> TO: Star2274
> FROM: LuckNGlass
> July 23
>
> Sorry about the other messages. I know I'm being pushy, but I'm going crazy here. I think I have to move out. I don't know what else to do. My dad's hoarding is out of control.

He's spent all the money we have.

I don't think I'm going to get to go to college anymore. Not the way I planned to, anyway.

Look, if you get this, can you please please reply? I'm losing my mind.

I hope cleaning out your mom's house is going well.

All the best,

Glass

Shit, I think, and toggle the mouse over to the reply button. I'm about to click it when I hear a familiar voice, and my spine turns to steel. I look up from the screen and there, walking in the front door, is Lacey. Luckily, she doesn't see me. She's chatting away into her phone, grinning widely as she makes her way toward the line, looking like she's on her way to spend the day at the beach. She's got her long hair loose, falling in big waves around her shoulders, and a pair of what look like designer sunglasses perched on her nose. I can't help but wonder how she can afford to look like that on a waitress's salary, but there's no way I'm going to ask. For one bright moment I think I'm in the clear. But then I realize that the line just happens to go right by my table. I stifle a groan and sink down in my seat. Maybe if I just don't look, she won't see me. Maybe she'll just walk right by.

No such luck. Even with the sunglasses obscuring her eyes, I can tell the instant she sees me. Her entire body flinches and she stutters to a stop and goes silent. I can hear the sound of the person on the other end of the call asking in an annoyed tone if she's still there, even from half a dozen feet away. She grimaces as she mutters, "I'll call you back," and ends the call, making a beeline toward me.

"Listen," she says, plopping down in the seat across from me. I'm starting to think that this is *kind* of a thing with her. This aggressive no-introduction form of communication. She reaches across the table and grabs my hand. It takes actual physical effort not to jerk away like I want to. But we're in a public place—*extremely* public, considering the way people are starting to turn and sneak peeks at us from the corners of their eyes—and it's not like I'm the town's favorite resident right now. Or ever, really. Actually, I'm pretty sure that I'm currently occupying the second-to-last spot in the popularity contest, as far as the town of Avenue is concerned. "I just wanted to say I'm sorry."

I blink at her, confused. *What the hell is she talking about?* "For what?" I ask.

"Well, for the car, of course."

What? I blink at her for a few seconds, certain that my confusion is clear on my face, but she doesn't say anything further.

Okay, subtlety isn't going to work on this girl. I lean forward and try to keep my voice low, so I don't attract any more attention than we are already getting. "What are you talking about?"

She pulls her hands back from mine, eyes widening.

"You don't know?" she says. "Oh my god. I thought for sure he would have told you?"

"What are you talking about, Lacey?" I ask. I don't like the sound of this.

"Your friend's car," she starts, and then suddenly stops talking. She looks away, appearing to gather her thoughts for a moment, and then blows out a deep breath and looks back at me. "Preston and the guys. They were the ones who messed up your friend's car."

What?

"What?" I snap.

"Listen, it's not what you think," she says hurriedly, as though talking faster is somehow going to make me *understand*. "Preston was just worried about me."

"How the *hell*," I say, "can you say that? What the fuck does one thing even have to do with the other?"

"Oh god," she says, reaching up and covering her mouth with her cupped hands. As I watch, her fingers curl in, and she's pressing her fists against her lower lip. "Preston was just looking out for me, okay? He saw that your friend was always hanging around me, and he got scared. He wanted to scare him off before he did anything. To me."

What.

The.

Fuck?

That's *it*. I've had it with this fucking town. I shove back from the table, my chair making a god-awful screeching noise as it scrapes against the floor. People are turning in their seats to look at us. I don't give a shit.

"And you actually bought that? That's a load of crap, Lacey. First of all, Ash *barely* goes into the diner *just because* of the shit he's gotten from people like your asshole boyfriend—"

"Hey!"

"I'm *not finished!*" I yell. *Everyone* is looking at us now. Good. *Good.*

"First of all," I repeat, more slowly this time. I lean forward, planting the palms of my hands against the table, to get in her face. "Ash never fucking goes near you. Second of all, Ash is not fucking dangerous. He made a mistake. He got in a car when he shouldn't have and he drove when he shouldn't have. He's not a murderer. He didn't go out there *intending* to hurt anyone. He made a *mistake*. And yeah, it was awful. It was heartbreaking. But that's life. But you, little miss perfect, and your boyfriend wouldn't know a thing about that, now, would you?"

Lacey's sitting there, dumbstruck. Her mouth sort of sags open as she stares at me. But then she pulls in a breath, and starts to push forward, moving as though she's going to respond. But I'm not done.

"Finally," I snap before she can say anything. *"Finally,* how the hell do you get from your stupid boyfriend thinking that Ash could possibly be threatening to you, to him and his buddies beating the shit out of Ash's car?"

Out of the corner of my eye, I can see the three teenagers behind the counter hovering together, whispering. One of them kind of sighs and then his eyes dart over to me, and when he sees me looking at him, his entire body actually *jerks.* Great. Now I'm the crazy one. Those poor kids are probably over there drawing straws for who has to ask me to leave. Fantastic.

I turn back to Lacey, but my eyes can't even focus on her. I'm just looking through her, like she doesn't matter to me anymore.

And as I take a deep breath and force myself to calm down, I realize that's exactly it.

She doesn't matter.

None of these people do.

Only Ash and I matter. And that's the way it should be.

"You need to get your life together," I tell her and pull myself back into a standing position as I scoop my laptop off the table and snag my bag off the back of my chair. I shove the computer inside and pull it over my shoulder. "Because no one should think that what you and your little boyfriend did was okay."

Then I pick my tea up off of the table, turn on my heel and walk out the door.

Ash

I hear Star's car pull up in the driveway and I wipe the palms of my hands against my jeans for the millionth time.

I can't believe how fucking nervous I am. We've been messing around for weeks, and just the thought of asking Star to actually *go out* with me has my knees shaking. My palms are sweating like I'm thirteen fucking years old and about to ask Jessica Kirkley to our first middle school dance.

But this is going to go better than that had. It *has to*. I am sure of it. Jessica Kirkley had laughed in my face and told me to try again when I got taller.

Bitch.

Star wouldn't do that to me. Not after everything we've been, though. Even if she hates the idea, she'd be nice about it. I'm sure of it.

Pretty sure.

I think.

"That stupid bitch!" Star groans out once she's in the door, and my head whips around to look at her. What the fuck happened while she was gone? She hauls the strap of her bag over her head, sending her hair flying, and dumps the bag on to the sofa once it's free. The living room isn't quite clear, but it's getting there. Soon we'll actually be able to use it for, you know, *living.*

Okay, for sex. The air-conditioning will be fucking glorious for that.

"What's the matter?" I ask, a million different scenarios running through my mind. "What happened?"

"Lacey," Star snaps, like that explains everything. It doesn't. I have no fucking idea who Lacey is. And after a second of me just staring at her, Star seems to realize that. "The waitress," she says, reaching up and rubbing a hand over her face. "The blonde from the diner that was rude to you when you applied for a job. That Lacey."

"Oh . . . kay," I say. Progress. We're getting there. "What happened?"

"It was her boyfriend that trashed your car," she says, and throws her hands up in the air. Unfortunately, the house is still a little too packed to be expressive in, and her hand knocks against a precariously-placed—and what appears to be empty—shoe box at the top of a pile, and it comes falling down. We watch it as it somersaults to the floor, knocking down a grocery bag full of grocery bags—why the hell are there so many of those in this house?—and a plastic Christmas tree topper in the shape of a star. Everything goes tumbling, and Star is standing there, looking like the goddess of fury and in that moment all I can think is *she is really fucking hot.*

She hauls in a deep breath, and, once the dust has settled, continues her rant like nothing happened. "She told me, at the tea shop that Maisie told me about. It was Preston and his brother and their stupid asshole friend. They're all assholes. And Lacey is the biggest bitch of all because she had the absolute gall to try and tell me that they did it for her protec— Wait. Ash? Why are you looking at me like that?"

I can feel the smirk tug at the corner of my mouth, and I don't bother trying to hide it any more. Instead I just look her up and down and take a step forward.

She, in turn, takes a step back. "Ash . . . seriously?" she says, eyes widening. But I can see the flush that's starting to spread up her neck, and I'm struck by the urge to see just how far down it goes.

"Mmmhmm."

"Seriously? This is doing it for you?" She takes another step back. But it's the last one. Now she's backed up against the row of boxes against the far wall, the ones we've been working up to going through. I grin and reach out and press my hands against the boxes on either side of her, bracketing her body against the stack of boxes with my arms. I lean closer and press a kiss to her jaw before pressing my lips against her neck and just breathing her in.

"You have no idea," I say, because *hell yes* this is doing it for me. "Somehow you're even hotter when you're all pissed off."

She scoffs, but her hands come up to spread against my chest. "Somehow I don't think you'd be so into it if it was you I was pissed at."

"Hmm, well we'll just have to see, then, won't we?" I say, and lean in for a kiss.

Afterward—way, *way* afterward—we're in the kitchen and I suddenly remember what I'd been meaning to ask her when she walked in the door all mad and hot. So while we're waiting for our macaroni to finish cooking, I swallow down my fear and say,

"So . . . you wanna go out dancing with me tomorrow night?"

Star kind of stares at me for a second, all deer-in-the-headlights, and I can't help it. I start laughing. She harrumphs out a sigh and reaches over to whap me on the belly with the back of her hand. "Stop laughing," she says. "It's not funny."

"Yes, it is," I say, reaching out and poking her in the side before stepping around her to poke at the noodles in the pot. *Another couple minutes,* I think.

"Well it's not like I was expecting it," she says, exasperation in her voice. But when I turn to look at her, she's smiling this soft little smile, and I want to wrap myself around her and never let go. "Why do you want to go out, anyway? You hate this town."

"Yeah," I say, "I do. But the place I want to take you isn't in Avenue. It's in the next town over. And besides, I want to take you out." I take a deep breath and blow it out, bracing myself a little. "You deserve it."

You deserve a hell of a lot better than I could ever give you. But I'm willing to try.

"But you told me you hate dancing," she says, but her little smile is turning full-fledged and I know I've got her. I knew she'd like this.

"I do," I say. "I suck at dancing, I look like a monkey on speed. But you told me you love to dance. So you and me, we're gonna go dancing. Besides . . . " I move up so I've got her right up against me. Her body feels so good, even when it's just barely brushing up against mine. I reach over and slide my hand around her waist, dipping my fingertips under the hem of her shirt so I can brush up against her skin. She shivers a little at my touch, but she doesn't move away. I grin and press my face into her hair, my mouth brushing against her ear. "I kind of like the thought of you rubbing that hot little body of yours up against me as we dance."

A full-on shiver runs down her body as I whisper to her. Then she turns in my arms, and pushes up on her tiptoes and nuzzles her nose against mine.

"I like the sound of that," she says, and I can't hold back any longer. I lean forward and wrap both my arms around her middle and lift her up a little bit, just so that her feet are off the ground, and I press my mouth against hers.

And, because right at that moment, I'm the luckiest bastard on the planet, she kisses me back.

Chapter 18

Ash

I ended up taking her to Gerard's for dinner first, a little hole-in-the-wall pub in the next town over, not far from where I'd planned on taking her dancing. I used to come here, not to get shit-faced like I normally did at bars, but for the food. It has the best damn chili on the planet, and just like I thought she would, Star fucking loved it. Not the best first-date food, sure. But it has always been my favorite, and I wanted to share it with her.

We got a little booth in the back, eating and laughing and having a good time. I'd wrapped my arm around her shoulders, snuggling up against her as I tried to shove my nerves about going dancing deep down so they wouldn't show. I'm going to look like an idiot. *But that's okay,* I tell myself. *You're going to be with the hottest girl there. No one is going to be looking at you. Not when they could look at her.*

And damn, does Star ever look good. I don't know where she even got those clothes, but when she walked out of the bedroom in those tight jeans and that little leather jacket, it took everything I had not to suggest just staying home and doing some "dancing" on the living room floor.

Well, if there was room on the living room floor, anyway. Which there wasn't. We hadn't gotten that far in the clean-up yet.

Soon, I think as I follow Star out to the parking lot, my eyes following every curve of her body as she walks ahead of me. *Soon.*

"Come on," she says, reaching back and snagging my hand in hers. Smiling, she raises her hand in mine and twirls her body underneath it like a ballerina. "You promised me dancing."

I smile and pull her close, wrapping my free hand around her waist, and press a kiss to her temple. "Are you sure you still want to do that?" I ask. "Because I can think of a couple other things we can do. By ourselves."

"Hey, mister," Star says, laughing and shoving me away from her playfully. I laugh and fake a stumble into the side of her mom's station wagon, clutching at my chest like she's wounded me. "You promised me dancing." She wags her finger at me. "And that means that we are definitely goi—"

"Well, look who came crawling back." A voice cuts through the darkness, and it makes something cold shoot up my spine and the hairs on the back of my neck stand up. I know that voice. I know it extremely fucking well, even though I haven't heard it in five goddamn years. My heart in my throat, I squeeze Star's hand and slowly turn around.

Fuck.

She looks different. Her hair's shorter now, up around her

shoulders instead of trailing in curls down her back, but it's still just as red. And her eyes are just as fucking cruel as they were the last day I saw her.

I take a deep breath, trying to brace myself, but my voice still sounds like a hormonal fucking teenager when I force it out.

"Hey, Gina," I say, trying not to wince at the sound. "It's been a long fucking time."

My ex-girlfriend just smirks at me and cocks her hip out to one side as she crosses her arms over her chest.

"Yes, Ash," she says, "it has."

Star

This is her, I realize. This is Ash's ex. The one that broke his heart and dropped him when the accident happened. The one who abandoned him when he needed her the most. I grit my teeth as I look her over. She doesn't even glance at me, even though Ash and I are still pressed close together.

I want to rip her eyes out.

"I should have figured I'd see you around here," she says. "After all, this is where you used to take me all the time." Her gaze darts over to me finally, giving me a cold once-over before dropping down to where my fingers are linked with Ash's. Then she looks back up at me and smirks before turning back to Ash.

"It's my favorite restaurant, Gina," he says. He's gripping my hand so hard that I'm going to have bruises, but I don't care. I squeeze back just as hard. I'm here. I'm his now, and he's mine.

This girl is his past.

And the past doesn't matter. Not to us. Not anymore.

But she just scoffs. "This dump?" she says. "Not exactly fine dining, is it?"

"I don't know what the hell you're complaining about," Ash says. "In case it has escaped your notice, you're here, too."

"Only because I saw you in the parking lot. Brenden and I are having dinner at the new French place across the street." She tilts her nose up into the air like that's supposed to mean something, like she's better than us, somehow. Yeah, right. Ash has told me all about her. Little rich girl who wanted to walk the wild side, wanted to get her parents attention by getting into drugs and drinking. But she's the one eyeing him like he's the worthless one. "You remember Brenden, don't you, Ash?"

Smirking, she takes a step closer, and Ash takes a step forward and tugs me behind him slightly, so that he's standing between the two of us, the line of his back stiff as an arrow.

"They should have let you rot in prison," she says. "You deserve it, after what you did."

I lay my free hand on Ash's back, trying to soothe him, but it's no use. He's tensed up completely, muscles coiled like he's ready for a fight.

But instead of snapping back at her, like I expect him to, his muscles begin to loosen. As I watch, Ash almost seems to shrink in on himself, becoming smaller and smaller as this horrible woman goes on and on, telling him how useless he is, how terrible. Her voice is like the scraping of nails across a chalkboard. It's killing him.

Then she draws her arm back, hand twitching like she's about to take a swing at him, and I can't take it anymore.

"Get the hell away from him!" I yell, stepping forward around Ash, and the girl jerks away from me, her eyes widening as I reach down and pull my phone out of my bag. I can't help the smirk that starts to tug at the corner of my mouth as I turn on the phone and waggle the screen in her direction. "You lay one finger on him and I'm calling the police and having you charged with assault."

She takes a step back, eyes darting back and forth between me and Ash, probably wondering who the hell I am. Good. Little redhead wasn't expecting anyone to actually say anything, even after she spewed all that crap where anyone could hear it. I can't imagine why. Did she think that she was so damn intimidating that she could just walk all over everybody?

I take a step forward and, hilariously, the girl—Gina, Ash said her name was—actually takes another full step back. "Yeah," I scoff, dropping my phone back into my bag. "That's what I thought."

For a split second, she fumbles, her perfect little persona slipping for an instant before she manages to shake it off and pull herself back together. But it's too late. I've already seen straight through her. She's weak. The worst thing that ever happened in her life didn't even happen to her. It happened to Ash. She's had nothing that hard in her life, nothing she's had to live through, to force herself to be strong just to keep breathing through.

But I have. And that makes me stronger than her.

Much stronger.

But she's the one who's crossing her arms over her chest and looking at me like she's the queen of the world, like I'm beneath her. Like Ash is nothing more than a bit of dirt on her shoe, and I'm no better, having associated with him.

How wrong she is.

She whirls on Ash, what little is left of her fire flashing in her eyes. "Are you going to let this little bitch talk to me like this, Ash?"

I can feel as much as hear the breath Ash takes and blows back out as he comes back into himself, and I smile as his hand lands on my waist, pulling me closer.

"She can say whatever she wants," Ash says, and I turn to look over my shoulder at him, feeling my belly flip at the warmth in his eyes when he looks at me.

I turn back to Gina, crossing my arms over my chest. "That's right. And what I want, right now, is to tell you to go to hell. So guess what?" I take a step forward, feeling Ash's hand drop from my side as I move into Gina's personal space, and whisper, "Go to hell."

I flick my hair over my shoulder and turn away from Gina, a grin spreading across my face. I can practically *feel* it as her glare burns into my back, smack dab between my shoulder blades, but I don't give a shit. She abandoned Ash when he needed her.

He deserves better.

"Ash, call off your stupid whore," Gina snaps, but I don't even turn around to look at her. She isn't worth my time. "You will listen to me or you will regret it!"

Ash is standing there, leaning against the passenger door of the car, grinning like mad. "I don't think so, Gina," he says, but he isn't looking at her. He's looking straight at me as he tells her, "You and I are done. For good. I'm with Star now, and she's right. You should go to hell."

Behind me, Gina's still screeching at us, but all I can see is Ash and how good he looks. He grins at me, and lets his gaze wander from my eyes all the way down to my feet and back up again, the suggestion clear in his eyes. I give him a saucy little wink and watch as he throws back his head and laughs.

It's the most gorgeous thing I've ever seen. All at once, I want to throw myself at him, wrap my arms around his shoulders and my legs tight around his waist, and French the hell out of him. The need is like a hook in my belly, just below my navel, and it tugs me straight to him.

Oh, what the hell, I think. And then I do just that.

Ash

That was fucking amazing. I'd never seen Gina's face look like that in my entire life. It had done some weird thing, like she'd sucked on a lemon while trying to shit a brick at the exact same time. And Star had been classy as fuck while she was putting Gina in her place.

It had been hot as hell, especially right afterward, when Star had wrapped her legs around me, pinning me to the car with her weight. She'd rubbed up against me like a cat, and it made me want to do all *kinds* of things to her. And judging by the things she'd whispered in my ear as Gina had let out a huff and stalked off, I'd be getting to do everything I'd pictured real damn soon.

Especially since one of the things she said was "You know what Ash? Fuck *dancing*. Why don't you take me home and fuck *me?*"

Goddamn, I think, replaying the scene over again in my mind. *So fucking hot.* I need to drive faster.

Luckily the streets are pretty empty. But it isn't surprising. It isn't like Avenue is known for its nightlife. But even though the drive is going pretty quickly, it feels like I've already been in the car for an eternity. I'm half tempted to just pull over on the side of the road and pull Star into my lap. Get started on the fun a little bit early.

But when I look over, the suggestion on the tip of my tongue, Star just smiles at me, and my stomach does that weird flippy thing it's been doing an awful lot lately.

Fuck, I'm in love with her. Every time I look at her, something moves through me, and all of a sudden I don't give a shit that she lives two states away. I'll follow that girl to the end of the earth, if she'll let me. I reach over and lay my hand on hers on the bench seat between us. Her skin is warm and smooth beneath mine. My hand's all rough and calloused, especially after all the work we've been doing on the house. But hers feels like silk. She flips her hand over under mine, and I link our fingers together. Then I tug our joined hands up, and, looking over at her, I press my lips to the back of her hand.

She squirms a little in her seat and a laugh bubbles up out of her. It sounds like music to me. "Watch the road, jerk," she says, and I wink at her as she tugs her hand away, and I turn back to the road. The sun is sinking behind the horizon, and the light is getting dim. As we drive, the streetlights start blinking on one by one.

It's a nice night.

But it's more than that somehow. It almost feels like a beginning.

Star leans forward and turns on the radio, and as I drive she fiddles with the dials, finally settling on an oldies station. She leans back in her seat, and as soon as she's out of reach, I reach over and switch it to a classic-rock station. Star turns and says, "Hey!" as AC/DC starts blasting through the speakers. I grin and glance over at her. She's glaring at me, but I can tell by the smile that's tugging at her mouth that she doesn't mean it. Soon enough her glare fades and she rolls her eyes, reaching out and twisting the dial, turning down the volume to a much lower level.

The song ends and the DJ switches over to Metallica and, from deep in the caverns of Star's bag, her phone rings. She leans forward, digging through it until she finds it, and sits back clutching the phone in her hand. But she doesn't answer it right away. It just keeps ringing. I look over her. She's staring down at the screen, her brow furrowing.

I reach over and touch her leg, but she doesn't look up.

"Hey," I say, glancing back at the road and then looking back at her. "What is it? What's wrong?" I trail my hand up her leg to where her free hand rests. I lay my palm over the back of her hand, then trail my finger down until my pinkie is linked with hers.

She just shakes her head and touches her thumb to the screen, answering the call. Bringing it to her ear, she murmurs, "Hello?"

And that's the last thing I see that makes sense. Suddenly, everything is a cacophony of noise and movement.

Everything around me spins, turning upside down again and again and again. Beside me, Star is screaming, and there's the sound of metal against metal. Tearing. Cracking. Shattering.

And then, suddenly, everything stops. The chaos is gone. And then there's nothing but silence and stillness and *pain*.

So much pain.

And then all I can see is darkness.

Sometimes, a single second is all it takes.

And everything changes.

Chapter 19

Ash

I try to open my eyes but I can't.
    I can't focus.

All I can see is flashes. Flashes of light and of darkness. All I can hear is the thunder of my heart and snatches of voices. But they're all talking over one another and it's like I'm in a dream, like they're all out of order, out of sequence. Or that I am.

"—other. We're his pa—"

"—e's crashing. We need to in—"

Someone's crying. Sobbing. I want to reach out, to move.

But I can't.

I'm trying so hard that the shock of the jolt, of my body jerking without my permission stuns me and I start to fall back in on myself.

"—eed to get—"

"—epped for sur—"

I try to follow the voices, try to make them make sense, but it's no use.

They're fading.

Everything's fading.

No.

No.

No no no, I think. I try to scream it but the words won't come out.

The light is gone now. The voices, too.

Fuck, I think as I slide into the darkness.

It's happening again.

Star

When I wake up, I do it slowly. I'm groggy. Sluggish. I feel like I'm deep under water, and it's a struggle to fight my way to the surface. To consciousness.

But slowly, I edge my way back, bit by bit. And finally, *finally,* I open my eyes.

The first thing that filters through my hazy mind is just how incredibly bright everything is. Walls gleaming white in the sunlight that filters through the window by my side, bits of metal catching in the light, sending off little glints that dance like fairies across my vision.

The second thing is the *pain.*

Everything hurts. Every last inch of me aches, and as I breathe in, I feel a shooting, stabbing pain in my side. I try to squeeze my eyes shut and breathe through it, but I can't quite stop the whimper that escapes my lips. Struggling, trying not to scream, I shift myself on my side and lay there, exhausted, just breathing. In and out.

In and out.

The machine next to me lets out a beep, and, once the pain has faded into the background, I open my eyes.

I'm in a hospital room.

What the hell happened to me? I wonder. *How did I even get here?*

And then . . . *Oh god.*

Ash.

Where's Ash?

I try to surge forward, to pull myself out of the bed, but I can't. The pain is so bad I want to scream and I have to grit my teeth and ease myself back down, and wait for it to pass again.

My heart is thundering in my chest.

Where is Ash?

I open my mouth to call out for someone. Anyone. But the haze that keeps threatening to envelop me is too great, and I can't quite get the words out. I still, squeezing my eyes shut and try to concentrate. I can do this. I have to do this. I suck in as much air as I can, and let out a yell before I collapse back onto the mattress. A moment passes, two, and I'm lost in the whirling, dizzying cloud of pain that surrounds me. There's a noise from the other side of the door, and my eyes blink open just in time to see the doorknob begin to turn. I reach out with my left hand to grasp the edge of the bed and push myself up into a more upright position, but as I set my hand down, my hand begins to hurt. Bad.

I look down and my heart catches in my throat. And as soon as

I lay eyes on it, the pain hits me in full force. My hand is wrapped in gauze, my fingers are trembling, from the pain or the fear, I'm not certain. But there's something wrong.

My hand is too small, too narrow to be my own.

I turn my hand over, palm up, just to be sure, and my throat starts to close up as I realize what has happened.

My pinkie finger, the one I've linked with Ash dozens of times as we made promises to each other, is gone.

It's just . . . gone.

Ash

I hear them talking before I open my eyes. My parents. I can't make out what they're saying, but I know their voices better than anyone's. And that's definitely my mother.

I groan before I can stop myself, and try to turn over to go back to sleep. It's early—what the fuck does she think she's doing, trying to wake me up at this time? But as soon as I shift, I can feel it, the pain, and I fucking *jolt*.

Jesus Christ. Everything fucking hurts. What the hell happened to me?

"Ash?" Mom's voice cuts through the haze. "Ash, are you all right, honey?"

Why is that familiar? Why have I heard those words before? Well, almost. I'm pretty sure there wasn't a *honey* attached to it last time.

What the fuck happened?

I grit my teeth and force my eyes to open. There's a flash of white, and then my vision clears. I'm in the hospital. Jesus.

All at once, I'm back there. I'm back in Gina's car, weaving back and forth completely wasted. I'm back at the crash, at the car I tried not to hit but did, anyway. I hear the horn, the scrape and scream of metal against metal, and then I see the white of the hospital room, the dark uniformed figure, reading me my rights before I'm hauled off to holding. To the courtroom. To prison. It all hits me all at once, and then over and over again. It won't stop.

It won't ever stop.

Crash.

Scream.

Darkness.

Light.

Crash.

Scream.

Darkness.

Li—

A hand lands on my shoulder, jostling me hard enough to jerk me back into reality. I blink my eyes open, even though they feel heavy and I'm sluggish under the weight that's pressing on my chest. What the fuck happened? Why am I here?

I must say it out loud, because Mom's face comes into view, and I feel her cool hand rest on my forehead. It feels good, relaxing, but I shake off that feeling. I have to. I have to stay awake. Stay alert.

"It's okay, honey. Everything is going to be all right."

"What—what happened?" I ask, trying to pull myself up into a sitting position even as the room starts to spin around me. Mom's hand is on my shoulder almost immediately, trying to push me back down against the pillows.

"Mom?" I say, desperate. I don't remember. I don't know why I'm here. "Mom, what happened to me?"

I manage to keep my eyes open long enough to see her glance behind her, and I hear the sound of footsteps against tile, and Dad appears beside her. They're silent for a moment, doing that weird mental communication thing that all parents seem to be able to do, the ones that stay together, anyway. But I'm fighting against the pain and the drugs—goddamn, what the fuck do they have me on? I feel like I'm flying—and I need answers before I pass out.

"Mom. Please. What's going on?"

She sighs and turns back to me, and I see her eyes are filled with unshed tears.

"You were in an accident. The car you were driving was hit."

Fuck.

Star!

"Star," I say, instantly more awake than I had been a moment ago. My hands are pulling at the blankets, trying to get them off me so I can sit up. "Where is she? Is she okay?" I fight back a wave of nausea as I swing my feet over the side of the bed and start to climb down. My parents' hands are on me at once, trying to push me back, but I just shove them off. I need to find her. I need to make sure she's okay.

Holy fuck. What if she's not? What if she's dead?

I think I'm gonna puke.

"Ash! Ash, stop!" Mom says, her fingers gripping the flimsy-ass hospital nightgown I'm wearing. I don't remember putting that on. I reach up and start prying her fingers off. I need to find Star.

"Let me go," I say, pulling her hands away. "I need to see Star.

I need to know if she's okay."

"She's fine." Dad's voice comes from the edge of the inky blackness that's hovering all around the edge of my vision. I shake my head, trying to clear it, but all that does is make it start to spin even worse. I lean back against the edge of the bed, and feel his warm hand come down on the back of my neck. "Ash. Did you hear me?" he asks, his voice deep and close. "Your friend is okay. She's banged up, but she's alive."

Jesus Christ. Relief spreads through me like a tidal wave.

Holy shit.

I lean forward, resting my throbbing head in my hands for a moment, trying to get the fog to pass. My entire body's shaking and I feel like I'm freezing and sweating my ass off at the same damn time. I don't remember feeling like this before. Not even the last time I was in the hospital.

But my relief is short lived. I feel like only seconds have passed before my body is thrumming again. I open my eyes to see both of my parents staring down at me, concern written all over their faces, clear as if it were tattooed right there on their skin for everyone to see.

"I need to see her," I force the words out, clenching my hands into fists as I struggle to stop shaking. "I need to see that she's okay."

I reach down and brace my hands against the edge of the mattress, and try to work up the strength to get back on my feet. My mother's hands are on me again in a heartbeat. "You can't," she says, trying to push me back onto the hospital bed. "You'll hurt yourself." Her voice is firm but her hands are gentle. Too gentle. I push past them easily.

"I don't care," I say. "I have to find her." God, she doesn't even have any family left. Both of her parents are dead and she's never really talked about any of her foster parents. She'll be all alone. I can't leave her all alone. I make it all of two steps away from the bed when I feel the painful tug and look down. My left arm is in a cast, and the other is hooked up to about a million different wires. Fuck. How bad had the accident been? I reach down and, using the half-numb fingers on my broken hand—at least, I'm assuming it's my hand that's broken. It's hard to tell when the cast starts close to my fingertips and goes nearly all the way up to my elbow—I tug the little heart-rate monitoring clip off my finger and then reach for the IV line.

"Don't touch that!" my mother snaps, reaching out and batting my hand away. "You need that medicine right now."

"Fine," I say, and reach out with my good hand and grab the IV pole next to my bed. It's not hooked up to anything else, and it wheels freely toward me when I pull it. Good. With my other hand, I reach up and start pulling off the monitoring sensors they've attached to my chest. Beside me, a machine starts beeping like it's doing some sort of end-of-the-world countdown, but I don't care. Finally free, I start heading toward the door.

"Ashley! Get back here! You need to rest."

My mother's voice keeps getting louder with every word, but nothing she says is going to stop me. I feel a smirk start to pull at my lips as I limp forward out the door. I don't even need to turn around; I know that behind me, Mom looks like she's about to blow a gasket, and Dad's looking helplessly around the room. They're never going to change. "At least let me get you a wheelchair!" is the last thing I hear from the room as I turn and start hustling down the hallway.

The hospital is surprisingly quiet. I keep expecting nurses to jump out of nowhere and drag me back to my room, to have doctors rushing by with gurneys of people bound for emergency surgery, shoving me out of the way. But it's calm out in the hall.

I don't know where I'm going. For all I know, Star could be in the room beside me or on the other side of the fucking hospital, if she's even in this hospital at all.

A million thoughts run through my mind at once as I approach the counter of the nurses' station. What if my parents were lying? What if Star isn't okay? What if she didn't survive the crash?

Fuck. I need to find her. Right now.

I take the last few steps a little too quick and hit the counter with an amount of force that I really didn't intend, and the pressure slams through my chest and makes black spots swirl in front of my eyes all over again. Fuck. I'm more hurt than I thought. I can hear the rapid clip of footsteps coming up behind me, and I know my mother is hot on my tail, so I have to make this quick.

"Hey!" I yell, leaning across the deserted counter, hoping against hell that there's someone in the room behind it. "Hey!"

A second later a guy in pale blue scrubs hustles out, his eyes widening when he sees me. "You, Nurse-Dude. I need to know where my girlfriend is." I've never called her that before, but damned if it isn't true.

"Uh, sir? I think you should be in bed," he says, blinking at me like he's never seen a fucking beat-up guy before in his life. Some shitty nurse he is.

"Not gonna happen, asshole," I say, and lean farther over the counter, shrugging off my mother's hand when it hits my shoulder. "Star Collins. S-T-A-R C-O-L-L-I-N-S. Look it up in your little computer there and tell me where she is." The guy looks back and forth between me and my mom, and for a second I think he's going to piss himself.

"Sir, really," he says. "I'm going to have to insist that you return to your room. The doctor will be in to see you shortly—"

"Fuck that," I snap, and push myself off the counter. The hallway spins around me and I have to stop for a second and breathe through it, get my feet under me again. After a second, I shake it off and open my eyes. There's probably a dozen people in the hallway now, and every single fucking one of them is staring at me.

"Ash—"

"No," I say and start walking—*limping*—down the hallway. "I'll find her myself."

I'm booking it down the hall, and I can hear my mom and the nurse whispering behind me, but I couldn't give a shit if I tried. I pull in a deep breath and start yelling for Star. Everyone who's got their eyes on me seem to jerk in unison, and a couple people actually turn and scurry back into their rooms like rats. Good. Stay out of my way.

"Star!" I yell, but other than my mother and the nurse, the hallway is silent. Fuck. Where is she? I move faster, half pulling the IV stand and half using it for balance when my knees start to get weak. My right thigh is aching like a bitch, but I don't look down. If I see it, whatever it is, it'll just hurt worse.

"Star! Baby, where are you?" I say, my voice dropping low. The hallway is fucking spinning around me, and I have to squeeze my eyes shut for a moment. I've got the IV pole in a death grip, but it isn't helping. If I don't sit down soon, I'm going to be going down, anyway. I have to find her.

"STAR!" I yell, my voice booming down the hallway. And for long, terrible seconds, there's nothing, and I can feel my body start to shake again.

"Ash?" I whirl around at the sound, afraid for a second that I've imagined it. But then it's back, louder this time. "Ash!"

Holy shit. It's her. It's Star.

I turn down the hallway to my left, limping as I try to keep as much weight off my right side as possible, booking it toward the source of the sound.

"Star!"

"Ash!"

I skid to a stop and turn to my right. There she is. Holy shit. I feel hot and cold all at once, and my throat feels like someone's got their hands around it, and they're wringing the life out of me. But fuck, it doesn't matter. It's her.

"Jesus," I say, the word barely making it out past the stranglehold on my throat. I don't know how I did it, but suddenly I'm right in front of her. She's got tears streaming down her face, and I reach out with my busted hand and touch them, wipe them away, just to be sure that she's real. She lets out a sob and reaches for me. One of her hands is bandaged up like a mummy, and she's all black and blue, but she's here. She's here and we're okay.

"Oh god," I fall forward and gather her up in my arms. The IV pole catches on something and goes tumbling to the floor. I feel it jerk the line attached to my arm, and it hurts like a bitch, but I don't care. I've got her in my arms. I can't stop shaking.

She's crying, but I realize that I am, too. Big, nasty sobs that I press into her hair as I try to breathe through the ache in my chest. I feel like I'm dying. I press my lips against her ear, and try to take in enough air to force words out, but I'm shaking so bad. We both are.

"Ash . . . " she says, and her voice is a fucking whimper and I can't . . . I just . . .

"Jesus Christ," I say against her hair, pulling her closer even though I don't have to. She's pressed as close as physically possible. Any closer and we'd be inside each other's skin. My face is wet, and I can't get the tears to stop, but it doesn't matter. It doesn't fucking matter. She's alive. I pull back just enough to press our foreheads together. "I love you," I say, and I press my mouth to hers. "You hear me, Star?" I ask as soon as I break the kiss, because she needs to hear it. I need her to hear me, to understand. "I love you so fucking much. Don't leave me, okay? Whatever you want. Just don't leave."

My eyes are squeezed shut, but I can feel her nod against the side of my face, the wetness of her tears against my skin. Her body is wracked with sobs, and I pull her closer, wrapping both of my arms around her back, even though every inch of me hurts. I want to wrap myself around her and her around me, and just get lost in her existence. I hear my mother come up behind me. I recognize the sound of her voice, but I can't make out what she's saying. All I can hear is Star as she cries, as her breathing slowly calms down enough for her to speak.

All I hear is Star.

"I love you, too, Ash," she whispers, and I squeeze her close and just breathe her in. "I love you, too."

Chapter 20

Star

"Now are you sure that you both don't want to stay with us," Ash's mother asks for the hundredth time since she first suggested it. "We have plenty of room."

"That's okay, Mrs. Winthrope," I say, and try to suppress a grin as Ash rolls his eyes and leans against my shoulder. "We'll be fine at the house."

"It's just that you're both still healing, dear," she says. "And I don't like the thought— Roger! Roger, turn here! I don't like the thought of the two of you being on your own at a time like this." She's turned around in her seat now, looking over her shoulder at us, her eyes soft as she catches a glimpse of Ash's arm around my shoulders, her son cuddled close to me. I wonder if she'd look so happy if she knew the things Ash has been muttering to me the entire ride over, low enough so she can't hear them.

He doesn't mean them, though. I can see how happy he is to have his parents around again. So I'm not going to blow his cover. "Really, Mrs. Winthrope," I say. "We'll be just fine."

"Well, if you're sure," she says. "And really, dear, call me Nadine."

"Okay," I say, and smile at her, even though I have absolutely no intention of doing any such thing. Just because Ash and I are together doesn't mean I'm ready to get all chummy with his mother. Not when I wasn't even that close to my own.

Maybe Brick was right. Maybe I do built up walls around me. But sometimes people manage to get inside them with me. Like Ash did. I smile and lean over and press my lips against his cheek. "Your mom is going to make me crazy," I whisper in his ear as Mrs. Winthrope argues with her husband over which is the best route to get to my mother's house. Well, she argues. He just kind of nods and phases her out.

"Join the fucking club," Ash murmurs back, a little too loudly, and I poke at him with my good hand, trying to shut him up before his mother catches us. Or before she catches onto the fact that he's faking sleep. One or the other.

"You keep quiet," I say. "We'll be alone soon enough."

I can feel his smile against my skin.

"I like the sound of that."

All told, we were in the hospital for just over two weeks, but it had only taken hours after we'd been reunited for us to find out what had happened.

It was Preston. Lacey's boyfriend. It was his car that hit us. An accident, they said. Both cars were totaled, my mother's old station wagon completely destroyed. And even though his buddy who'd been in the car with him had messed his back up real bad, my injuries and Ash's had been far worse. The doctor had come in while Ash's mother was explaining what happened, and he'd confirmed what I'd known to be true. The pinkie finger on my left hand was gone. Amputated. Too destroyed to even try saving. On top of that I had some bruised ribs and a black eye to end all black eyes. Ash had made out only slightly better. Broken wrist, deep puncture in his thigh and another in his lung that they'd managed to get to before it got too bad. That wasn't even counting the innumerable bumps and bruises between the two of us.

All things considered, though, I figure we made out okay.

And Preston? That bastard had walked away without a scratch.

"Gonna beat that guy's ass into the ground if I ever see him again," Ash had muttered into my skin, snuggling closer to me on the hospital bed. Despite what the doctors and his parents had said, he'd refused to be budged, and for the past two weeks, we've barely been out of each other's sight.

To be honest, I'm kind of starting to get used to it.

It's . . . *nice.*

"Now," his mother says, turning around in her seat to look at me as the car pulls into the driveway. "Are you sure that you and Ashley will be all right here? It's perfectly all right if you want to stay with us." She turns around in her seat again, and orders her husband to move the car up farther in the driveway. "No, farther! There. Was that so difficult?"

"She says that now," Ash mutters against my shoulder. "But the second she catches us doing more than holding hands, her brain will explode."

"Shut up," I murmur in his ear, but I'm smiling as I do it. *"Ashley."* I get a poke in my side in response, but it's in one of my—very few—uninjured spots, so it doesn't bother me all that much. I turn back to face his mother. "Honestly, Mrs. Winthrope—*Nadine*," I correct myself before she can do it for me. "We'll be fine here. We'll just clear a couple extra paths and—" *and take it easy,* I'm about to say, but as I turn and look out the car window, the words catch in my throat. There, on the front porch, is Autumn. And Roth. And as I watch, Maisie and York and about half a dozen other people I've seen around town but have never actually met begin filing out the front door to stand with them. *What on earth?*

My heart is slamming in my chest as I shake Ash into sitting up, and I can feel the second he sees it by the way his body jerks against mine. Slowly, I turn back to look at Ash's mother, and I'm blinking through tears to see that she's smiling at me.

"We wanted it to be a surprise," she says. And that's when I really start crying.

They cleaned it. Autumn and Roth and York and Maisie. Ash's parents. Them and a handful of people they'd recruited, they'd cleaned out the whole house.

Ash and I walk through the house in a daze, leaning on each other for support. It's not perfect, not by a long shot. There's still work to be done, walls to be painted, boxes of things they deemed *important* to go through. But those are stacked up neatly in the corners of the rooms, and the color of the walls was never my problem. My mother's hoard was. And it's gone.

I'm crying again, and I've shed so many tears lately that my face actually aches from it. But Ash is gripping my hand like a lifeline, and every time I turn to him, he's smiling at me.

"I can't believe it," he says. "I'm thinking maybe I'm still in the hospital, and they've got me on the really, *really* good drugs."

I laugh and sniffle, reaching up with my injured hand to wipe away what I can from my wet face. "Then how do you explain the fact that I can see it, too?" I ask. He smiles and leans over to press a kiss to my temple.

"Don't worry," he says. "I'm pretty sure it's real. And if not, then it just means I'm sharing the good drugs. Win-win."

My laugh comes out like a sob, and I feel a gentle hand land on my elbow. I turn and see Autumn and Roth, and I drop Ash's hand briefly so that I can reach out and wrap my arms around them both. "I can't believe you did this," I whisper.

They squeeze me back, Roth a little bit uncomfortably, and I'm struck by a sudden urge to reach up and ruffle his hair. He's so bad at being a real boy. Instead, I just lean into them both, and Autumn nuzzles into my shoulder.

"What else were we supposed to do?" she asks, and when she pulls back I can see that she's been crying, too. "Just leave it while you guys were in the hospital? There was work to be done."

I pull out of her embrace, but reach down with my good hand and squeeze her hand in my own. "Thank you," I say, but I have to force the words out through the boulder in my throat. She squeezes my hand back, but then she doesn't let it go. I look up at her through aching, tear-damp eyes, and she tugs on my hand. "Come on," she says, pulling me gently forward. "There's something I want to show you, something we found."

I let her pull me through the house, down hallways I haven't seen the floor of since I was a little kid, past pictures on the walls that I barely recognize. Finally, we stop at a door. It's the door to my childhood bedroom. Even after months of working on the house with Ash, we'd never even gotten close to making it this far. Keeping my hand in hers, Autumn reaches out and opens the door.

And the bottom drops out of my world.

The walls. They're murals. Image upon image, layered together to form a single story told in pictures. Horses and pigs with wings, unicorns and princes and even a princess with her very own sword, wielding it against a fearsome fire-breathing dragon. I want to look everywhere, all at once, but instead I'm frozen, standing sagged against the door jam, my heart in my throat.

It has been so long, so long that I had forgotten.

My father had painted these.

He'd painted them for me.

And now they're mine again. I sag back against Ash, who'd followed after us, and I'm caught between laughing and crying. I never thought I'd find any of his art ever again. Now I have a whole room of it, a thousand images to choose from.

"Thank you," I whisper, turning and burying my face in Ash's shoulder because I don't know what else to do. His hand comes to rest on my back, rubbing up and down and I see Maisie come up behind him, tears in her own eyes.

"There's one more thing," she says, and for the first time I notice the shoe box she's holding. She looks down at it, strokes her fingers over the top of it. "We found it when we were cleaning."

She holds it out to me, and I pull away from Ash just enough so that I can reach out and take it. It's lighter than I expect, but still my arm sags, exhausted. "What is it?" I ask, holding it out to Ash so that he can help me remove the lid. But I don't need them to answer. As soon as the lid's off, I can tell what it is.

It's letters. Dozens of them.

I turn to Autumn, confused, and she gives me a sad little smile. "They're from your mother," she says. "They're for you."

All of a sudden, I can't take it anymore, and the gentle stream of tears that has been escaping my eyes turns into a torrent, and I collapse against Ash.

These people, right here. They've given me everything. Their time, their care.

Their love.

They've even given me the impossible.

They've given me my parents back.

Ash

"Are you sure you want to do this?" I ask as Star settles down next to me on the bench. It's not even dark out yet, but the campfire York built before he and the others left for the evening is already crackling away in front of us.

"Definitely," she says, and shifts around so that she can drop the box Autumn had handed her from underneath her good arm into her lap, without using her injured hand. Not gonna lie, I'm so so glad that we both survived the crash, and that we managed to do so without any life-altering injuries, but I'm fucking gutted that she lost her finger. And no matter what a brave face she puts on, I know she is, too. The pinkie-swearing was kind of our thing. But I'd rather have Star with me than just about anything else, even our stupid little ritual.

I've been turning it over in my mind ever since I woke up. The crash. Maybe if I'd done something different, we wouldn't have been hit at all. Maybe if I had just taken her dancing, or not taken her out at all, or not looked at her or not gotten distracted, or a million other things, then we'd both be okay. Star caught me thinking about it once. It must have shown on my face, the guilt, because she asked me what was wrong. And after a token of resistance, I told her. I don't know what I expected, I guess that she'd be pissed off at me or something, having realized I've messed her up permanently.

But all she did was roll her eyes at me.

"You're an idiot," she'd said, leaning over to give me a kiss to ease the sting of her words. "If you'd done anything different, yeah, we might have been okay. But at the same time, we might have died. So don't be stupid and think about *what-ifs* okay? You're here with me now, and we're okay. That's what matters."

Then she'd stolen my Jell-O and winked at me. So that was that.

"But seriously," I say, nodding down toward the box, reaching over to help her tug the lid off when she starts to struggle a bit. "These were from your mom. Are you sure you don't want to keep them?"

She looks up at me, and there are tears in her eyes, but she nods. "I'm sure," she says. "I can't turn into her. I can't keep everything. If you keep everything, you end up losing what's most important." And it's true. Her mom kept everything, but lost Star. I feel my own eyes start to prick at the thought of what that woman must have gone through, and reach over to wrap my arm around her shoulders. "Okay," I say. "If you're sure."

"I am," she says. "Besides, this way, I get to say goodbye to her on my own terms. Not anybody else's."

I lean over and press a kiss to her mouth, holding her tight until I feel her start to relax, then I pull away. Her eyes are shining with tears, but she nods and reaches down into the box and pulls out the first letter.

"Dear Daughter," she reads.

One by one, she reads the letters her mother had written for her. And one by one, after she's done and has read aloud the last line *Love Mommy,* I watch as she places the letters into the campfire, and says goodbye. After the first letter, I can tell she is starting to get choked up, so I reach over and wrap my arm around her shoulders, and hold her as tightly as our injuries will allow. After the second letter, tears are flowing freely down her face. She doesn't even try to stop them. After the fifth, my own face is wet and my throat feels like it's strangling me from the inside out. After that, I stop counting. I don't know how long we sit there, but by the time she's read the last letter, the one her mother had written just days before she died, the sun is staring to dip behind the horizon, and the light is beginning to fade, making the fire cast little dancing shadows around the yard.

I press a kiss to her temple as she finishes reading the last letter, her voice so choked up that the sounds she's making are barely even words anymore. Then, instead of leaning forward and placing it into the fire as she had with the others, she takes a deep, shaking breath and carefully refolds the last letter, placing it back in the box. She sets it down gently on the ground next to her. Then she turns and wraps both of her arms around my middle, and burrows her face into my aching chest.

"It's okay," I murmur into her hair. "It'll be okay."

"I want to keep that one," she whispers, and I can feel the moisture from her tears seeping through my shirt. I bring my good hand up and slide it down her back gently, nodding.

"Okay."

"I want to get it tattooed, too," she says. "Her handwriting.

Dear Daughter, Love Mommy."

I press a kiss to her hair, my heart aching for her, for all she's lost. "I think she'd have liked that," I say. "I know I would. It's really nice."

She pulls back just enough to look at me. Her eyes are wide and shimmering with tears, so I reach up and use my thumb to brush them away. She blinks and presses the side of her face into my palm.

"I love you," she says, her voice still choked up.

I lean forward and press another kiss to her forehead.

"I know," I say. "I love you, too."

We sit there silently, just us and the fire, and together we watch the last of the letters burn into nothing, sending little bits of ash up into the darkening sky like stars. I take a shuddering breath. I need to do this.

I need to move on.

I pull my arm from around her shoulders, and reach deep into my pocket, pulling my wallet free. Star looks at me, questions in her eyes, but she says nothing. Slowly, heart in my throat, pain in my chest, I open my wallet and pull out the slip of paper I stashed there what seems like forever ago, but really it was only a matter of months. I unfold it gently, and try not to flinch when Star reaches out a hand to tilt it toward her. She needs to see this. She needs to understand.

FATHER OF TWO KILLED IN CAR CRASH the headline reads.

She tilts her head back, reaching up and raking the fingers of her good hand through her dark hair, shoving the strands away from her face. "It's about that night," I tell her. "The crash."

"The accident," she says, and for the first time, I nod at the word, instead of brushing it off. That's what it was, after all. Beyond anything else, it was an accident. I didn't mean to hurt anyone. Not that night, and not any night before or since.

"I . . . " I let out a breath and tilt my head back toward the sky. Why is this so hard?

Letting go shouldn't be harder than holding on.

"I think I want to burn it," I tell her.

"Are you sure?" she says, but it's not a question, not really. I can see it in her eyes. She just wants me to be certain, like she was. I reach out with my free hand and link my fingers with hers.

And then I nod.

"I need to," I say. "Holding on, it's killing me."

"Then do it," she says, and nods toward the fire. "Let go."

It's as easy as falling. I reach out and let the fire take it.

I have something else to hold on to now.

Star

It's late and everyone has finally gone home, and I just...
My heart feels so full right now. So thankful. I can't believe everyone came out to help us like that. It . . .

It doesn't feel real.

"So," Ash says as he eases down onto the porch swing next to me. The swing shifts a little, and I'm worried about how sturdy it is. I mean, it *looks* good, but it's been out of use for a long time, and I have no way of knowing if it's going to stay attached to the porch ceiling. I'm having visions of it suddenly giving out on us, sending our already-injured bodies sprawling across the porch, covered in debris. But he manages to make it down onto the swing without incident, even though his movements are slow and stilted by pain. I wince in sympathy. I know the feeling.

"So?"

He kicks his feet out in front of him, and the swing begins to sway back and forth.

"Are you ever going to tell me what your other tattoo means?"

A smile sneaks across my face as I realize which tattoo he's talking about, and before I know it I'm grinning so hard my face hurts.

I reach over and link the fingers on my good hand with the fingers on *his* good one, and squeeze them tight. And in that moment, I know that no matter what's headed for us, we're going to be okay.

Better than okay. We'll be *together*.

He glances over at me and catches me smiling at him like a maniac, and his eyebrows raise a touch in confusion, a little furrow burrowing between them. But then he's smiling, too, and Bruiser trots up and settles at our feet, shifting with a groan and then I can hear the thump of his tail against the wooden planks of the porch floor.

Still grinning, I lean over and press a gentle kiss to Ash's mouth, careful of the bruises on his face. His free hand, the one with the cast, comes up to cradle the back of my head gently and our lips slide together until we find just the right spot, and his mouth opens under mine.

Long moments later, we ease apart, gentle as breathing, and the streetlights start to blink on in the distance. "That's not an answer," Ash murmurs, and presses a kiss to my forehead.

And I just shake my head and smile, closing my eyes as I lean back into him. "I don't have to tell you what it means," I whisper against his skin. "You're going to figure it out on your own."

Ash lets out a soft chuckle and tugs me forward to kiss me again. "Okay," he says. "I can do that. After all . . . " He presses another kiss to my neck.

"We have the time."

Acknowledgements

To C, for being the best writing buddy ever. Thank you for all your help and support. You're still my favourite.

To D, for helping me fix it. Thank you so much. You're amazing.

To A, for reading it first. Literally. I forgot to read parts of it before sending it to you. You're wonderful.

To K, for just being amazing. You're one of the best friends I've ever had. So just thank you.

To Jennifer Ellision, Megan Erickson, and Jennifer Armentrout; thank you all for your kind words and for all the encouragement. It means more than you'll ever know..

To all the bloggers out there, thank you for all the work you do. I really hope you like it!

And to everyone else. No matter who you are, what you've done, or what you've had done to you, someone out there loves the hell out of you.

Let them

Sadie Munroe has been dreaming up stories for as long as she can remember. She is often found staring off into space, brainstorming her next plot, even when she hasn't quite finished the one she's currently working on.

It's a problem.

She lives in Ontario Canada with her family and her dog Trips, as well as what some people would consider far too many books (they're wrong).

All it Takes is her first novel